WHEN WE WERE US

Patricia Caliskan

SAPERE
BOOKS

WHEN WE WERE US

Published by Sapere Books.

24 Trafalgar Road, Ilkley, LS29 8HH

saperebooks.com

ISBN: 978-0-85495-237-3

CHAPTER ONE

Erika's nail polish was chipped. It was David's favourite shade, a deep, dramatic red called *Sortie Française*. It had happened somewhere between yesterday's manicure and the countdown to tonight's dinner. David would take it as a personal slight, his wife not looking presentable.

Presentable. That was how he phrased it when, years ago, she'd asked for his advice on what to wear to one of these events. Once or twice a year, Erika was introduced to a handful of business associates along with a few carefully curated fans of David's work. The setting was usually an in-store event or, as was the case that night, a gathering held at his literary agent, Monica's place.

Erika had found it endearing initially, him taking an interest and picking something out for her, and so it had become a tradition. A tradition which meant, despite the warm evening, she was dressed in a black, cowl neck dress with opaque stockings and stilettos. She'd have preferred something light, a maxi dress maybe, but whenever she made an appearance at one of these bookish things, he insisted on a little black dress.

Someone once asked, back at the beginning of his most successful series, if it was a turn-on, being married to the writer behind the Finn Schuyler novels. She laughed it off, amused by the assumption David spent his nights seducing her, behaving like his famous secret agent, instead of staying up late, struggling to commit to a compound adjective. During those first few years of his career as a novelist, she'd been nervous of how people might scrutinise the wife of a successful author. She felt the same anxiety getting ready for tonight. A silly kind of wife, dressed to complement her husband's achievements, like one of the clichéd femme fatales in his novels.

As the car slowed towards the lights, Erika tucked away her unkept nails, and clasped her hands neatly in her lap as they turned past the flagship Waterstones branch. There it was, front and centre. An entire window promoting pre-orders for the release of David's latest novel, *Code Name: They*. The jacket illustration featured the jawline of a man wearing a shirt and tie, with a slightly lipstick-smeared mouth. Erika thought it looked cheap and schlocky, but David was fixated on injecting some "semblance of contemporary relevancy" into his work, after his last book was deemed outdated. "*A slow-paced noir, harking back to the tired conventions of the author's heyday...*" That was the quote he threw around the breakfast table, frustrated with himself and everyone around him, quietly expecting to revisit the best-selling status he hadn't quite reclaimed during more recent years.

His first novel drew attention from critics. The second hit all the right lists in all the right places. As a former creative writing teacher turned playwright, then novelist, David had become a literary success, and Erika had been entirely flattered when he'd declared her his muse. But recently, she thought, gazing ahead as they neared the avenue of listed buildings, each successive failure seemed to erode the man she had married. Her husband was alternately invigorated by praise and depleted by criticism with each new publication. She missed her husband. The original version who was perhaps in love with the assumption that Erika was going to make him a better person, a better partner, a better writer. A better everything, really. She'd clearly failed as some sort of emblem for this life he wanted, especially after their son arrived.

Erika slipped her feet back inside her heels — leather stilettos. She wasn't doing this again, she decided. *Dressing the part.* Only a man of David's age would appreciate a stiletto, dressed up like a Cluedo character. As Erika glanced around the table, everyone else was wearing the regalia of the achingly underground or pseudo sophisticated, as if attending some upscale, fancy-dress party.

Monica's dining room lent the event an air of subtle decorum that David himself was at pains to cultivate. Imposing candelabras stood tall. White china was framed by ornate cutlery and heavy crystal glassware. A gentle symphony drifted through the air with fresh plumes of peonies along the table. The apartment boasted high ceilings and original fireplaces, paired with an Art Deco-inspired eye for design.

Erika sipped her drink, leaving too heavy an imprint of lipstick. She was glad to notice her husband enjoying himself, and was relieved to find the guestlist seemed to strike him as impressive. There was George someone, who headed up the UK publisher, and the digital marketing guru, Clara, along with an assistant who went unintroduced. Most notable was the lauded independent film director, Nate Petersen; his girlfriend, Ingrid, a Gothic artist; and Halo Jones, the non-binary feminist writer who ran a website dedicated to cult classics. Sadly absent was Monica's husband, Victor, who'd passed away almost six months before.

'The next thing,' David was saying, sharing one of his favourite anecdotes, a story Erika had heard many times, 'Gary Oldman leans across the table —' here came the usual pause — 'and says, "I get your point, Dave, but I still need you to take off my hat!"'

Erika smiled on cue, tilting her head in a charming fashion as her husband scanned candlelit faces for mirth. Monica, equally familiar with the story, smiled patiently as the caterer arrived to clear the first course.

David briefly met Erika's eye, his expression slipping into an altogether more familiar look of tired resignation. Erika looked away, sensing a long night ahead. He looked good, she decided, wearing his cashmere sweater over his chambray shirt. She'd steered him away from his original choice of polo neck, which he thought lent a debonair appeal, but instead drew attention to his double chin and awful taste in jumpers.

'A toast to *Code Name: They*,' George announced. 'And the return of Schuyler.'

'To Finn Schuyler,' Monica said, as David joined the toast, looking as he always did ahead of any new release: like a man on a ledge.

Erika knew how apprehensive he was. She remembered him once confessing how that initial decade of high praise seemed to have done nothing but set him on a steady course for subsequent failure. Desperate to concoct something edgier, the latest novel found David resuscitating Finn Schuyler from a fictional death. Now undercover, presumed dead, Schuyler worked as a non-binary assassin.

Erika struggled with the concept and had told David as much, but when she'd suggested there was no defeat in returning to the existing formula, his simmering panic had turned to indignation. Erika didn't understand his need to rejuvenate, to re-evaluate the last twenty years. Funnily enough, as his wife, she was more than in tune with that concept. As she watched him charming the guests, Monica caught her eye and leant over. 'Outside for a break?' she suggested.

Draped in a russet, wraparound dress which accentuated her figure-of-eight curves, Monica closed the door behind them. The guests' glasses had been replenished, and the staff had been advised to hold back for a few more minutes before serving the main course. Erika wondered how it must feel to be the kind of woman who lived in a perfect home, threw elaborate dinner parties, and hired staff for the occasion.

'So, how's our baby boy doing?' Monica said, brushing back thick ringlets that almost reached her waist as they stood in the jasmine-scented courtyard.

'Which one?' Erika said, sharing a smile. 'Matt's fine. Doing great. How are you, more importantly?'

'I'm good,' Monica said, somehow managing to make vaping seem elegant. 'And, not so good,' she admitted, 'depending on which day you catch me.'

'Well, we're always here,' Erika said. 'Doesn't have to be so formal.'

'Yes, I know that,' Monica said. 'Thank you. Both of you. David's been great.'

'Tonight means a lot to him.'

'Means a lot to me, too,' Monica said. 'He was one of the first writers we signed — the only one to turn down a much bigger option. I've learned to appreciate loyalty like that. I'm hoping tonight might lead to a few interesting opportunities. Nate's looking for a new project.'

'You think he'd be interested in adapting the book?'

'I think it could be worth a conversation, and having Halo here might help,' she said, with the confident air of the card table. 'This could mean a new era for David. Although...' Monica lowered her voice. 'I wanted to give you a heads up. I've had some indication, early reviews — nothing we didn't expect with the redirection of an established character.' It didn't take more than a second for Erika to understand the subtext. 'Too early to predict if they reflect the general consensus, but he may be feeling a little bruised.'

'Thanks for letting me know,' Erika said, wondering whether it was worth David carrying on under this kind of pressure.

Monica offered her a hit on the vape, and she took it. 'You know, David's a talented writer, but it can be difficult to evolve. Don't get me wrong, people still anticipate his work, but courting that same level of recognition at this stage?' Monica took a drink. 'He deserves to find his joy.'

Erika nodded, but joy wasn't an emotion which came naturally to David these days.

'Anyway,' Monica said, one bejewelled arm briefly patting Erika's wrist. 'Let's not spoil the evening. We both want what's best for David.'

As they returned to the table, an almost accusatory silence greeted them. David's self-righteousness was palpable.

'All I'm saying is,' Clara continued, flushed, both from the wine and her words, 'you have to question what kind of message we're sending to the non-binary community, using that artwork.'

The cover. Erika hated to agree, but she was hardly surprised by the objection.

'It's an illustration of the protagonist as depicted in the work, Clara,' David said, at once dismissive and, Erika recognised, shaken by the possibility. He then addressed the table, throwing the argument out there. 'I mean, on the one hand, if we continue to write these kinds of … heterosexual, leading men, we're antiquated. Perpetuating stereotypes.' He was sounding increasingly erratic. Erika shared a look with Monica. 'But if we're brave enough to make the work … *inclusive*, we're deemed exploitative. I mean, maybe someone has to take that first step. Defy expectations of the genre.'

Erika knew this was exactly what David was banking on, that his new novel would be heralded as a breakthrough. David

Daniel Forde, the man who turned secret agents into sexual pioneers.

'I think what Clara's trying to say,' said Nate, casually resting the crook of his elbow on the back of his chair, 'is that, taken out of context, the artwork could seem … insensitive? I mean, can you imagine Eon Productions putting James Bond in stockings and suspenders? Experimenting with his sexuality?'

'I think that's unfair,' Erika said, interrupting the growing amusement. 'The issue of identity — isn't that the whole point? To challenge expectations, broaden representation? An author holds as much creative license to deconstruct as they do to define their characters.'

'Creative licence to thrill,' Nate said, sipping his wine. 'So, Erika, are you responsible for inspiring David here to experiment with this brave new, non-gender-specific world?'

'Finn Schuyler's not experimenting with his sexuality,' David clarified, heat creeping up his neck. 'As I said, he's undercover. *Code Name: They.* The clue's in the title.'

'How the fuck's he going undercover?' Nate fired back. 'Walking around with a gun and a face full of bronzer?'

'I'm fairly sure Schuyler's doing no such thing,' Erika said, trying to keep the debate friendly as the guests grew uncomfortable. 'And I doubt David finds inspiration from me. I don't use bronzer, for a start.'

Nate grinned and started clapping, one of those awful gestures people made when trying to gain favour.

'Have you even read the book?' David snapped.

'That was my next question,' Monica said. 'Did you pick up the advance copy, Nate?'

'Guilty as charged,' Nate held up both hands in surrender. 'Just fucking with you, man,' he added, as David attempted something resembling a smile. 'You know, I still have your first book from way back when I was a pup. First novel I ever read, *Darkened Days*. Should've brought it with me for you to sign.'

'Now,' Halo said, perpetually typing into their phone, 'the jacket artwork for that, was it…?'

'Mort Louis,' David said.

'Of course,' Halo said, calling up the image. 'So iconic.'

'Beautiful,' Ingrid agreed as Halo shared their screen. 'Love the holographic element.'

'That kind of duality could've worked perfectly with this novel,' Nate added.

'Well, I must say, this is marvellous,' said George, mustering goodwill. 'Already provoking this level of discussion.' He raised his glass in David's direction. 'Exactly the space we need to occupy.'

'Exactly,' Monica said. 'David's been incredibly brave with a much-loved character.'

'So, Erika,' Nate said, practically cross-legged on his dining chair. 'What is it you do?'

'Do people still ask that question?'

'Only the truly obnoxious.'

'I'm in advertising.'

'Ah, a fellow masochist! You're in good company. Who're you with?'

'Lingua Franca,' she said, as David tucked into his sea bass.

'Lingua Franca,' Nate said, considering the name. 'Why's that so familiar?'

'Stix & Stones?'

'Get out of town!' He almost leapt from his seat. 'Stix & fucking Stones? Brilliant!'

'A-*may*-zing!' Clara fixed on Erika as if sighting a UFO.

Stix & Stones had been Lingua Franca's finest hour: a skincare brand which had launched a range of sustainable, cruelty-free cosmetics for men. The campaign had gone viral, winning the agency an All Talk award the year before, along with accolades rippling across the industry.

'You do know,' Nate said, 'that I pitched for that and ended up working with your competitors.'

'What competitors?'

'Ah, come on, now,' he said, clearly enjoying the joust. 'It was a valiant attempt.'

'Well, it was an attempt…'

'I *fucking love* this woman!' Nate slapped the table, turned to Ingrid, who was looking suspiciously vacant. 'No wonder you're in favour of David sticking lippy on his famous spy. You clearly do inspire the man.'

David remained silent, and it occurred to Erika that Nate might be right.

'Exciting times,' Nate said, shaking David's hand as their taxis arrived. 'Erika, great to meet you. Forgive the formality,' he handed over a business card, 'but I'm entirely serious about that future collab.'

As they sat in the darkness of the backseat, Erika reached across to take David's hand, finding his arms folded as he huddled in the corner.

'Great night,' she said, brazening it out, attempting to break the silence.

'Were we at the same table?' David huffed. '*That bastard*, Nate Petersen. Doesn't even write his own scripts, for God's sake! That last film of his was utter dogshit. Finn Schuyler wearing bronzer! Did you see that Nate was wearing eyeliner? *Guyliner*, or whatever they call it. Facetious prick.'

'Forget it. It wasn't his night, it was yours,' Erika said. 'I'm very proud of you.' She reached again for his hand, and this time, he took it.

'Your nail polish is chipped,' he said.

CHAPTER TWO

Erika parked up, double-checking door handles and wrapping her jacket around her before taking a right onto Church Street. She enjoyed the solidarity of fellow workers, unloading vans and raising shutters. Once she reached the high street, window displays caught her eye. It was as if someone had raided her wardrobe from twenty years ago. There were crop tops, high-waisted jeans, clumpy ankle boots and short, quilted jackets.

It reminded her of being Erika Karter, poised to take over the world in a shrunken T-shirt and bootcut jeans. Who was she now? She paused at the pedestrian crossing, striding across at the insistent bleep. She was David's wife, and Matt's mum. She didn't resemble the original Erika anymore, not even close —

Her mobile rang.

'Fuck me, Erika!' said Richard Harrington, part-time bastard and full-time agency director. 'Did you not get my text?'

'What? No. I've only just got out of the car.'

'We've got Stable Denim in at ten,' Richard said. 'William's brought the meeting forward. You know what that means? They're getting ready to oust us, fob us off.'

'Not necessarily,' Erika said, narrowly avoiding a collision with a Deliveroo rider.

'We *need* this account, Erika.'

'Yes, I'm aware of that.' She was well acquainted with Richard's semi-permanent state of panic. 'I'll be there in five minutes,' she added, but he'd already hung up.

Stable Denim had been incredibly cool when she was a teenager. They'd had great-looking ads which she'd cut out from her favourite magazines and stuck on her bedroom wall. They were currently looking at ways to regain some credibility after suffering a midlife crisis, which was something Erika could relate to. Stable Denim still designed and manufactured great products, and she was confident that after today's meeting, Lingua Franca would get the chance to change customer perception.

The world of advertising was saturated with creative agencies far slicker than Lingua Franca. However, Richard being Richard — despite threatening to quit roughly once a fortnight since the day Erika had joined the team — remained hungry for that next big campaign, even if that meant nursing frequent, belligerent hangovers.

Despite the constant search for their next client, theirs had been a pretty successful partnership. Kissable Organic Lip Balm had been their first national campaign. After that, they'd won Cupboard Love, a range of eco-friendly cleaning products, and had gained valuable coverage promoting the recycled aspects of Lounge Around sofas, too. Those smaller wins had become steppingstones towards the heavy hitter, their biggest win, Stix & Stones. The only problem was they hadn't won anything nearly as lucrative all year.

Erika made her way into the offices, located in the converted building of a former theatre. The motion sensor lights snapped awake as she made her way up three floors. A ground floor of dazzling white space featured abstract artwork and small, adjoining rooms of airy, glass-encased spaces. Floor two was home to the production studios, run by Gareth, and the digital department, run by Ursula. Her main domain was in the converted attic, with low ceilings still coated with peaks of Artex. It had just enough space for her and Richard's desks, a corner couch and a humble kitchenette.

Richard was getting up from the sofa almost vertebra by vertebra as she made it to the top of the stairs, avoiding the lift to make use of the impromptu cardio. She'd gone up a dress size since January (she hadn't shaken off the Christmas weight) and worried she'd reached the point when things like that were beyond her control. Now she was over forty, she'd grown quietly suspicious of her own body, which seemed hell-bent on doing exactly as it pleased, like a teenager throwing an unsupervised party.

'Good God,' Richard said, rubbing at his face. 'I thought you were never getting here.'

'Will you please stop? It's not even nine yet, Richard. Everything's prepared.'

'It's called taking my job seriously,' he said, popping a couple of painkillers.

Erika had met Richard a lifetime ago, when she'd written for *Vista Magazine*. He'd been the show business reporter for the *Mitcherton Gazette*, renowned for drinking like a fish and shagging like a Trojan. Since then, the only thing he'd quit was the reporting.

'Late night?'

Richard was infantile, arrogant, and highly irresponsible, but somehow they'd become firm allies. During the time they'd worked together, he'd flirted with an addiction to prescription painkillers, been sued for inciting a fistfight in Studio Two, acquired six points on his licence, gone through an acrimonious divorce, and was currently dating Ursula, the twenty-seven-year-old digital marketer and part-time makeup artist and influencer, who also acted as his PA, which Erika decided must unofficially stand for Piece of Ass.

'Ursula's parents came over,' he said, crunching on the pills. 'I spent three hours shockingly sober, getting grilled on my intentions.'

'Christ, I hope you didn't tell them,' Erika said, calling up the Stable Denim account.

'I polished off two bottles of a very decent Malbec back here, and despite what they tell you about it being a decent bottle, it does nothing to deter feeling like shit.'

Richard's relationship with alcohol was his most enduring one. His taste in wine was in direct contrast to his taste in women, whom he preferred younger and not so full-bodied.

'Ah, it's just like the old days,' Erika said. 'Cheer up, at least you're not slumped in a sea of sweat and regret at an unknown address. You're still okay to take this meeting?'

'Will be,' he said, pressing his palm against his forehead. 'Ursula brought me these.' He gestured to the tablets.

'Ah, so true love won, then?'

'For now, until the next wave of insanity.'

'Oh, well, if all else fails, I'm sure you and Malbec will be very happy.'

'Exactly. Malbec doesn't want a diamond ring or baby Malbecs.'

'Why would anyone want baby Malbecs with you?'

'For my own good, apparently. Kids are what's missing to make me grow up.'

'Really? I think you might have that the wrong way round.'

'Nothing to do with me. I know my limits. Mostly,' Richard replied, still cradling his forehead.

'Shame. You'd make a lovely dad,' Erika said, firing up a coffee. She used to hate the smell of it, but now, like everything else, coffee was inevitable. 'You'd be forgetting birthdays. Turning up drunk to the nativity. Ditching them for some younger, cuter kids, as soon as things got too heavy.'

'I'd never turn up drunk to a nativity. I wouldn't turn up to one sober. Anyway, this is a good sign, me being hungover.' Richard stretched as he stood, opened his drawer, engulfing himself in deodorant. 'Think about every big pitch we've ever won.'

'Absolutely.' Erika cleared her way through the scented cloud. 'If it wasn't for you, sweating through your shirt, where would we be?'

'Am I that bad?'

'Well, you're not good. Don't suppose you've got a razor and a clean shirt handy? You look like you've been living in your car.'

'The car would've been more comfortable. Since Ursula moved in, I seem to be spending more time going out. Bastard,' Richard glanced at his phone. 'We're up. William Torrence. He's early.'

'In an increasingly competitive market, Stable Denim has fallen out of favour with the original demographic of males aged eighteen to twenty-five,' Richard said, tapping one jaunty finger on the keypad and running through the folio of Stable Denim's previous campaigns. 'While the quality and ethical manufacturing of Stable Denim is undisputed, rival brands have emerged to disrupt the marketplace.'

Disruptive marketing. Erika wasn't sure Richard entirely knew what the term meant, but he was fluent in jargon. *Transparency. Measurable data.*

'Current trends have been particularly damaging,' Richard went on, as the wall-mounted screen switched to an assortment of young blokes wearing skinny-fit jeans. 'Today's styling isn't in keeping with the Stable Denim brand aesthetic. And, in the name of authenticity, we have to agree.' Richard held one hand up, bearing witness.

'Yes, yes,' said William Torrence, the man behind the Stable Denim empire, his gaze fixed on the presentation over bifocals. 'No better than elasticated leggings, those things.' He nodded at the visuals. 'We discussed all this last time, Richard.'

During their first meeting, at Stable Denim HQ, William had presided in front of a Blu Tack-ed yearly planner filled with stick-on stars, an assortment of tea-stained cups, and dust-covered fabric samples. Erika had expected the man behind the brand to be some kind of denim-clad, urban cowboy. Instead, he was a short, egg-shaped man who wore suits with sleeves slightly too long and trousers slightly too short, so you could see his socks but barely his hands as he sat.

'I'll explain why I'm recapping here,' Richard said, springing into his signature move and pacing the room like a modern-day Sherlock Holmes. He scrolled through the assortment of former Stable ads. 'For these men, wearing a pair of Stable Denim jeans *meant* something, and, brilliantly for us, *it still can*. Stable Denim was a *real partnership* between a guy and his jeans. And that guy is still in the marketplace, but he's opting for a lower price point that compromises on style — *and he knows it*. William —' Richard prepared for the big reveal by perching on the edge of the boardroom desk — 'I give you the Dad Jean.'

Richard hit the button, loading up a slideshow of sad-looking, middle-aged men in sad-looking, shapeless jeans. 'What we mean by the Dad Jean is everyday denim offering a loose, unflattering fit, mistaken for comfort. This slightly wider-hemmed leg is *appalling*, and it's paired with a bleached, sagging knee.' He was visibly offended. 'Mostly purchased at supermarkets or discount outlets, the Dad Jean is the standard offering of store-only brands.' He reported the devastation like a retail war correspondent.

William reached for his tea, bordering on disinterested as he dunked a Digestive.

'The great news is,' Richard continued, 'according to our focus groups, the current generation of Dad Jean wearers form approximately seventy-six per cent of your former demographic. That's an *incredible* stat!' He whipped back his head like a heavy metal drummer. 'They're nostalgic: they still associate Stable Denim with a former sense of independence. *Freedom!*' He raised a fist. 'Bonds of youth. Credibility with women. They know to expect quality, durability, and unlike other brands, there's the possibility of recapturing those positives with a return to the classic cut of Stable Denim.'

As Richard was about to debut an audio treatment of Erika's script, William brought about a pause, removing his glasses and rubbing at the pink indentation marks on the bridge of his nose.

'So, your solution,' William said, 'is to promote our jeans to the fellas who used to wear them? Older customers who can't afford them anymore because they have families now?' He slid his glasses into place, clearly unimpressed. 'Isn't that the whole point of them wearing *that rubbish* in the first place? Walking round like that?' He flickered a dismissive look towards the imagery. 'You said it yourself, Richard. These customers, their priorities have changed. And if those slides are anything to go by, they don't care what they look like. Am I missing something?' William turned sharply to Erika, who was trying to dry the sweat patches rapidly forming beneath Richard's armpits using only the power of her mind.

'William,' she cut in, giving Richard the chance to pour himself some water, which she hoped wasn't vodka, because he'd been known to do that before. 'These men, our Dad Jean wearers, they still want to look good, the same way women their age still want to look good. Women are incredibly loyal to brands who remember we're still out there, still spending on looking stylish.'

'What have women got to do with it?' William said, gruff now, resting his elbows on the desk. 'We're a young man's fashion label,' he said, underscoring each word with one stubby finger. 'At least, we were, until they started dressing in jeans that are no better than two legs of elastic.'

'My point is,' Erika said, 'women have more options. So many ways to affordably flatter their figures and replicate trends. Men and dads — we don't expect them to care. Women care. Men give up. That's the presumption, and it's outrageous. We believe Stable Denim can step up and fulfil an unspoken demand, because men do care, and so do their partners.'

'Fair enough,' William said, still unconvinced, 'but are they bothered enough to spend money they haven't really got?'

'Some customers will be priced out, yes. It's maybe thirty or forty pounds more on jeans than they are currently spending,' Erika said, finding the appropriate slide, 'but, according to our research, if they're confident that they're getting a longer duration of wear and a better quality fit, like the Stable Denim they wore years ago, they're going to at least try on a pair for old time's sake. And that's exactly what women have got to do with it. They want their men to look good,' she added, as William started to look engaged. 'The fact is, for a lot of men in this demographic, it's their partners influencing their wardrobes — buying their clothes, picking out what works. Our campaign, it's important to remember, isn't solely aimed at the wearer. Sexy is in the eye of the beholder.'

Erika gave Richard the nod to play the demo. William was growing curious now.

'*Dad Jeans? There's a dark horse in town. Calling all medium-rise guys. Remember those days, in your favourite blue jeans? That straight-talking, slim fit, button-fly. We're older, wiser. Distinguished denim with added stretch and lift designed to last. Go along for the ride. Stable Denim. We're back in the saddle.*'

William sat up a little straighter, slightly invigorated.

'This percentage of the market is hugely overlooked, but we can speak to them, loud and clear, and reappoint Stable Denim as a trusted, statement brand,' Erika finished.

CHAPTER THREE

Erika had no idea what she was expecting to find. A hostage? A makeshift sex dungeon? Her husband, crouched inside the chest freezer, dressed as his mother?

She honestly wasn't the type to go poking around in other people's business, not even her own husband's, but as she eased the skinny brass key into the garage door, she was determined to find something.

When David had announced a trip to the theatre, she assumed he meant with her, but he explained, it was a work thing organised by Monica. She was keen to introduce him to the theatrical director, who was apparently interested in his work. For some reason — maybe it was the heavy note of apology, or the aroma of the cologne she'd bought for him, suddenly territorial — her wife senses were piqued.

For the past couple of months, the garage had become David's makeshift office. He had initially started using the space for a new exercise regime. David hadn't visited a gym in years, not since he'd nipped in to use the vending machine, waiting to pick Matt up from swimming. Next, in went the desk, finding it peaceful, he said, to edit his final draft. A few weeks ago, she dared knock, offering him a glass of wine, conducting their entire conversation from behind the half-propped door, with only his Crocs visible. Erika suggested he might be more comfortable indoors in his actual office. He mumbled the usual gripes about needing to compose his thoughts, but to all intents and purposes, her husband had left her without actually leaving her, and where was the fairness in that?

Matt left her with spare keys to the garage and shed when he left home, and for some reason, she'd not said a word about them to David. David had the other set. She'd been thinking of doing this, taking a look inside the garage, since the weekend. So, as soon as David left, Erika knew exactly what she was going to do. The overhead mechanism yawned in protest as she lowered her head and entered the space.

She pictured David hurtling around the corner, somehow aware of a breach in security. Could he have it wired up? The thought had never occurred to her, but with his interest in mail-order gadgets, it was a possibility — exactly the kind of precaution her husband might reasonably take if he was up to something. And Erika definitely thought he was up to something.

At the centre of everything was Matt's old weights bench. She was glad it was being used, no longer a clothes rack, but hadn't expected her husband to put it so steadily to work, given it a week or two before he went back to slouching over his keypad.

Despite her sweater, there was a tomblike chill inside the small space, but she knew David could deal with the lack of natural light and heating. Winter had been an almost fight for survival. The climate inside their house so adverse that she wouldn't have blinked if Sir David Attenborough had made his way into the lounge, narrating their journey towards hypothermia. One evening, she'd stifled a laugh at the sight of David wearing a fleece and a beanie, sipping from a thermal flask, his breath visible in the kitchen. Erika tried pretending they were glamping instead of cutting down on utility bills. For a couple of nights, when temperatures plunged below zero, she thought he might realise he was taking things too far as she slept in thermal gloves. Instead, he gave her a scathing look, wrapped himself in his dressing gown, while she counted the hours until she could luxuriate under the office hand-dryer.

Erika caught her reflection in the full-length mirror from their old wardrobe, propped up against the half-wall of storage boxes. Is that what he did? Lift weights and worked out while admiring himself? She stopped and looked more closely at her reflection. She looked okay, and she could think that if she liked. Matt said she looked amazing for her age, but even from her own son, she resented the disclaimer. *For her age.* Totally destroyed the sentiment.

When Erika was younger, she'd been quietly excited by the thought of getting older. She imagined her future self as a wise, accomplished figure who knew things which, one day, she would know too. Those invaluable pieces of wisdom would be of great importance to the future Erika. She would finally belong to the mysterious world of the grown-up. A world she couldn't wait to explore; anything was better than being at school, living in what she sincerely believed to be the most boring place on earth, with little more to do than walk around the park with a friend and a full face of makeup. And so, by the time she reached her twenties, it was the thought of starting out on the road to figuring it all out which caused a murmur. Erika passed the exams, and that had passed the time. She finally got the job she wanted, so that had kept her optimistic. Her latest line of work was perfectly fine too, but David had always been the more ambitious one. Now Erika was older, she tried not to care about getting older, which was a similar feeling to walking into a room and completely forgetting what she expected to do once she got there.

She put her hand to her face, leaning towards the mirror. There was barely a crease, barely a laughter line, maybe some advantages to life with David. *You look good*, she thought to herself, *and not just for your age.*

One day, she promised herself, one of those useless pledges borne of regret, she would find an excuse to wear a bikini. Show the world Erika Karter wasn't looking too bad at all. She surprised herself. *Erika Karter?* That was her maiden name. She'd been Erika Forde for the last couple of decades.

The thud of a car door almost stopped her heart in her chest. Erika scooted back a couple of steps, sure David must have forgotten his ticket, back in time to catch her, and he'd never let her forget. She glanced out, relieved to spot the woman from across the road unpacking shopping. *Look at me*, she thought, *practically burglarising my own home.*

She took in his desk, complete with the bedside lamp from Matt's room, and a leaflet for dental veneers. She picked it up. Didn't veneers cost thousands? And why the sudden fixation with his teeth? David thought £12 was steep for a haircut, and now he was concerned with the radiance of his smile? He didn't even smile that often.

On top of a tower of Perspex storage boxes were a couple of cardboard packages, lids left half-open. She wasn't doing this again, snooping around, so the search had to be thorough and final. Reaching up, Erika grabbed the first box, disappointed to find a tooth-whitening kit. It looked expensive, though, with one of those UV light-packs and half a dozen syringes of brightening gel. She had no idea why he hadn't just put the stuff in the bathroom, but it was hardly the worst thing she could've found. There were no discarded items of women's clothing lying around, and no evidence of people-trafficking or an arsenal of homemade weapons. Not yet, anyway. Maybe she was just genuinely curious about what made her husband happy these days, because she knew it had nothing to do with her.

Erika looked at the time. She needed to finish this quickly. She eased the next box towards her, her head stooping as the plastic lid gave way. There were assorted printouts, and odds and ends from Matt's studies. A wooden box filled with pastels and charcoal slipped over her shoulder, followed by her brother, Josh's, old notebooks. She slid the box back into standing position, unable to resist a quick look at her brother's work. He'd been such a talented artist, even then. As she closed the book, on the floor, she noticed her old Zippo. Holding the heavy brass weight in her hand, flipping the lid, that strangely sweet smell. No idea why, but she put the lighter in her pocket. Feeling stupid now, she opened the last box, resigned to finding nothing in particular.

Inside was a box: The Man Mower written on the front with a male model, oiled chest, giving it his all. It was an electric razor with a clump of hair caught in the mechanism. She realised what it was — pubic hair — and dropped the thing, brushing her hands free of fuzz. David treated Radox like some kind of aphrodisiac, but he was buying specialist equipment to preen his groin? Why would he be doing that to himself? The guy on the front looked like some kind of fire-eater, for God's sake. He might not be having an affair, but her husband was having a Midlife Crisis — either that or auditioning for Magic Mike.

She picked up the discarded razor, only as she did so, she noticed a mobile phone had fallen out of the box. She didn't recognise it. David usually made sure to trade-in his old phones, and Matt upgraded his handset constantly. This was your bog-standard, unremarkable mobile, exactly the type of nondescript phone David would choose for himself. Her suspicions were reawakened, but maybe the whole thing looked worse than it was? David was perfectly entitled to want whiter teeth and a shaved groin. She dithered for a second, but before she could put down the phone and walk away, the screen slowly blinked awake to request a pin code.

She typed in the year. *No, you idiot*, she scolded herself. *That was a waste of a go. Did you get goes with these things?* She keyed in her date of birth, but knew, deep down, that he wouldn't be using that. Then she typed in his birthday. Nothing. She tried Matt's birthday, and the damn thing went right ahead and woke up.

She was aware of every breath, her heart thundering as she clicked on Messages. As she scrolled through, she realised David had only been messaging one number. No names. The level of subterfuge was chilling. She read the texts, which promised things she'd never thought David capable of. Grabbing lunch, his treat. Going for walks, holding hands. Gifts, which he apparently loved to buy. Generous, considerate. Romantic, even. Who was this man? And did this other person know that she, Erika, *his wife,* existed? Did they care?

Shaking slightly as she switched the thing off, she shoved it back inside the box, already tempted to reread the messages. Instead, she made herself calmly reassess the space for evidence of intrusion. A quick once-over, and you'd never have known she'd been in there, but then again, what did she care? Was he planning to waltz in with a mouthful of ceramic teeth while she ignored that too? A tummy tuck? Peck implants? An attractive assistant working out there with him at all hours? Knowing there was someone else, Erika was reminded of how it felt when David Forde first turned his attention on you. Her wedding dress must still be in the garage somewhere. She hadn't seen it in years and probably should've sold it, like David suggested. He'd hired his suit, but then, that was typical of David. The only thing he got sentimental over was his pension plan.

She remembered him as the person he once was, when she'd still had him on a pedestal. He'd had that lovely gentleness and a soothing intensity. The sentimental part of her, or maybe the stupid part, wished she and David could go back to how they were. When Matt had been born, David had loved being a dad, but he'd been so distracted around that time. She understood it now. The pressure to be successful and take care of his family was inbuilt, as was his need for undivided attention. Erika supposed she might've struggled to be there for him while taking care of Matt, but the truth was, there was no contest. She'd chosen her baby and wished David had chosen their family too. Instead, he'd pulled away, and as he did, she'd held Matt that tiny bit closer.

You never thought you'd make so many compromises. It was beyond disappointing, but the things you thought you'd do, differed greatly from what you actually did, once you become a family.

Life got things spectacularly wrong sometimes, and there wasn't too much you could do about it, not until, maybe one day, you decided you finally must.

CHAPTER FOUR

Erika wandered into the kitchen, enjoying the cold tiles beneath her feet. The space lit up as she opened the venetian blinds, heaped coffee into her cup and added a teaspoon of sugar, just for the hell of it.

She squinted out of the window. David was already out there, patrolling the garden and raising his hand to acknowledge her presence. He dispensed with what looked like a rogue crisp packet from the depths of the borders. She was surprised he hadn't kitted himself out with a hi-vis and whistle, with that look on his face. The upholding of gardening duties and recycling routines were conducted with an almost military precision. It was even worse at the weekends, when he'd fire up the strimmer at first light, priding himself on getting to it before next door's gardener arrived. Turning his attention to the flags, he weeded the patio with that gizmo he'd bought from one of those mail-order catalogues only the elderly subscribed to. At around ten, he'd settle in front of one of his Natural World documentaries, slurping tea from his metal gardening mug and dunking toast. It was an ugly habit; the butter formed an oily sheen on the surface, coagulating on his top lip. He'd stay there until lunchtime, because that's exactly what he'd done every Saturday for the last several years.

Erika watched as David removed a cereal box from the plastic bin, inspecting it as if handling forensic evidence. He had to reorganise the recycling on an almost weekly basis, he reminded her, because Erika did it wrong, apparently. It seemed that recently, she did most things wrong according to David. She couldn't remember how many times he'd demonstrated his recycling system — not so much QVC as *WTF?* Packets were to be folded in a certain configuration before joining his filing system in the depths of the green bin. A filing system which, she regretted ever pointing out, was a complete waste of time, if it was destined to end up in a heap at the bottom of the big bin. Plastic symbols were to be consulted, glassware washed until almost too pristine to throw out. She'd stuck a bunch of daffodils in a mayonnaise jar a few weeks back and put it on the windowsill just to take the piss, and he'd almost thrown a fit. It was childish, but she couldn't begin to describe the thrill she got from throwing an unwashed tin into the wrong wheelie bin.

David always found things to do around the house before settling down to work. When he was writing, he'd go hours on end, calm and remote as an ocean view. When he was stressed, in between ideas, he homed in on the most boring household non-events with the quiet indignation of the prematurely retired. That particular morning, the publication of his new book, *Code Name: They*, had finally arrived. This was his eleventh release, so Erika knew the drill. He'd be wading through the first batch of reviews, checking his messages, with Monica updating him on press requests. Years ago, on the release of his fourth or fifth novel, David's favourite review had described the work as: *The place where Arthur Miller's tragic Willy Loman meets Chuck Palaniuk's trail-blazing Tyler Durden.* At that point he'd started wearing hats whenever he left the house, using his full name of David *Daniel* Forde, and loudly denouncing every paperback Erika picked up as 'Bloody chick lit *inanity*!'

She took a seat at the dining table, one eye on the time, sipping coffee while leafing through a pile of junk mail about to be lovingly constructed into origami creations and released into David's recycling basket. There, beneath an assortment of pocket loot from the depths of David's combats, she noticed a copy of *The Rough Guide to Denmark*. Another international publisher was interested in his work, most probably. He already had Paris and Barcelona under his belt, having met with their publishing houses to sell translation rights. Erika nursed her cup, browsing the guide before the back door opened and snapped her away from the *picture-perfect villages and sandy beaches of Odense*. David walked in, his mint green Crocs swiping against the coconut fibre doormat.

'Gorgeous day out there!' said Erika, a little too brightly.

He sighed, bland as celery, as if he'd somehow taken issue with summer now.

'Checked your emails yet?' she asked.

'Not yet, no.'

'Leaving it a bit late, aren't you? Thought you might've sneaked a look.'

'I decide my own hours,' he said, opening the cupboard.

'Oh, come on, aren't you excited?' she asked, speaking to the back of his head. 'Publication day!'

'Something like that...' he said, shaking out a sachet of porridge.

He was on a diet. So far, the only thing he'd lost was his sense of humour.

'Denmark?' Erika held up the guidebook. 'Sounds lovely.'

'It's work, Erika,' he replied dismissively. 'Not some holiday.'

'God forbid, David...'

He met her eye, smirked, and relented. 'All I'm saying is that I'll be sat in meetings in Denmark, not idling away on some beach. You've no idea how much pressure I'm under. It's not some sort of novelty excursion.'

There was no chance of the two of them getting away anytime soon, David reminded her every time a sun-drenched location filled the TV screen. Not that Erika was complaining. From the moment he'd sat on a beach applying athlete's foot lotion during their last vacation as a family — the year Matt got his GCSE results — she'd lost any desire to travel with David. She'd have preferred a holiday without him. Her mind flashed to the mobile hidden in the garage. If he was taking an extracurricular vacation from their marriage, maybe she was allowed a break too? Except she'd go alone and tropical, racking up her credit limit on tacky souvenirs and near-lethal cocktails, and wearing next to nothing in the heat.

They hadn't always been that way, of course. There was a time when they'd provided each other with romantic respite from the mundane. Erika thought David was intriguing, back then. She considered him the perfect balance between anchor and aviator. He was a daydreamer, but focused and driven. Fascinating in his depth of thought, spontaneous in action. They'd got engaged on a whim after David whisked her off to Paris at a moment's notice. He strode through Charles de Gaulle carrying their luggage, revealing his surprise plans for the duration of their stay. A friend of his, a former lecturer teaching English in Paris, had vacated his apartment especially for their trip. They taxied straight to the Eiffel Tower, sitting on the lawn of the Champ de Mars, David pouring warm red wine into plastic cups. The famous tower suddenly lit up, a sight met with gasps and affectionate applause. Erika settled against David, her head against his shoulder. As they kissed, it felt like New Year's Eve to her. A time of resolutions, fused into existence with the woman she was to become, in this life with David Forde. No matter how much the voice in her head urged caution, she dared herself to jump into their new life together without hesitation.

They made their way along the 16th arrondissement, the air sweet and full of unspoken feelings. There were beautiful, ornate streetlights and cobblestones, as if they'd stepped back in time. As they turned the corner, everything looked so perfectly French, as Erika had been imagining on the flight. People were smoking cigarettes, talking and laughing under striped canopies after midnight. David came to a halt.

'I think this is us,' he said, looking up at the imposing façade of an aged, stone building. He put down the luggage, sliding his hand around her waist and giving her a quick kiss, before reaching behind an ivy-strewn trellis, where keys had been left. He led the way up several flights of stairs and found their apartment number, opening the door to reveal the tiniest space, perfect for two. Erika walked across the darkened room, opening the glass doors to a balcony. Accents and traffic rose around her. Clear, bright stars shone above. David's kisses were at once innocent and unnerving, sending shivers across her skin like the shimmering lights a moment before.

'I'll never hurt you again,' he whispered. 'I will never, ever, hurt you again.'

Erika, alert to his words, fought to subdue the fear of that unknown place where loving David would finally lead her. And now, here she was. She thought of her Sat Nav telling her *You have reached your destination* as David clattered one hand around the cutlery draw. Before long, he'd be ordering orthopaedic tin openers and shoehorns from those catalogues they kept receiving. In some ways, David was very consistent at being David, but Erika didn't feel very consistent about being his wife anymore.

'Matt texted this morning,' said Erika. 'He's going to give me a call later.'

'I should think so,' David said, futzing around in an overhead cupboard and setting down his old soup bowl. It was beige and chipped at the top, with "Yum Yum!" written on the side in green bubble letters. She'd tried to throw it out countless times — to recycle it, the way he liked, but his standard retort was that they couldn't afford to be frivolous, not at their age.

Erika grabbed her packed lunch, the food staple of small children and horribly sensible adults, from the fridge. She and Matt texted each other pretty much every day and caught up properly with a call every week or so, but David couldn't help himself nowadays: he seemed compelled to issue some kind of reprimand with every other comment.

Erika rinsed her cup as David had a brief tussle with a built-in rack. 'Root vegetables live on the third, not the second shelf,' he said, wrestling with a bag of potatoes. 'I know you think I'm being petty, Erika, but this is how we end up throwing away good food.'

He uncrumpled a receipt from behind the pepper mill, sunlight falling on his newly dyed hair, tufts sticking out at geometric angles. An unnatural shade of dark brown, like something a child might have coloured in with felt-tip.

His latest domestic system concerned reorganising kitchen storage and price-checking grocery items. She watched as he ran his eyes down the receipt, angling his reading glasses with the same anticipation most people reserved for lottery tickets. David had become almost religious about not spending money on anything he didn't consider a bare essential, and was eager to keep her updated on household outgoings. Shower cream was out in favour of soap, which lasted longer and didn't have environmentally detrimental packaging. Dessert was pretty much consigned to birthdays and Christmas, and not something his cholesterol levels would thank her for, anyway. She'd splurged on a trio of luxury ice creams the weekend before, hiding them at the back of the freezer in case he thought he'd forgotten their anniversary.

'And, for the last time,' he said, casting aside the receipt to pull on rubber gloves and retrieve debris from the peddle bin, 'could you please remember to put eggshells in the compost?'

'Are you actually going through the bin, now?'

'Yes.' He let the lid fall shut for dramatic effect. 'Because I knew you wouldn't bother to remember. It's not that difficult—'

'— Erika. I know.' She pulled on her coat, picked up her bag and made her way into the hall, where she took out her keys and retrieved her lipstick, hastily applying it in the mirror. '*I know*,' she called. '*Nothing's to be wasted, not even the waste.*'

She wiggled her hips, trying to loosen herself up. She was getting those aches again. Google said it might be early onset osteoporosis, but Erika knew exactly what was causing it: boredom. She was bored to the bone. She glanced upstairs, zipping her bag. There was nothing to do, not a thing out of place, not with Matt gone. The entire house was polished and gleaming, vacuumed to showroom-levels. She longed to spy a rogue cobweb, just for the endorphin rush.

'*Erika?*'

'Yes?'

The truth was, as David had explained several times, recycling was an entirely necessary obligation, contributing to the greater global good. But her dissatisfaction had nothing to do with the recycling. It was about David. Erika was beginning to wonder if it was worth recycling yet another year with her husband.

'Before you go,' he said, wandering towards her, eggshells resting in one rubber-gloved hand. 'Happy birthday.'

CHAPTER FIVE

'Happy birthday!' Richard sang, a jaunty cardboard crown covering his eyebrows. He was inflating a party blower as she found him downstairs in the studio. 'Surprised?'

A takeout coffee, a bouquet of flowers and a birthday card sat on the production desk.

'I am, actually,' Erika said. 'Especially since I forgot to remind you.'

'That's what I'm here for,' Ursula said, as Erika leaned in, hugging her.

'Happy birthday.' Gareth pulled his headphones around his neck, digging into his usual bag of Space Invaders for breakfast. 'I got you the coffee. Two-for-one on a Wednesday.'

'Thanks, Gareth.'

'And we're all going to lunch today. My treat,' Richard said, nodding towards the flowers. 'Look, I got your favourites. See? I do listen.'

'This is so nice, guys. I hope you remember my birthday more often.'

'There are Hobnobs here, too,' Gareth said, offering her the packet.

'Thanks.' She took a biscuit and picked up the long-stemmed roses, admiring the scent. 'They're lovely.'

'It's the least we could do after you bloody *wowed* William yesterday.'

'Please don't say wowed, Richard…'

He stretched his arms along the back of the couch as if surrounded by a bevy of invisible Playboy bunnies. She'd had to put up with his insufferable gloating since the minute

William Torrence had left. Realistically, they'd come up with a steady concept for Stable Denim. Unrealistically, Richard seemed to think they'd hit the big time. And yes, that was how he put it.

William Torrence had been swayed by Erika's logic, admitting he hadn't bought so much as a new pair of socks without his wife's involvement for the last couple of decades. They'd need to make a few changes and that could take a bit of time, he said, but time was exactly what Lingua Franca needed. They were looking to cast a forty-something man who encompassed everything the Dad Jean wearer wanted to be.

'We've pulled in a few names, who will be arriving shortly,' Richard said. He hadn't looked this smug since he'd backed the winner at last year's Grand National. 'Gareth's playing around with some potential soundtracks, and Stable sent over the branding package for Ursula to work on some visuals. I'm thinking that we rent some space, go big, and pitch OOH.'

'What's OOH?' Gareth asked.

'Out-of-home,' Richard said, his hands clasped behind his head. 'Y'know, big screens, big launch. We just need our guy.'

'Richard, I hate to tell you, but this Stable Denim Guy idea?' Erika shared a cautionary look with Gareth. 'William's expecting us to cast some bloke who rocks up, causes a frenzy, and shames men into incinerating their jeans. Meanwhile, women have to find him attractive, while the blokes find him cool enough not to boycott the brand. This isn't what we do, Richard. We're not Models One.'

'Well, if we do get stuck,' Richard said, trying to keep it casual, 'William did say how much he liked my voice on the demo.'

'You really think you're the guy we're looking for?'

'I didn't say that,' he said. 'We'll find him. I've been through the books —'

'You've been through our books? Because I can tell you right now, the guy we're looking for isn't on our radar. Trust me, I'd remember,' Erika said. 'I mean, we've got older names, but I can't think of anyone who's going to sound right and turn heads in a pair of Stable Demin jeans, can you?'

'Well, excuse me for not having Chris Hemsworth on speed dial.'

'We couldn't afford Chris Hemsworth. And how are we supposed to deliver an iconic campaign from a selection of people who haven't been in front of a camera for the last century?'

'The guy I put forward wasn't bad,' Ursula said. 'Quite hot, actually. He's in at eleven-thirty.'

'See?' Richard assured her. 'And if we don't score the right guy today, we'll hire a model. Dub him over if we have to.'

'We're not dubbing over anyone. That's the whole point,' Erika said. 'He has to be real. That's what William wants, and it's what he's expecting, after you told him we can deliver someone credible with a non-existent budget at very short notice.'

'I told him that's what we'd do, because if we don't, we'll just end up charging for some piddling concepts.' Richard stood, smoothing his shirt. 'We're better than that. This place is running on audiobooks and those fucking divorce lawyer ads I'm sick of hearing.'

'Chill out, Richard,' Ursula said. 'You're not married anymore.'

'Yes, which is why I'm trying to shit out something big enough to pay off my car loan, while I'm still shelling out for my last wedding.'

'The wedding that means you won't even consider marrying anyone else,' Ursula said, picking up her mug and heading to the door.

'Ursula,' Richard said, 'if we get Stable, you can have three weddings.'

'Wow,' Erika said, sipping her drink. 'Was that a proposal?'

'Just not to me!' he shouted after her.

They settled into the production suite, the three of them forming a row behind the soundproof studio window as potential candidates for the role of the Stable Denim Guy took to the mic.

'Dad Jeans! There's a dark horse in town,' said Howard, who usually voiced ads for Balls Up Bingo. 'Calling all medium-rise guys! Remember those days in your favourite blue jeans? A straight-talking —' he pointed to the left, some weird attempt at *Saturday Night Fever* — 'slim fit, button-fly.' He tilted his crotch slightly, revealing a couple of safety pins holding his jeans together across an opulent belly. 'We're older. We're wiser.' He delivered this as a chant. 'Dis-ting-u-ished denim with added stretch *aaa-nnd lift*! Designed to *last*,' he went on, hooking his thumbs into his waistband. 'Go along for the *riiide*… Stable Den-im. Get back in the *sad-dle*.'

'That was great, Howard, thanks!' Gareth said, obviously as keen as they were to end this misery. Erika and Richard sat grinning in an increasing state of barely subdued panic.

'Are you sure, mate?' Howard hovered in the booth. 'I can do it again, with maybe a bit of a sexier voice this time?' He searched their faces. 'I'm getting into it now.'

'No, no, that was great, Howard. Thanks,' Erika said, buttoning-in to the sound booth as Howard took off his headphones. 'What the hell have you told people?' she asked Richard.

'You know what I told them,' Richard said. 'Maybe wear some jeans, get into the role.'

'Richard, we want sexy and natural. We're not auditioning for *The Full Monty*. Over forty is what we're after. Age, not waist size. Sorry.' Erika shot a look at Gareth, chomping his way through a Snickers. 'But I'm thinking of the client.'

'The right guy's got time to shape up if we find him.'

'Time to shape up? How long? Imagine William's face if he could see this lot! We need to cast this professionally, Richard, with the right candidates. There's no point trying to save a few quid by cutting corners. We'll still get paid for our part, but we need a guy who can model jeans, which means at least being able to fit into a pair.'

'Yes, I know,' Richard said, admitting defeat. 'I knew this was a longshot, but we start with our own talent. Imagine the uproar if this thing with Stable Denim goes as big as we think? I'd never hear the end of it.' He glanced at the clock. 'Only two more to go. We'll head out to lunch after that, and if no one fits the bill —'

'If no one fits the bill,' Erika said, 'we'll work with a casting agency to put together a pitch starring someone who absolutely does fit the bill.'

They sat in silence, with Richard sulking and Erika wishing she'd intervened earlier, as the next candidate appeared.

'Good to see you, Tommy,' Richard said, as Tommy Merchant, a sixty-something, former stand-up comic, moseyed in. He stood behind the mic with an inane grin, waiting for their hilarious reaction to his costume of a Stetson, leather waistcoat and water pistol.

'Ready when you are, Tommy,' Gareth said, before counting him down.

Erika pinned a look of polite amusement on her face as the studio atmosphere grew thick with desperation.

'Dad Jeans?' Tommy said, pushing his glasses up his nose. 'Bit like mum jeans, but never any cash in the pockets, is there?' He put one hand on his hip. 'No cash.' He searched his pockets. 'Spend it all, don't they? Kids.' The three of them made all the right moves, offering agreeable nods from behind the glass. 'Bit of observational comedy for you there, but anyhow, here it goes: Dad Jeans? There's a dark horse in town.' He directed his routine at Gareth. 'Have I told you the one about the horse who walks into a pub? This horse walks into a pub…'

By the time Tommy had ended his cabaret stint with a bawdy joke about a milkman getting saddle sore, Erika never wanted to hear the script again.

'Right, bit of a long shot next,' Richard said, checking his email.

Erika gave a snort. She hated to think exactly how long a shot this was going to be if Howard and Tommy were in the running.

'This one came through Ursula, G-man,' Richard said, fist-bumping Gareth's shoulder. 'He's about the right age. You said he'd done some commercial stuff before?'

'A few years back, it says,' Gareth said. 'I've never worked with him, though.'

Erika was already trawling commercial agencies for good-looking guys over forty, wondering if this was how Tinder worked. They only had a couple of weeks to pitch back to William. She wasn't prepared to embarrass herself or be accused of wasting his time. As the studio door opened, Erika put on her headphones and stared intently through the glass.

This guy was a definite improvement. He was over six feet, with long, denim-clad legs. A reassuringly slack amount of denim hinted at a compact butt. He wore a crisp, white shirt and his shoulders were slightly too large for his body, almost like armour, she thought. She found his face and recognition hit. The new addition of a salt and pepper beard made her doubt it was him at first. But as they locked eyes, she felt his recognition.

'Bloody hell,' Richard muttered, folding his arms as he took in Erika's reaction. 'You okay there?' He turned to Gareth. 'Our Erika's gone bright red. Let's hope the guy can read, hey?'

'Erika?' said Enzo Morelli. His eyes were beaming blue, his expression all the more intriguing with that still-boyish smile. 'Is it really you?'

'It is me,' she said, pulling herself together as she buzzed in, taking in every detail, as if any momentary lapse and Enzo might slip back into the recesses. 'Is that really you?'

'Something you want to tell us?' Richard asked, enjoying every moment.

'No.' She held Richard's gaze. 'Can we get on, please? Concentrate on the read?'

Richard buzzed into the booth. 'You two, do you know each other?'

'From way back,' Enzo said.

'Very well, by the looks of it…' Richard said, releasing the mic.

'*Fuck off*, Richard…' Erika hissed.

'Says here that you've done a bit of commercial stuff before. Him & Hair,' Richard said. 'There's a blast from the past. I used to swear by the Handsome Head Sculpt-it Stick.'

'Yeah, well,' Enzo said, running his hand along his shaven head. 'Didn't we all?'

'So, Enzo,' Erika said, buzzing back in. 'Whenever you're ready...' She rested her chin on her hands, trying to concentrate.

'Ready when you are, my friend.' Gareth gave the nod.

Enzo smoothed out the script, cleared his throat, and stooped slightly to reach the mic: '*Dad jeans...* Sorry...' He adjusted the mic so that it matched his height and cleared his throat again.

Erika grew tense, not only on his behalf, but on behalf of the whole campaign. Her Stable Denim script felt so dumb, with him about to deliver the lines. Enzo Morelli was reading her homework.

'*Dad jeans, there's a dark horse in town. Calling all medium-rise guys... Remember those days, in your favourite blue jeans? That straight-talking, slim fit, button-fly...*'

Erika pictured Enzo back when he was about fifteen, calling at their house for her brother. He was always in blue jeans and a long-sleeved top, usually white, pulled down over his knuckles. She was thirteen and left him stranded on the doorstep, busy watching *Beverly Hills 90210*, engrossed in Jason Priestley. All the boys she loved were cut out from magazines then, and the worst you got was a papercut.

'*We're older, wiser. Denim designed to go along for the ride. Stable Denim. We're back in the saddle.*'

'Nice one.' Gareth nodded, giving his first genuine smile of the day.

'Yeah, didn't want to interrupt your flow there, mate,' Richard said, eyes on the script, using the blokey voice he affected, 'but I think you may've skipped a few lines —'

'Yeah, I did. I know,' Enzo said. 'I read it, and I thought, do blokes really talk about stretch fabric? If that was me, I don't know, I'd find that a bit —'

'Yes, I agree,' Erika butted in. 'He's right.' She turned to Richard, still assessing the script. 'It's better.'

It was better because his was the voice, the pitch-perfect tone she'd been trying to capture. The Stable Denim Guy. Enzo had nailed it, and though part of her didn't want it to be the case, Lingua Franca had their contender.

CHAPTER SIX

Less than an hour later, Richard invited Enzo along to Erika's birthday lunch. Despite the fact they worked together, away from their usual setting, Erika found something slightly unnatural about socialising with the gang from work. As their number increased from a party of four to five diners, Enzo edged his seat closer to hers. Her knee occasionally jerking back when it made contact with his, as if avoiding a hot surface.

'So, Enzo,' Richard said with a clap, as if he'd be awarding prizes for the best answer, 'how do you know our Erika, then?'

'Mind your own business,' Ursula said, giving Erika a wink as she spooned smashed avocado onto her ciabatta.

Sitting there in the local Italian, Erika remembered how she'd become besotted with Enzo Morelli. Her secret crush, who took thoughts from her head, words from her lips, with one sullen look. The trivia she'd stored included the fact that his family were Italian. Blue jeans, electric blue eyes and thick, dark hair, closely shaved at the back. The nape of his neck used to render her speechless. The crush had hit like a force of nature that summer. Enzo had taught her about love, sex, and breaking up, an unavoidable earthquake, not once, but repeatedly.

'I've known Erika since school,' Enzo said, as she tried to look preoccupied with her chargrilled salad. 'I was best mates with her brother, Josh.'

It had started on election night: May 1997. The three of them, Erika, Josh and Enzo were planning to stay up as votes cast were finally counted. Erika had been monitoring coverage the same way she usually listened to the charts, because for the first time, politics felt like theirs. Brit Pop. They were it. The election played out like some kind of festival; an unmissable, political Woodstock. They pitched their tent accordingly, making a hub in the lounge, an intense trio of amateur analysts. Their generation was going to change things, shoulder-to-shoulder, with their favourite bands providing the soundtrack.

Initially, Erika and Enzo sat at either end of the couch, with Josh on the floor, resting against the settee. Enzo and Josh, both eighteen, were drinking Budweiser. Erika, sixteen, was drinking contraband Bacardi Breezer. Following a series of promising yawns, she was thrilled to watch her brother admit defeat. Josh launched a sleeping bag at Enzo's head and left the two of them alone.

Enzo had moved to the floor, eating the last of the crisps, eager to witness the potential redesign of the country. Erika dreaded him saying he needed to get some sleep after he commented how tired he was, but she felt fate was on her side as he took her up on the offer of coffee.

'What are you doing for your A-levels?' Enzo asked once she'd handed him his mug.

'English Literature. Classics. Media Studies. Suitably vague…' Erika shrugged, trying to sound compellingly nonchalant.

'I wish I'd taken English,' Enzo said, as she felt the thrill of validation. 'I almost did. I have no idea what I was thinking, signing up for a Film Studies degree. Doubt I'll even last it out.'

'You will,' she said, trying not to wince at the bitterness of her first ever coffee. 'Film Studies is cool. It's not just the films, is it? It's the context — the history and politics. It's about representation, as well, isn't it?'

Enzo nodded, hopefully impressed. 'Josh said you want to study in London, too?'

'Maybe,' she said, avoiding her usual raptures at the thought of living as an independent young woman in the capital. 'That's my first choice, if I get the grades.'

'Of course you will. You're the whole package.'

She didn't reply, but blushed, tummy-first, aware of some silent conversation taking place between them, as she tucked up her legs on the couch. 'I think you'll end up a famous director, or an actor, or something.'

'An actor?'

'Yeah, you're good-looking enough,' she said. The courage it took to say it almost gave her a head rush. 'But maybe you'll be a director, or a writer — a *screenwriter*, I mean, because you're onto things, aren't you? When we watch stuff, you get what things mean, what they're trying to say.' She knew how clumsy she sounded. 'You're going to do something good. Better than good.'

'Better than good?' He smiled into his cup.

'Yes,' she said, smiling back.

Erika sat watching the rest of the election, imagining meeting Enzo on a rainy afternoon in London, sheltering beneath a shared umbrella. They'd watch a European movie, probably something he'd studied, and halfway through that fantasy afternoon, Enzo would whisper: "Let's go to bed." Right there, in the middle of the day. He'd been at their house a lot, but that summer something had shifted into urgency when he was around. They both laughed at the same bits from the shows they watched with her brother. They both loved independent movies and music. A huge indication of compatibility, Erika had thought at the time, but as conversation flowed that night, the urgency slowed. She was happily resigned to a warmer level of friendship, feeling she'd made a respectable impression, until he tilted his head and his lips met hers.

The future of Britain could wait. Despite imagining his kiss so many times, the change in altitude to her sixteen-year-old gravity, she couldn't possibly have predicted. They lowered the volume on the TV to avoid interruption. Then they locked eyes as she unbuttoned her shirt, proud to reveal her new Wonderbra, not the usual prim-looking numbers her mum picked up. He forgot to unbutton the cuffs of his shirt and knelt up, attempting to remove the check flannel, arms locked behind his back as if under arrest.

'I think I saw David Blaine do this once,' she said, as he struggled. 'Want me to time you?'

'That would be brilliant, yeah,' he finally freed himself, lay next to her on the carpet, kissing, as his hips moved against her. She grumbled slightly at the grind of his belt buckle, and as Enzo took it off, she wondered if that meant doing more, but he didn't try pushing things any further. She appreciated this all the more after she made it to university and discovered how horribly entitled some boys could be, as if taking something back which belonged to them.

Erika and Enzo remained semi-clothed but were undone that night, both aware, she later thought, of her inexperience and of her brother's potential reaction. She convinced herself that if Josh knew how she felt about Enzo, he'd understand. She also knew this was exactly the kind of stuff that could bust up a friendship. He slumped slightly as she sighed against his neck and her hand found its way beneath his T-shirt. The baby-fuzz of dark hair leading from his navel was the best thing she'd ever seen. The way he seemed to sense how she felt about things. Studying each other, gauging reactions, she realised, it was that quality which captivated her more than anything. They were wordless, breathless, as he kept his eyes on her. Her reactions almost involuntary. Tiny shocks stung like bitter kisses as he touched her, laying on the couch, clothes half-removed, legs entwined, as if washed up like castaways.

Time passed and they heard the creak of a floorboard above. They exchanged glances and buttoned back up. Enzo put his hand around her waist as she went to leave the room. One last kiss. She felt him hard against her again and gave a victorious smile as he jokingly looked wounded, pulling her back towards him.

'I'm glad,' he whispered, and she left him with a peck on the lips.

Back in the present, chairs scraped against the floor, snapping Erika out of her reverie. Someone noticed the time, and Richard signalled the waiter. After bringing up football, imported beers and German car manufacturing, topics he leaned on when trying to determine the social tribes of other men, Richard insisted Erika take an extended lunch to catch up with her friend.

'We've got this,' he said, handing over his card as Enzo offered his. No wedding ring, Erika couldn't help but notice. 'Nice to meet you, man. We'll be in touch, as they say.'

'Sure,' Enzo said. 'Good to meet you.'

'See you again,' Ursula said, steering Richard to the door.

'See you around,' Gareth added, already engrossed in his phone. 'I'll send you the take.'

'Erika Karter.' Enzo brushed one hand over the top of his head. She couldn't have pictured him without his dark, wavy hair, but if anything, that face of his was all the more distinctive. 'This never happens,' he went on, leaning his elbow on the table, scrunching up his napkin, letting it drop straight from his hand to the plate. 'I haven't been inside a studio for years, not since I did Him & Hair.'

'Him & Hair,' she said, with a half-laugh, remembering how cool that brand had been at the time. 'That was about twenty years ago?'

'Don't I know it,' he said. 'Couldn't do much for them, now.' He ran his hand along his head again, perhaps self-conscious.

Erika wondered what changes he noticed in her. She'd needed her glasses to look at the menu, and wished she'd put in her contacts that morning.

'You've changed your hair.' Enzo broke into a slight smile, studying her. She cut a quick pose, holding her glass.

'And look at you,' she said. 'All grown up with a beard.'

'All grown up with a grey beard,' he said, running his fingers along his chin.

She glanced at the finer details of his hands, the half-moon cuticles, for a few seconds. 'So,' she went on, 'are you still a photographer, moonlighting as a pin-up?'

'I think we can both see,' he said, looking at the table with an almost-smile, 'that I'm no pin-up. I'm not much of a photographer these days, either.' He slouched forward, arms folded on the table, toying with the salt.

'You're running your own business now?'

'I co-own the place with my brother.' He sipped his espresso. 'Dad died. Mum went back to Italy, where she runs my grandparents' restaurant.'

'Sorry about your dad,' said Erika, then she remembered something. 'Ah, not just Italy, but Nerano — birthplace of the sirens! You told me all about the mythology.'

'Did I?' He looked nostalgic. 'I was trying to impress you, no doubt.'

'I think you're going to get hired for this campaign.'

'Do you? Richard likes to talk a lot of talk…'

'Oh, he does, but I think he's right,' she said. 'Are you really up for doing this?'

'Why not? It's a good gig for an old bloke like me,' he smirked. 'But yeah, I think so, and if nothing comes of it, at least I got to see you.'

'Yes,' she agreed, not entirely sure how she felt. 'It was lovely to see you, Enzo.'

As they made their way outside, Erika became flustered all over again.

'Why are you offering me your hand?'

Keeping you at arm's length, she thought.

Enzo leant forward. 'Happy birthday,' he gave her a quick kiss on the cheek. 'And hopefully, I might get that call,' he said, without much conviction.

CHAPTER SEVEN

Erika could hear David on the phone, hiding out in the garage, as usual. His tone was intermittently discordant and celebratory. Now she was home, she swapped jeans for joggers and her blouse for a sweatshirt. She fixed her hair with a band, poured herself a gin and added fresh lime, going wild on the ice cubes, treating herself for her birthday. *Enzo Morelli.* She was still reeling slightly at the way he'd appeared in the studio. She hadn't thought about him for a while, no contact for almost two decades. Then he'd casually walked in as if he'd forgotten his coat on the way out of her life. How did that happen? The whole thing knocked her off-kilter.

But it wasn't the first time he'd reappeared like that. When they'd still been in their early twenties, they'd crossed paths in almost the same way. He'd shown up at her workplace, fronting that haircare range. She'd been writing magazine features back then and had been sent to interview the face of Him & Hair. He was working as an assistant photographer at the time, wanted to eventually run his own studio. He never enjoyed the modelling bit and hadn't done anything since, not as far as she knew. Now, twenty-odd years later, he was putting himself back out there. The whole thing seemed strange. She wondered if Enzo was as fazed by seeing her … but maybe men didn't think that way.

'*Erika?*'

She almost splashed gin against her chin as David called, and she heard the familiar swipe of Crocs.

'Sorry,' he said, dressed in style-defying, three-quarter length combat shorts with his socks pulled up, looking like an overgrown boy scout. 'It's been non-stop — I've been stuck in meetings all day. I take it you've seen the reviews?'

'Some,' she said, keeping it noncommittal, although the truth was she'd spent the afternoon wincing at comments as she hopped from site to site. *Code Name: They* had incited a mixture of lukewarm reviews and bewildered commentary. 'They're only initial responses, don't forget. Those people are paid to critique; they're not real readers...'

'That's what Monica keeps telling me,' he said, handing her a card. 'Sorry about your birthday. I've not had a minute's chance to —'

'David, honestly, it's fine,' she said, noticing that the envelope was barely glued. The card had most probably been written moments ago. 'It's my fault for being born on the same day you released your new novel.'

'I know it's a practical gift for a birthday,' he said, at least having the decency to look slightly embarrassed as she studied the enclosed voucher. 'But I know how much you hate cleaning the car, and I've not had chance to shop around, so...'

'It's very thoughtful,' she said, thanking her husband for the car valet he had been given by his brother last Christmas.

Later that evening, she answered her mum's standard questions about work, although she wasn't entirely sure her mum knew what she did for a living. At a family wedding a few years before, a clutch of relatives had intermittently enquired about her job as a speech writer, some kind of television producer, and the new voice of Hovis. Lynda, her mum, had been PA to a firm of accountants, and was more than happy to let them think her daughter was doing something that sounded far more glamorous.

'Doing something nice with David?' Lynda asked.

'His new book came out today, so we've nothing planned,' Erika said, trying to sound bright. 'He's been so busy.'

'You've got to make the effort, love,' her mum said. 'It's your birthday.'

Make the effort, Erika thought. They should include that in your wedding vows. *I promise to love, respect, and make the effort.*

'I'm not too bothered,' she said. 'It's not a big one or anything.'

'All birthdays are special, Erika. It's a gift, getting older,' said Lynda. 'It's your brother's birthday next month, don't forget. And Ewan's, two days after Josh.'

'I know,' Erika said. 'I don't forget. I'm good with birthdays.'

'Ewan sends his love. He's in the middle of a merger. That man never fully retired.'

Her mum was seventy-one now. She'd met Ewan when Erika was taking her GCSEs and Josh was starting his A-levels. She and her brother were both surprised by the emergence of a boyfriend. It had only been the three of them after their mum and dad had split up. Erika was four and Josh was six when it happened, and she could barely remember it. Their dad had drifted in and out of their lives for a year or so, until, like the Easter Bunny or Santa Claus, appearances became reserved for special occasions. He eventually went to live in Australia and made some noise about having them visit at first, but they were both so young and the journey so long. Then he met Betsy, his wife, and it seemed easier to let things slide. Josh kept in contact with him, but Erika was too distracted by their mum, alerting them to the penance that came with being a woman, becoming a single parent. Men were free to leave responsibilities behind, was the basic translation of her disaffection. There'd been one guy, very briefly, before Ewan.

Erika couldn't remember his name, only their grandma babysitting and letting them stay up way past their bedtime. She'd been close to Grandma Karter, and from what little she'd said about her son, Erika never felt she was missing too much from her dad. Thanks to his absence, Erika couldn't wait to grow up and felt tremendous guilt as a child for needing any kind of parenting at all. Josh, she could see, was trying to become the sensible, dependable man of the family, making up for the fact that their father was neither of those things.

'How's that grandson of mine?' Lynda asked.

'Matt's giving me a call tonight.'

'Well, tell him he owes me a call, too.'

'We'll come and see you, or you can come here,' Erika said, 'whichever's easier once he gets back. Only a couple of weeks now.'

'I'll look forward to it. Maybe you'll do something nice for your birthday, you and David, over the weekend?'

'Mum,' she said, slightly hesitant, 'do you like David?'

'Do I like David?' Lynda said, bemused. 'It's a bit late, asking me this now, isn't it? What difference does it make if I like David? Do *you* like David?'

'Yes, of course I like him. I just —'

'Life's not like *The Notebook*, Erika. That's why they make films like *The Notebook*,' Lynda said, with a cautionary tone. 'We're only human; none of us is perfect. Anyway, happy birthday. I'll let you get on, and remind Matthew about that call, won't you?'

'Will do,' Erika said, wondering why she'd tried to initiate a deep and meaningful conversation with her mother, when they didn't have a deep and meaningful relationship.

'And, yes, Erika. I do like David. Not many women can say they're married to an author.'

'Happy birthday, doll!' Matt appeared onscreen, making her day. 'I'm toasting you with a Frappuccino!' He raised his reusable cup to show her the slogan: *Hot Boy, Hot Coffee.* 'Cute, aren't I?'

'Very,' Erika said.

'Not that you're biased,' he said. 'Can you see this tan? I'm hoping the sheen on these cheekbones isn't causing too much screen glare.' Erika laughed as he swept his hands across his face. 'You'll be proud to know that this cup is one of the babies from my new online side hustle.' He lifted a succession of designs into view: *'Nice Tight, Flat White.'* He wriggled his eyebrows. *'Americanos Do It Better.'* Erika laughed. *'Caffè Latte Gets Me Off. Kiss My Cappuccino. Macchiato Makes Me Hard. Sip, Slurp, Suck.'*

'Are people actually going to use those in public?'

'People do worse things in public, Mum,' he said. 'And twenty per cent of all orders goes to the Terrence Higgins Trust.'

'I love you.'

'I love you too. Now,' he said. 'Open your presents!'

Erika had been under strict instructions not to delve into the parcel that had arrived a few days before until their birthday call. 'Oh God,' she said, noticing the logo on top of the box: *Drink Up Coffee Cups.* 'Is this one of your designs?' she asked, unwrapping the cup. It was covered in lip-blot patterns, with a '50s-style illustration of a woman giving a theatrical wink. The slogan read: *MILF. No Sugar.*

'Matt! You can't give this to me. I'm your mother!'

'Facts is facts,' he said. 'All the boys love my momma. You're spectacular, remember?'

'Ah, yes, I'm spectacular. I knew I'd forgotten something,' she said, making him smile. 'You're unhinged, you do know that?'

'Bad genes,' he said, as Erika made a mental note to look into the possibility of launching a younger range with Stable Denim.

'This is so nice,' she said, holding up an olive-green sweatshirt. 'So soft.' She was about to try it on when she noticed the small, cursive letters on the left-hand side of the chest, subtly sewn in the same shade: *One Beautiful Bitch*. 'What is it with you and these logos?'

'It's a cool brand! And it's cute. And you're smiling already, so let's get it on!'

She went offscreen, swapping tops and checking herself out in the mirror. 'I love it!' she said, snuggling against the warm fabric. 'I look so trendy.'

'Don't say trendy, Mum,' he replied, as if issuing a health warning. 'Say, hot. You look *hot*.'

Erika pulled a face as she was overcome by a sudden rush of emotion.

'Oh my God!' Matt covered his mouth. 'Are you crying? You're crying! See why you're adorable? Promise me you're going to use that cup, loud and proud.' He blew a kiss.

'I promise.'

'And you're one beautiful bitch, so you're entitled to wear a sweatshirt that says so, okay?'

'I will. I love it,' she said, relieved that the logo was discreet. 'Thank you, Matty. You've made my day.'

And every other day, she thought, watching her son.

'So, where are we going? Why aren't you all zhushed up with a blow-dry?' he asked. 'I thought I'd be able to smell the Lancôme from here.'

'Dad's busy,' she said, pulling the face they shared when David was being high maintenance. 'Publication day.'

'Oh shit, yeah,' Matt said. 'Totally forgot.'

'You'd better send him a text.'

'Might send him a mug.'

'Please don't,' she said, as they both sniggered.

'Put him on?'

'You've got no chance. He's been on calls since I got home. It's all systems go.'

'Oh well, good for him,' Matt said, and she didn't have the heart to contradict him.

She and Matt were well aware of David's eccentricities when it came to his work. There was David, and then there was David when he was writing. Constantly distracted, his mind performing laps, running up against so many deadlines, you could practically hear him ticking. When they'd first got together, she'd been the first one to read his work, suggesting revisions and listening to his frustrations. She loved storytelling; it was something she'd grown up with, thanks to her brother. Josh collected graphic novels and illustrated his own imaginary worlds. Erika had edited and bound the pages, unaware that she was in training for her writing career. She and David had used to talk about work for hours, but these days he found her advertising role rather juvenile, a tiny bit beneath him. "You'd be better paid in a shop if they've got you *selling jeans*," he'd said, as she sat at the dining table, preparing notes for the Stable Denim pitch.

The more insecure he was about his novels, the more pretentious he became as his alter-ego, The Novelist. Take Matt out of the equation, and Erika wondered if either of them really knew who they were to each other anymore. Recently, it was as if they were both being played by actors in some low-budget TV reconstruction. David Forde was petty, distant and irritable. The role of Mrs Erika Forde was played by a much older actress who'd forgotten her lines. She remembered how uncomfortable she'd felt at his stuffy dinner, dressed like Joan Collins in that too-tight dress. She'd embarrassed herself by going along with it. It was the same with the house. They lived in rural Silverage, a place she still loved, but how much say had she ever had in her own home? David had insisted on keeping his family's antique furniture, and there were framed pictures of his book jackets leading upstairs. His literary awards were also on display, as if they were living in his personal museum. The more Erika thought about it, the more it seemed as if she and Matt simply slotted into David's existence. But surely that was what family was — the messiness of personalities underpinned by acceptance, if not by understanding.

She wondered if he'd been as aloof with his first wife. His first marriage wasn't something she thought about anymore. David and Anya had both been young and had barely lasted three years. Erika was young enough, after she and David married, to see herself as some kind of winner. The True Love. The One. He never went into too much detail about the split, nothing beyond the standard sentiment about them not being the right fit. So, after twenty years together, were Erika and David the right fit? There were times when they'd popped the odd button, but nowadays there was a straining at the seams of their life together as Mr and Mrs Forde.

After Erika asked about arrangements for Matt's journey home, he told her he had great news. He'd applied for a few things and had had an unexpected response from a promotions company offering paid work during the summer break.

'That's brilliant. Well done,' Erika said, artificially buoyant as the runner-up in the contest between ten weeks with your parents, or spending the summer with friends. It was a ridiculous response, but the thought cast a long shadow. Matt wasn't coming home, and although they skirted the issue, he wouldn't be home until his next break.

'Shall we watch a movie?' Erika called from the kitchen, loading the dishwasher.

No response. She dried her hands. There was no sign of David in the lounge, where he'd been on his phone a few moments before, annoyingly delighted by Matt's news about the work placement. She went to draw the curtains and paused to wave at the guy from next door, walking past with his dog. They hadn't exactly gone out of their way to make conversation since David had demanded they cut down the laurel tree on their side of the garden, since the branches were encroaching over the fence. Erika had been mortified as David ignored her advice, spluttering orders on their doorstep in some T-shirt from his student days. A few days later, Matt had ushered her into his room as the bloke caught David hacking away at the tree under cover of night. She remembered what he'd said as David droned on about plumblines: 'You've obviously put a lot of thought into this.' Needless to say, David learned to live with the tree.

Thelma and Louise was on TV. Erika hadn't seen that movie in years, but her timing was perfect as Brad Pitt lay on a bed with Geena Davis. Erika loitered as he ran through his hold-up speech, brandishing the motel hairdryer and barely wearing his blue jeans. She thought about Enzo Morelli and Stable Denim as Brad seduced Geena, then finally noticed the time and wondered what her husband was still doing in the garage. Checking his secret texts, presumably?

'David?' she said, venturing out to the garage.

'Bloody hell, Erika!' He stood in front of their old wardrobe mirror. 'I'm flossing,' he said, pulling dental string between his teeth.

'Right,' she said. 'Well, there's a perfectly good bathroom upstairs you're more than welcome to use. We've got plumbing, fresh towels, a sink, everything you could possibly need.'

He pulled the floss from his mouth. 'Do we really need to discuss this now?'

'Not at all, David,' she smiled. 'Floss away!'

'Always have to be so sarcastic, don't you?' he said, arms slumped. It never failed to amaze her how easily she managed to antagonise him lately. 'That's exactly the kind of comment I'd expect from Matthew, and for your information, I come out here for a bit of space. Do you wonder why?'

'A bit of space? Standing around, brushing your teeth, pretending you live out here?'

'I'm not brushing, I'm flossing, Erika. And if you don't mind,' he said, eyes bulging with indignation, 'I'm perfectly entitled to stand in my own garage, enjoying my own space, flossing my own teeth, whenever I like!'

'Take all the time in the world,' Erika said, calm and compliant. 'I'll be having a choc ice with Brad Pitt.'

'Please, Erika, don't try and be intriguing…'

'Wouldn't dream of it, David…'

CHAPTER EIGHT

Erika went straight to the bathroom and sat on the side of the bath with tissue pressed against her eyes. She gave in and cried over being so selfish, trying to keep hold of her son, but maybe it wasn't just Matt she was missing. She cried a while longer because her mother was right, birthdays were special, but she was basically home alone with a shitty voucher she'd never use. She wasn't expecting anything extravagant, but her husband was spending her birthday flossing his teeth. What did that say about her?

She calmed herself. It wasn't exactly the first time David had disappointed her. And, let's face it, it wasn't the first time she'd suspected him of cheating. *Don't confront him now,* she told herself. Not on publication day.

She noticed her new sweater as she took off her makeup. *One Beautiful Bitch*, it read, when she felt more like One Ugly Cow. It wasn't Matt's responsibility to make her happy. He was about to complete his first year at the Liverpool Institute for Performing Arts; she should be used to him being gone by now. Things had improved since those first few months when she could barely eat, feeling full of undigested sadness. She reminded herself that Matt was having the kind of experience she'd dreamt of when she'd set off as a student.

Erika had expected student life to bring a non-stop carousel of flirtations, instant affinities with photogenic flatmates, and meaningful conversations with new loves by candlelight. Instead, her old English Literature teacher would've been proud to note that her initial experience had been an altogether more Dickensian affair. Her frugal means had made Erika doubt her choices, hating the enforced anonymity of being alone in the city. She'd spent most of her time circling words like *assonance* and drawing crude renditions of Heathcliff, while reading daunting tomes such as *Dante's Inferno* and being forced to dwell in the nine circles of hell: 9 a.m. lectures surely being one of them.

Another irrational thought, she regretted not having more children — a big old thing to admit once you were on the wrong side of forty, but it was something they'd tried unsuccessfully to make happen for a long time. At one point, almost optimistic over her recent hot flashes, Erika wondered if she might be pregnant? She stood in the Women's Health section of the chemist, sexual evolution mapped out by contraceptives stacked alongside homeopathic menopausal remedies, as if it was that simple. Erika was vaguely self-conscious, like a nun buying condoms as she picked out a pregnancy test, all digital displays now. You could probably check-in on your social accounts while you waited, post the result to your followers.

Joining the queue, Erika hid the test under a facecloth she didn't need, ashamed to be a woman her age needing a pregnancy test. The girl at the checkout looked about fourteen. She'd be labelled a geriatric mother, as if she'd committed a crime against nature. She couldn't recall much talk of geriatric fathers and there were plenty of those about. Erika imagined well-wishers assuming she was a proud grandparent, any fertilised ova considered medically prehistoric.

She'd been in denial when she'd first realised she was carrying Matt; having a baby was not remotely part of her plans. Her symptoms started during that trip to Paris, when she decided that whoever concocted the term "morning sickness" was either an optimist or slept a lot. Erika was travelsick, which had never happened before. She and David had to leave a couple of restaurants, as the aroma of food turned her stomach. She felt delicate and couldn't wear anything cinched around the waist. Thankfully, despite going out of his way to organise the trip, David wasn't put out. When she apologised for ruining the holiday, he reassured her it wasn't her fault. What neither of them wanted to discuss was the stress she'd been under during the weeks leading up to their official reunion in France. They posed for pictures around the Arc de Triomphe, along the River Seine, and at the Basilica of the Sacré-Coeur as if nothing had happened. But Erika sometimes caught herself remembering that, only a month before, she'd sworn they were over.

There had been an actress David was working with at the theatre, named Chloe. Erika had disliked the name ever since. When she commented on Chloe's odd behaviour, he assured her that that was just how Chloe was: wracked with nerves in between performances. Erika had never been the jealous type and was embarrassed by her reaction, but this feeling of distrust resulted in a series of petty arguments that avoided the real reason behind her irritability. Maybe that was how it felt, to be in love? Once the show came to the end of a six-week run, she regretted ever saying a word, settled with the thought that Chloe was gone, and she and David were doing great. If she wanted to be the kind of girlfriend he deserved, it was time to grow up. David was mature, thoughtful, and smart. A serious relationship required restraint from childish attacks of insecurity.

She broached the subject one last time, speaking openly. David insisted she was protecting herself after that last guy she'd told him about, Enzo — the one who'd messed her around. She needed to learn how to trust and allow herself to be happy.

Only a few nights later, David nipped out to pick up drinks, leaving Erika to warm up some snacks. She opened a few kitchen drawers in search of a tea towel, then noticed an envelope. There was a heart drawn around David's name, and she found a thank you card inside:

Darling David,
  Time wasn't on our side, but I won't forget a moment.
  Thank you for the hand-holding and encouragement.
  Chloe X

Erika slid the card back into the envelope, shutting the draw as if the secret hadn't already escaped. How old was this woman? Was she some kid writing fan mail? But that was David — courting attention, loving nothing more than being adored for his academic prowess and creative sensibilities.

As David let himself back in, unloading shopping, she barely said a word. They settled on the sofa, Erika casually asking if Chloe had a crush on him. Her mind was still open to the possibility that an actress could be prone to dramatic gestures, flights of fancy. If David had given a plausible reply, suggesting it was a possibility, Erika might have been able to push everything to the back of her mind, but instead, he was resolute. He said he barely knew the girl, but she had a boyfriend she talked about at every opportunity. While he was flattered by Erika thinking other women found him irresistible, he assured her that simply wasn't the case. He continued nibbling on tapas until she retrieved the card and read it aloud, as he grabbed for it. She ignored his attempts to turn the thing into her mistake, an innocent misunderstanding, and decided to draw a line under David Forde's name for good.

She ignored his calls and deleted his texts. Warned by one of her colleagues that he was waiting outside the office, she left through the parking bay. She threw herself into work and reorganised her flat. On receiving news from back home that Claire, her old friend, was marrying her childhood sweetheart, Erika decided it would be good to escape to Claire's hen do in Dublin. On her return, she found a letter addressed to her in David's writing. She read his words twice over, her suitcase abandoned in the hall.

Erika,

I write this letter with little hope of you reading my words, but to offer a sincere apology and explanation. It's the least I owe you.

Erika found herself as flattered by the intensity as she was irritated by the flourish.

Firstly, I assure you, nothing progressed further than flirtation. The thought of you, of us, would never allow anything further. Secondly, I lied to you. Anything I say will be difficult to believe, but please know I truly love you. I lied only from fear of losing you.

He sounded as if he was clutching a quill.

After my divorce, I swore I'd never get lost inside another relationship. Finding myself doing exactly that with you is the only pathetic excuse I have for hurting you. I understand your decision, how terrible this looks, but please consider this my final attempt to tell you that I have not betrayed you. I would give anything for the chance to regain your trust.

Erika didn't respond. She'd almost texted to say she'd read the letter but stopped herself. She was done with apologies, done with guys who needed to offer explanations.

Almost a fortnight later, she ducked into a café she'd never visited and noticed David at a table. She felt her resolve slip. The part of her that wanted to believe in him was instantly resuscitated. She decided their meeting was fate. The least she could do was talk to him, after bumping into him like that. He'd quit the theatre, he said. He was determined to finish his novel. Would she read his first few chapters? Glasses emptied, and almost an hour passed before he asked about the letter. The hurt on his face convinced her she must be wrong.

Less than a week later, David surprised her with that trip to Paris. By the second night, Erika was sitting on the bathroom floor, staring at two distinct pink lines. After taking several more tests, she faced up to the news. David was knocking at the door. She'd expected him to treat it like some kind of medical emergency at best, but instead, he'd been thrilled. In an instant, she and the baby became the most precious things in the world to him. They strolled the next day, Erika unaware he had a destination in mind. After a simple, very plain lunch of hard cheese baguettes, shared at the apartment for fear of her queasiness, he took her to a vintage jewellery store. Which ring would she choose as soon as he could afford to propose? She picked out a Chopard solitaire, not for one moment expecting him to get down on one-knee on those palatial steps. She put her hands to her face, making him laugh, and shouted, "*Oui*!" to a ripple of broken applause.

Matt loved hearing that story and made her re-enact the moment during playtimes as soon as he was old enough to understand. When he was about four, she and David talked about giving him a brother or sister. They decided to let nature take its course, as David put it, but nature wasn't listening. By the time Matt started school, she was convinced something must be wrong. She wondered if they should talk to someone or take some tests, but David insisted that her fixation was becoming unhealthy. Erika needed to stop being so obsessed with fertility cycles, which was probably the reason why nothing was happening.

He was right, of course. Their sex life had turned into a botched DIY project. Erika was mortified when he caught her, pelvis tipped and legs up against the headboard, after the afternoon romp she'd instigated. She took blood tests, her GP assuring her that everything was fine and she needed to relax: sometimes these things took time. By the sound of it, she was driving her husband away with this fixation on a second child. Was she spending enough time enjoying her son? Her child needed her full attention, even more so if a new baby might be entering their lives. Erika returned home wracked with guilt, so grateful for her little boy, always happy and unknowingly hilarious. Matt loved making her smile with silly dances and nonsensical songs. He hadn't enjoyed school initially. That first year had been full of tears and tantrums most mornings.

"Let's go to the zoo!" he'd say, appearing with Voom-Voom, his cuddly elephant, under one arm. He'd stand there with his sunglasses on, trying to tempt her away on a daytime jaunt. "Picnic time!" he'd announce on other days, unpacking lunch and blocking the front door, hoping Erika would forget about school.

In the end, after countless days during which Erika had been left running late to the office, David took over the morning drop-off as well as the afternoon pick-up. David's first novel had done better than either of them could have anticipated, but he was feeling the pressure, working on his second with a renewed sense of purpose. It was set to become a common theme.

'Erika?' David called now.

'Yes?' Erika nipped halfway downstairs to find David waiting for her in the hallway.

'Look, I'm sorry. I shouldn't have lost my temper like that, especially not on your birthday,' he said, looking at the floor like a child sent to apologise after a telling-off. 'I'm sorry if you're disappointed we're not out celebrating, like we should be.'

'I'm honestly not,' she said, meeting him at the bottom of the stairs. 'I went out to lunch with my colleagues. If I'd had to dust myself off and head out to dinner, I don't think I'd have made it to dessert.'

'We'll reschedule,' he said with an unmistakable lack of enthusiasm. 'I mentioned your birthday to Monica. She said we could have delayed publication if she'd known earlier. My fault.'

'Don't be daft. It's just a birthday,' Erika said, tired of hearing herself saying that. Next year, maybe she'd throw herself a party. 'Remember Monica's fiftieth? Victor hired the entire restaurant. I can still picture that topless guy playing sax for the ballet dancer.'

'Typical Victor. All a bit much.'

'Well, you would say that,' Erika retorted, relieved when he didn't take offense.

'Matt's going to be fine, you know,' said David. 'We all have to spread our wings eventually. I know you think I don't notice as much, but I miss him, too.'

'I know you do,' she said, placing her hand on his arm. Just as she thought they'd called a truce, he flinched.

'Right then,' he said, patting her shoulder, the way you might bid farewell to an uncaged lion. 'Best get back.'

Erika left him to it and decided on a bubble bath followed by an early night. She never would've thought it, but these days, her idea of fabulous was being in bed before ten with fresh sheets and a few new chapters.

The next morning, when she opened her eyes, she felt rested for the first time in weeks. Her first thought was of Enzo Morelli.

CHAPTER NINE

Erika and Polly were dining at Mitrata, which Polly said meant "friendship". They occupied a chic, canopied booth in a lantern-lit setting. Erika had thought the cocktails were a little strong when she'd arrived, but now she was on her third daiquiri, they tasted just perfect.

Meeting Polly was always a rather fantastic combination of dressing up and sharing confidences, and about as close to therapy as Erika could get. Polly had left a career in graphic design to retrain as a counsellor. She was forty-four, with wide grey eyes and a full, downturned mouth: features that reminded Erika of Bella, the Persian cat she'd had as a child. Polly was stylishly understated, with a wonderfully wicked sense of humour and a brilliantly sharp mind.

'David's obsessing over the latest book,' Erika said, chewing a stuffed olive. 'Buying himself designer underpants. All I get are weekly reminders of how to recycle plastic, bouts of empty nest syndrome and a car valet voucher for my birthday.' She took another drink, putting an end to the tirade. 'I'm being a brat, but that's how I feel.'

'You need to loosen the reins,' Polly told her, sipping on a negroni. 'I know exactly how you feel. Now Tyler's at university, I look at Logan, counting down to when it's his turn. And then it will just be me and Steve,' she said, referring to her husband. 'That's it. What next?'

Erika and Polly had met shortly after Matt and Tyler, Polly's eldest, started year eight and began meeting up, going through a phase of visiting the cinema every Friday during the summer holidays. She and Polly had picked the boys up and chatted on each other's doorsteps. This gradually progressed to having lunch and then dinner together. When it came to playground politics, Polly was a great friend, one of the few mums who never made you feel judged, no matter how frayed around the edges you felt.

'Well, with me and David, I can't even remember what we used to do before Matthew.'

'You had him quite quickly, didn't you?'

'I got married while I was pregnant.'

'Well, you've been together a long time,' Polly reassured her. 'You must be doing something right.'

Polly once asked Erika what she would prefer in a man: funny, sexy or smart? Erika chose funny without hesitation. Funny *was* sexy and smart. Words barely escaping, she realised that she and David never had fun anymore. Fun wasn't a word that came to mind. Since Matt left, their son had packed up all the fun with him. David seemed stilted, nothing spontaneous, not even amusement. He used to be witty, light-hearted. Erika had been equally light-hearted back then. There was nothing as compelling as that initial spark between lovers. They never used to struggle with sex or conversation. Erika thought David an altogether exotic proposition, with his passion for writing rendering him poetic.

'Persevering?' Erika suggested, spooning coconut rice onto her plate. 'Anyway, it's not just about me and David. I just feel like the only thing I've got to show for an entire *forty-two* years is Matthew, and the fact is, we're not really part of his life anymore. He's never going to live back home.' She was anticipating the sporadic phone calls, annual greetings cards and social media stalking which would likely form the basis of any future claim to motherhood.

'It shows incredible drive. He's got a paid placement. They're like gold dust,' Polly said, which provided small comfort. 'He's a straight-A student. The world's his oyster. Same with Tyler.' She selected the chickpea masala. 'I can't believe my little boy's going to be a lawyer. I might hold off a few more years, so he can make sure his mum does okay in the divorce…'

'You're actually thinking of —'

'Oh God, no,' Polly said, more resigned than resolute. 'But you've got to have something to look forward to, haven't you? No matter how unlikely.'

Polly and Steve made an unusual couple from the outside looking in, and from what Polly said, they were just as unlikely a match from the inside looking out. Steve was a real man's man. Erika would never have picked him out as Polly's type after meeting him at a school sports day, where he'd been encouraging Tyler to use brute force and questionable tactics at every opportunity. He'd been a bit of a lad in his time, he'd frequently remind anyone who'd listen, always wearing the latest combination of duck-down jacket and pimped-up trainers.

'How is Steve?' Erika asked, more out of politeness than genuine interest.

'He's good, I think,' Polly said. 'Oh, wow, you must try this.' She passed a dish across the table. 'People are still buying into the dream of household shutters, so that keeps him busy. Still gets a thrill, hearing his voice on the ads.'

Happy Homes, Steve's window and door company, had bought into the trend for colonial shutters. Polly had prompted him to hire Erika's advertising agency for a regional campaign. The slogan had been: *Happy Homes. Making homes happier.* Shakespeare must've been kicking himself.

'So, David's new novel,' Polly said. 'That's exciting.'

'Sort of. It's getting mixed reviews. He's so stressed and constantly sniping. Did I tell you he's been spending entire evenings out in the garage?'

Erika had no intention of mentioning the phone, the texts, not now. *If ever*, she thought.

'Doing what?' Polly picked up her glass.

'He's got his desk set up, along with his home gym. He lifts weights in there like something off *Prison Break*.'

'If only,' Polly said. 'Sweaty T-shirt, shaved head, hands all taped up…'

'That was incredibly vivid.' Erika paused mid-sip. 'Do you know what's annoying?' She put down her cocktail glass. 'I feel like a cliché, even talking like that since he made that comment about our *Sex and the City* dinners. *Girls' talk*, he called it.'

'He's a man. They diminish female get-togethers because they know we've actually got something to say,' Polly said. 'Yes, I like talking about shopping and things, as well as putting the world to rights, but who's to say clogging up the bar, talking about sport or cars, carries more intellectual merit? Patriarchal claptrap, but the world's changing, and the conversation's shifting along with it. Bravo, I say.'

'David can be so pompous,' Erika said. 'Pompous isn't good.'

'Try a homemade meal and a hand job,' Polly said. 'Trust me, he'll be fine.'

'A hand job?' Erika said, remembering that line from Oscar Wilde. 'He flinched when I touched his arm, the other day.'

'I caught Steve watching porn on his phone yesterday morning.'

'Really?' Erika said, not altogether surprised. Steve seemed like the adolescent type — the kind of bloke who'd exchange porn alongside homophobic jokes over WhatsApp.

'We know men don't think about sex the same way; they don't tend to romanticise it. It's either technical or dirty, but for us — well, for me, it's the thought that counts. I think most men just feel a general urge to empty their balls. Steve's always had a bit of a competitive edge — double points if he makes me come. Even after a few failed attempts, he still thinks he's Man of the Match,' Polly said, as Erika tried not to look too concerned. 'I was changing the bed while he was going on about the pros and cons of convector fans, and when I looked over, he was watching a couple of women fighting over a cock with the volume turned down. Next thing, he'll be taking a dump with the en suite door open.'

'David used to come in and pee while I was taking a bath,' Erika said. 'I kind of liked it at the time. I thought it made us closer.'

'I used to sleep with my face in Steve's armpit. Nothing could induce me to do that now, but at least David's looking after himself by working out, right?' Polly said in her most diplomatic tone. 'Steve practically lives at the gym, so at least he cares.'

David certainly cares about impressing someone, Erika thought. There was the diet, the new underpants, the flinching. It all seemed so obvious, the affair, the more she thought about it. They hadn't had sex for…

'The sex is still okay, though?' Polly said, as if reading her mind.

'It would be,' Erika said, 'if we were still having it.'

'So, what? Once a month? That's not too bad, as long as you don't make a habit out of it,' Polly said. 'Or has it been longer?'

'Last month, maybe,' Erika cast her mind back. 'There was a Super Moon.'

'A Super Moon,' Polly said. 'You're charting your sex life by lunar cycles? Possibly a bad sign?'

'I mean, it was on the news,' Erika said. She realised it had been closer to three months but was too embarrassed to say. 'And we had sex that night.'

'Well, a Super Moon, who can blame you?' Polly smirked. 'Listen, sometimes all it takes is a couple of early nights. Buy yourself some of those outrageous little knickers from that boutique I told you about. Walk into the garage in those and a pair of slutty heels. That should take the weight off his barbell.'

'No chance,' Erika said. 'I haven't done anything that obvious since we tried role play.'

'French maid?'

'Air hostess,' Erika said. David would be furious if he knew she'd told Polly; it had taken her a while to coax the fantasy from him in the first place. 'It was years ago. I was carrying a tray and everything. We were supposed to pretend the plane was about to crash, but I got fired. I couldn't deliver my lines properly, apparently, and it was putting him off,' she went on, as Polly howled with laughter. 'He was giving me feedback like I was in one of his bloody rehearsals, except they didn't have to audition in crotchless panties and a peephole bra. Hopefully not, anyway.'

'Steve told me the idea of getting caught turned him on. Do you know where he took me? ESSO forecourt,' Polly said, as Erika laughed into her napkin. 'Not a fucking chance.' She dished out the pomegranate salad. 'How are things at the agency?'

'Really good, actually,' Erika said, perking up as she thought of Enzo Morelli. Despite a sudden dart of adrenaline, something stopped her from mentioning him. It seemed juvenile, as if she was looking for something that wasn't there.

Maybe she just wanted to keep the quiet, harmless thrill of it to herself. 'We're working on a pretty big pitch at the moment. David still wants me to leave. He makes me feel as though I have this dumb little job, best left to the youngsters.' She smiled. 'Since I work in advertising, I can't say I entirely disagree with him.'

'Some people, usually the ones with penises, have an inflated sense of their own self-worth,' Polly said. 'And let's not forget, even if David can't bring himself to admit it, he couldn't have done any of it without you. Behind every man, there's a far greater woman. Every time Steve makes a big sale, I think, that's my boy. I shouldn't joke, though. Those shutters paid off our mortgage.'

'You've paid off your mortgage?' Erika wished she hadn't sounded so astonished. If David knew Polly was mortgage-free, he'd have them barefoot and nil-by-mouth before Christmas. 'That's incredible.'

'And according to Steve, it's all down to Happy Homes,' Polly said, narrowing her eyes in frustration. 'Needn't have bothered working my arse off all these years, in that case.'

'Ignore him,' Erika said. 'Steve knows full well that everything you've achieved is based on your *joint* income. That's fantastic, by the way. Paying off the mortgage is the ultimate goal, isn't it?'

'Apparently, not.' Polly reached for her drink. 'A bigger place on Sommersville Lane is Steve's new goal. Not mine, though.'

'Sommersville,' Erika said, considering it. 'It is a really nice location.'

'It was, before the new-build lot swept in. They've demolished perfectly lovely properties in favour of slabs of glass and concrete. Nowadays, your neighbours are likely to be money-grabbing bigots,' Polly said, interrupting herself with a shard of poppadom. 'Zero integrity, dubious business interests, born without some essential part of their soul.'

'Are you quoting that direct from the estate agent?' Erika asked, not wanting to point out that Polly was essentially describing Steve.

'The couple next door gave us their entire dating, financial, and career history in solar panelling as soon as they noticed Steve sizing up the swimming pool,' Polly said. 'I feel a joint merger coming on.'

'There are worse things.'

'I know. I'm very lucky,' Polly said, investigating her handbag. 'I should be grateful to have a husband who works so hard, but you know, Steve used to be in social housing. He used to care about single mothers and fight for the elderly. Somewhere along the way, he started dreaming in pound signs.' She retrieved an envelope from her bag. 'Anyway, tonight's about celebrating! I wasn't sure if you'd be into this, but after everything we've said tonight, I hope you'll be pleased. Happy birthday.' Polly handed over the envelope with a shimmy of excitement.

Erika mustered her sincerest look of anticipation, knowing that no matter what lay in that envelope, she was going to have to go along with it. 'Oh wow,' she said as she read the card. 'This sounds fantastic.'

'Do you think?' Polly grimaced. 'I know you can be resistant to this kind of thing…'

Resistant? Even the word put Erika on edge.

'I think it's the perfect time for both of us to just spend some quality time with ourselves.' Polly let out a sigh. 'And it's not a spa. I know that kind of thing's not for you, and then I remembered someone mentioning this place…'

Erika read the card more carefully:

Divinity Wellbeing Retreat

Anything claiming to be a retreat left Erika feeling horribly claustrophobic. She pictured herself surrounded by dense woodland, and possibly a moat, with no means of escape. She wasn't a spa or retreat kind of person, not unless retreat meant being left to your own devices.

Welcomes you to a weekend of rebirth…

Hideous. She could almost feel psychological forceps being lovingly forced around her most private thoughts by well-meaning vegans. *Sharing.* There was going to be lots of sharing with complete strangers.

…and refocusing of your divine energies…

Oh God.

…in our safe and welcoming, 5-star, luxury home, far from day-to-day reality…

It was trying too hard, all of this. She didn't want to be sent far away from day-to-day reality — not unless they meant experimental drugs. If this was actually happening, she may well need them.

…which may be restricting your ability to nurture the happiness within you.

We look forward to welcoming you, Erika.

She drew back at the inclusion of her name. It felt as if she'd been enrolled in a cult.

'You've got to admit, it's got us written all over it,' Polly said, bright with their forthcoming adventure. 'It's in three weeks' time. Is that okay?'

'Of course! No plans, that's perfect…'

Tempted as Erika was to get out of it and encourage Polly to take someone else, there was no way of graciously backing out. The place must have cost a fortune, Erika thought, looking at the photograph of the aristocratic country house. Polly was excited, and there she was, faking enthusiasm. What kind of reaction was that to a generous gift from a genuine friend?

'Polly,' she said, racked with guilt, 'this is so lovely of you.'

'My pleasure,' Polly said, leaving her seat to hug Erika. 'I wanted to cheer both of us up and do something special for your birthday.'

'Well, it is special. It's great,' Erika said, newly humble, picturing Oprah, reminding her to practise gratitude. 'Thank you.'

'I've booked us in for the two-day Mastering Menopause detox.'

'Well, you don't get that from a herbal teabag.'

It was Polly who first diagnosed Erika. She just hadn't been feeling like herself, and if that didn't sound too bad, imagine having a newly malfunctioning thermostat and a nervous disposition luring you into decrepitude. Polly sent a link to Gwyneth Paltrow's website, featuring a blog on perimenopause. All that money the EU spent on medical research, and it took an Oscar-winner to provide vital answers. Erika had been thrilled because she knew the truth when she saw it. A conclusive link to the mysterious symptoms her GP insisted didn't apply. The only thing she was depressed about were her symptoms, but the doctor had offered her antidepressants as soon as she'd walked into his surgery. She'd left feeling worse, hopeless, in fact. The doctor hadn't listened, offering no compelling answers. She'd been entirely disregarded due to her lack of reproductive usefulness. That was what it felt like, she decided, indignant at the thought. David's balls hadn't even begun to sag, and there she was, shunned by modern medicine. Perimenopause made perfect sense. Nothing happened overnight, ruled by the moon, determined by tides, females were pro-surfers of hormonal changes. Perimenopause was the new puberty. The major difference being, Erika had been overly prepared for puberty.

'It's fully accredited,' Polly said, cracking the rest of her poppadom. 'There's yoga, one-to-one mind swim sessions, meditative chanting, and the moon bathing's meant to be incredible. I mean, there's a bit of fasting and group work involved, but hey, it's only a couple of days — all in the name of feeling good.'

'Sounds great,' Erika lied, almost swallowing her lime as she threw back the remainder of her cocktail, ready to order a fourth as her mobile rang.

Richard. She could guess why he'd be phoning out of hours. In the back of the taxi on her way home, the news was confirmed.

"*Er-ik-a!*" Richard sang into her voicemail. "*Why wait 'til Monday, because… We got it! Stable Denim. Signed, sealed, delivered for Mr Morelli. Thank you very much! Woo-hoo!*"

An initial spike of excitement was rendered mute by the thought of working with Enzo. Too many memories of him were resurfacing from the past, where they belonged.

CHAPTER TEN

In the days before iPads and smartphones, Erika had sat in front of a computer the size of a beer crate at a bank of desks that housed an island of solely female writers, headed up by editor-in-chief, Des. And they really were something of an island. Lesbos, if the predominantly male staff had any say in the matter. The newsroom lads took care of the grittier stuff, as Des called it, or the real work, as far as they were concerned. They were a blur of blue shirts, gripping phones and chewing the ends of pens. They had no time for Erika and the team, not beyond following their arses at desk height. The women focused on revenue rather than reporting. They wrote commercial pieces alongside the advertising team, giving clients far more decent coverage than newsprint. They featured them in glossy lifestyle magazines, including the one Erika headed up: *Vista: The VIP Vantage Point.*

Her mum had sold the house and married Ewan before Erika had graduated. Therefore, by the time she hung up her cap and gown, she was committed to staying in the city. She accepted a succession of dead-end jobs in shoddy bars and downtown restaurants, remembering that every slob she worked for, every creep she served, and every emaciated pay cheque she received was a step towards her real ambitions. After Des gave her a shot, hiring her from a slew of similarly plucky applications, she'd gained enough perspective to appreciate the red-roped launches, exclusive events, and celebrity parties in town. It was an era that brought a couple of unexpected twists: namely Enzo Morelli and David Forde.

Erika joined the usual Friday dispatches one morning, with Des distributing core pieces to be filed the following week. Gripping her notebook and pen, she scrawled notes as he broached the topic of the next front cover.

'Erika, I'm going to have to spring this on you, I'm afraid,' he said, his mouth moving beneath a moustache as substantial as a draught excluder. 'Last minute, I know, but Him & Hair have taken the back page. Full price, nice-looking ad.' He assessed his clipboard. 'And you've got yourself an exclusive.' He handed over the press release. 'All very arty. This afternoon, one p.m.,' he added as she speed-read the blurb, her eyes darting in disbelief to the accompanying image. 'Nice, national product for us, causing quite a stir, apparently. It's a behind-the-scenes sort of thing we're after. You know the score.'

Beth, fellow feature writer, sat elbow-to-elbow with Erika, taking a closer look at the photograph of Enzo, who was starring as the "him" in the Him & Hair campaign. 'He's a bit of all right, isn't he?' she said. 'Nice bit of coverage for you there…'

Erika could barely concentrate, wishing she'd done her nails and given a shit about what she was going to wear the night before. Thursday night was usually dedicated to prepping for the big Friday night out, but she'd been planning on staying home with an old *Ally McBeal* boxset and two-weeks' worth of ironing. As soon as it was close enough to lunch, she commandeered the ladies' bathroom, emptying the entire contents of her makeup bag into the sink and trying to repair her end-of-the-week face. She doused herself in Ralph Lauren, smeared on a layer of Lancôme Juicy Tube lipgloss, applied Frizz Ease to her thick popstar highlights, supposedly caramel but closer to rust, as if she'd been left out in the rain.

Erika rang the lift and stood next to Richard, a.k.a. Shagger Harrington, who was talking loudly on his mobile. She ignored him, checking her watch as Beth approached.

'I hate it when Des does that,' Beth said, as Shagger Harrington faked gentlemanly courtesy by stepping aside as the lift arrived, probably taking a good look at their bums. 'We need prior warning if we're interviewing someone fit. Lucky cow! I'm stuck with that fat bastard property guy who spends all his time trying to look down my top while he pulls his jockeys from his crack.' Beth faked throwing up. 'I hope yours doesn't turn out to be a total prick,' she said, eyes instinctively drawn to Richard. 'Some of those model types are snotty fuckers. That one who wore the suit for my racecourse feature could hardly bring himself to look at me. Then his co-star showed up. She was a right stroppy cow — moaned about the clothes, the camera angles and even the bloody weather, but she was all tits and teeth, so he was all over her like a rash. *Gobshite.* Just don't take any shit.'

'It's okay,' Erika said as the doors opened. 'I know him.'

'You know him?' Beth stopped in her tracks. 'Fuck off! Is he single?'

Enzo Morelli was reading a comic when Erika arrived. He wore a pink shirt with a fat, check tie loosened around his neck. He'd worn his school tie the exact same way, Erika remembered. Top button undone, white T-shirt beneath, tie loosened like a puppy straining on a leash. He ignored the mirror, his long legs splayed as he bit into an apple. His former mass of slightly overgrown waves had been shaved and sculpted for his new role as the Him & Hair guy. Erika loitered, feeling as if she was back at the school gates.

'Hi there, I'm Angie,' said a good-looking, skyscraper-tall woman. '*Vista Magazine*, isn't it?' Angie consulted her notes. 'Erika Karter?'

Enzo's gaze snapped up.

'Enzo? You okay to do this now?' Angie asked as he sat up a little straighter.

Erika had an urge to call her brother, because wherever there was Enzo, there had to be Josh. Erika remembered the last time she'd seen him. Josh had been getting ready to go to the pub for farewell drinks with his friends, while Enzo had stood in the kitchen, waiting for him. He'd given Erika a nod and a zip-locked smile, as if nothing had happened between them. Right then, after weeks of paranoia, Erika had known for sure that her brother suddenly hanging out at Enzo's place was more than tragic coincidence. Enzo was letting her know that election night had been a mistake. Nothing would ever happen between them again, because he wished nothing had ever happened in the first place.

'Sorry,' Enzo said, scratching the back of his perfect hairdo and jolting Erika out of her memories. 'This place is a bit of a mess.' He opened the fridge and took a reluctant sniff of the milk, then snapped back as if he'd been stung.

The interview was professional and straightforward, conducted without either of them mentioning their previous acquaintance. Then Enzo asked if she fancied a proper catch-up, inviting her back to his place, which turned out to be in Albany Buildings.

'You obviously weren't expecting company,' Erika said as she walked into his flat, and he threw his jacket along the back of the fatigued-looking couch. 'Unless this is all part of your dazzling, new image.'

'And is all this scathing observation part of your dazzling new image, now you're an intrepid reporter, Erika?' he asked.

'Yeah, I'm going undercover to reveal you use curling tongs. And look, dinner candles in *champagne* bottles. How decadent,' she said, giving everything a quick once-over with a critical eye. 'And a framed *Amélie* poster.'

He opened the blinds, rattled about in a cupboard and selected a bottle of wine. 'What's wrong with *Amélie*?'

'Absolutely nothing,' she said, toying with the idea of cutting her hair like Audrey Tautou. 'Us ladies love that movie, as you well know,' Erika said, enjoying the chance to unveil him as a player. 'And there it is in pride of place, suggesting you might just have the romantic sensitivity we've been searching for.'

He threw back his head and laughed, so she knew she had him.

'And as for the unmade bed with the bedroom door left enticingly open? Well, unmade mattress, I mean,' Erika corrected herself, pulling up a dining chair. 'It's set on the floor to remind us of your nomadic, slightly elusive, existence.' She gave him a mock-wistful look.

'You got me,' he said, deadpan. 'Or maybe I've got great taste in films and haven't had time to buy a bed, or so much as a lightshade.' He looked up and Erika noticed the bare bulb hanging from the ceiling. 'There's no food in the place, either. I hope you're okay sharing garlic bread and a bottle of wine. It's a very nice bottle of wine.'

'Of course it is. You're trying to be French, like Amélie. You'll be wearing a beret next, like that Kangol thing you used to have. Remember that?'

'Don't be daft. It'd ruin my hair. Since when did you get so cynical, anyway?'

Since you, Erika almost replied, but she was long past wearing her heart on her sleeve.

'Josh would piss himself if he could see you like this, you know?' she said, flicking through a magazine as he stuck a baguette in the oven. 'Galivanting round with your ridiculous quiff, and smoking.' She tapped the cigarette packet that was lying on the table. 'Or at least carrying around a packet of Camels to accessorise your fancy threads.'

'Let's face it,' Enzo replied, setting the timer, 'Josh would take the piss anyway.'

'So,' Erika went on, 'is Angie a friend of yours?'

'Angie?' Enzo frowned, pulling the cork from the wine bottle. 'No, Erika. I'm not seducing my way in front of the camera, in case you're planning an exclusive.' Despite his protests, Erika knew he was enjoying the interest. 'Angie is Christian's ex-wife. Christian runs the photography studio where I work sometimes, and Angie put me forward for Him & Hair.' He grabbed some plates. 'This is all off the record, by the way.'

'Off the record?' Erika slid a cigarette from the pack. 'You're not famous, and I don't work for *The National Enquirer*.'

He grinned, took two wine glasses from the cupboard, and gave them a quick polish with his T-shirt. Erika caught a glimpse of his stomach. Wasn't this the guy she always knew he'd become? She'd recognised everything enticing about Enzo Morelli, even as a teenager.

'Hey, brainbox,' he said. 'What are you thinking?'

'Nothing, just that I knew you'd do something cool.'

'Better than good, you said.'

'Yes, and I was right. In all seriousness, Him & Hair is better than good.'

He offered her a glass and lit the solitary candle. 'I hate being in front of the camera. I prefer to be behind it, but the money's good, so I took the job.'

'So, what do you want to do?' Erika asked. 'Photography?'

'Portraiture,' he said, serving up their bread. 'There's real skill involved. Capture a mood, a look you're being paid to achieve, all in a matter of minutes. There's more to it than technicalities.' He took out a cigarette, leaning over to catch a light from the candle.

'Bloody hell, Enz! Mind the quiff!' She sniggered. 'Your fringe is your fortune.'

'Anyway,' he said, pulling a lock in front of his eyes and assessing it before he took a pull on his cigarette, 'what about you?' He exhaled, slouching over and folding his arms along the table. 'Come on.'

'There's nothing much to tell,' Erika said, hoping the statement sounded intriguing as opposed to completely accurate. 'I finished university and worked in some restaurants and a couple of bars. I wrote here and there, had a few things published, and then got this job.' She put out her cigarette.

'So, that's the CV sorted,' he said, taking a bite of garlic bread. 'Any boys I need to scare off?'

'You mean, men? No one special, as they say.'

'And you're okay with that?'

'Completely okay with that. I'm busy with work.'

'How's your mum doing?'

The non sequitur made her pause as she reached for her glass. 'I keep promising to visit. She's fine. She married Ewan.'

'Sorry if I haven't been great at keeping in touch,' he said. 'It's nothing personal.'

'Who says I wanted to keep in touch?'

'Fair enough.'

They eventually gravitated towards the couch.

'I know it was years ago, but do you remember that night?' Enzo asked.

Erika finished her wine. 'I think I do, but do you want to be a *bit more* specific?'

'The night we messed around.'

'Messed around?' She smiled, enjoying his discomfort.

'Well, the thing is, I felt shitty about it.'

'It's okay.' Erika nudged him with her foot. 'I think I'm just about over it.'

'I wanted to tell you that I did want to see you again.' He almost stammered. 'I would've asked you out. I don't know if you already know this, if Josh told you?'

'Told me what?'

'He knew about that night,' Enzo said, wincing slightly. 'He saw us.'

'No!' Erika sat bolt upright. 'He *saw us*? How?'

'Dunno. I didn't ask for details. He wasn't exactly happy about it, which is completely understandable. I crossed a line.'

'Oh, come on,' she said. 'I mean, yes, I get it, but male bravado…' She rolled her eyes.

'No, it's not that,' he said. 'You wouldn't have liked it, if Josh had done something with one of your friends. We properly fell out for a while. That's why I stopped going round to yours. It wasn't the same after that.'

It hit her now, the summer she'd thought Enzo was fleeing the scene of the crime.

'He never said anything to me. He just said he was going to yours, so I assumed you were avoiding me.'

'Well, I wasn't. And he wasn't at mine. That was his cover while he was with … what was her name?' Enzo paused. 'Sonia Mills! Jesus, she was rough.'

'What about Layla Deane?' Erika said, enjoying the chance to finally confront him. 'You did it with her.'

'Josh told you that?' He shook his head. '*Bastard…*'

'So, it was true? The panic to do it, lose your virginity, before you left for uni?'

'I wanted to get it over with,' he said. 'I can't believe he told you that. Made damn sure he put you off me, didn't he?'

'You did that all by yourself.' Erika nudged him again. 'Shitbag. But we were kids, anyway.'

'Yeah, I know,' he said. 'It's fine now…'

'Oh, really?'

'Sorry, I didn't mean…'

'I know,' said Erika. 'It's okay.'

A moment later, Enzo knocked red wine across the carpet as they slipped from the settee, kissing their way onto the floor.

The next morning, Erika woke up with her head on his chest, surrounded by discarded clothes, beneath *Amélie*'s fairytale gaze.

Erika continued waking up with Enzo for the next couple of months. Eleven weeks and four days, to be precise. They took a trip to the movies, catching a midnight showing of *Lost in Translation*. Erika struggled to hold back the tears at the end, while Enzo laughed and put his arm around her. They spent a few afternoons touring galleries. Erika felt his quiet transcendence as he examined the photography and artwork, recognising her feelings for him in a more tangible appreciation of every moment.

It also turned out that when he had good reason, Enzo could cook. He introduced Erika to pesto, bruschetta, and creamy goats' cheese on a bed of linguine. His grandparents owned a restaurant in Southern Italy. 'Birthplace of the sirens,' he told her, relating the story of the mythical temptresses who guided sailors to their doom according to local legend. In return, she introduced him to Jay McInerney and Dennis Lehane paperbacks, and, in keeping with his desire to merge his Italian heritage with an adopted French sensibility, the music of François Parisi. He made occasional daytrips to different cities, doing promotional work for Him & Hair, but he was eager to get back behind the camera, toying with his Pentax K1000. Erika knew the show-off in him loved wearing it, the camera hanging from a thick black strap around his neck. Once, he convinced her to let him photograph her.

'Go on,' he said, lowering the lens. 'Let me! I won't show anyone.'

'You pervert!' Erika said, covering herself up with his sheets. 'Talking women into taking off their clothes…'

'Just one,' he said, kissing her. 'Please? You look so good. I want you to see what I see.'

'Let me fix my hair first.'

'No, that's the whole point,' he said, adjusting the lens. 'I like it like that.'

'Of course you do,' she said. 'You're really interested in how my hair looks, right now.'

As he took the pictures, Erika relaxed, watching him work. Enzo was sexier as a photographer than he was with a head full of wax, posing for the camera.

'Let me take your picture,' she said, but instead, he lay down, turning the camera on them.

He studied her for a moment, blue eyes shining. 'I love you,' he said, cupping one hand around her face.

'I know,' she said.

Erika tried not to presume anything this good was too good to last, but she couldn't shake the sense of an imminent ending.

One morning, while Erika was using the toothbrush she had begun keeping in her handbag, she overheard Enzo answering his phone and recognised a tone of shock and concern.

'That was Christian. Angie's not good.' He sat on the edge of the bed. 'It's breast cancer.'

'Oh, God.' Erika sat beside him. 'I'm so sorry.'

'She started treatment last month, but didn't want anyone to know,' he said. 'I need to see her.'

'Yeah, of course,' Erika said. 'Can I do anything?'

'Thanks, but it's…' He sat forward, rubbing his face in his hands.

'I know it must be a horrible shock.'

He stood, distracted, and then lifted his suitcase from the top of the wardrobe.

'You're going today?'

'As soon as I can. I've got some work coming up with Christian, anyway,' he said. 'Probably makes sense for me to be there.' Then he was on the phone, booking his train ticket as Erika buttoned her blouse.

She heard him confirm that he was leaving at midday. 'You're staying there?'

'Yes,' he said, rattling from room to room. 'I used to live there.'

'Oh, right,' she said. She'd had no idea that was the case. 'So, how long are you going for?'

'I'll see how Angie is, how long she's up for me staying.'

'Will that be okay?' she asked, ashamed that she was saying this as much for her own benefit as out of concern for Angie. 'I mean, with her having treatment?'

'Christian's been with her the whole time. I think it'll help,' he said, calling from the bathroom over the sound of him peeing. 'She's been asking after me.'

Erika stood, trying to work out what this meant. Christian was Angie's ex-husband. Enzo was … what? The whole set-up seemed strange, being friends with exes who didn't behave like exes. The history between him and Angie was platonic, he insisted, but why had he lived with her? And why was he planning to stay at her house in the middle of a serious illness?

'Right, then,' Erika said. 'Keep me posted.'

'Hey, hey.' He appeared from the bathroom. 'Where're you going?'

'Work.'

'Without a kiss?'

'I'll save it for when you get back.'

'Don't be like that,' he said, turning her shoulders. 'I'll see how things are, how Angie is, and I'll get back whenever I can.'

'Whenever you can?'

He looked bemused. 'Christ, Erika, I just found out my friend's got cancer.'

'I know, and it's horrible. I know she's your friend, but I don't understand why you're moving in.'

'I'm not moving in.' He went back into the bathroom, running the tap. 'I'm not getting into this now.'

'How convenient,' she said. 'Well, your *friend* here will see you when you get back.'

Over the next few days, Erika wanted to text to ask how Angie was, but it felt insincere after how she'd reacted. As their silence reached a second week, she stopped waiting to hear from him. This was the ending she'd been so afraid of.

Erika had gone to interview David Forde expecting a fusty, beige sock-wearing eccentric who'd drone on about dramatic symbolism, rhapsodise over a recent production of *The Seagull* and name-drop Kenneth Branagh. Instead, David was resolutely down-to-earth and self-depreciating as they sat on the edge of the stage with her cassette-loaded Dictaphone between them. He talked passionately about playwrights — Tennessee Williams, Arthur Miller — with the same enthusiasm Enzo spoke about Kathryn Bigelow or David Fincher. A week later, she found herself with a free ticket to his play, sitting in the front row.

She was a little in awe of David and marvelled at the performance. After curtain call, she'd watched him thank other journalists as he made his way over to her. He wanted to have a drink, just the two of them. This was around the same time Erika accepted the fact it had been over a month since she'd last heard from Enzo. More than that, every part of her felt his complete absence, knowing it was over. Erika willingly fell under David's spell, appreciating his persistence while she recovered from the loss of Enzo. Tired of being cynical, David made her feel secure. If she had a chance with this man, why spoil it, quibbling over David's political opinions, questioning his whereabouts, and harbouring suspicions about some of his female friends?

The night Enzo finally called, weeks later, her hair was wrapped in a towel and her toes were in separators as she answered her phone.

'Sorry it's been a while,' he said, as she half-laughed.

'How's Angie?'

'Coping,' he said. 'I've been covering as much stuff as I can for Christian, running the studio.'

'You're still there, then?'

'I'd have been in touch sooner if I was back.'

There was a pause. Erika was unconvinced. 'You're a good friend.'

'Trying to be. Have you been okay?'

'Fine.'

'You don't sound it.'

'What do you expect?' she asked, towel slumping from her head. 'I haven't heard from you. You do get how that's not normal?'

'It's not a normal situation I'm in.'

'Yeah, exactly. That's what I thought.'

'What does that mean?'

'It means,' she said, thinking of David and knowing how quickly things could change, 'I've no idea, Enzo. One minute, you say one thing…'

'And I meant what I said. Look, I'm sorry.'

'So am I,' she said, wanting to get off the phone. 'I really hope Angie's okay.'

'This isn't just about Angie, though, is it? I can't change things. I can't change how your family feels about me.'

'I don't want to talk about this right now.'

'Maybe we should,' he said. 'Maybe we need to.'

Erika knew Enzo was right, but for some reason that would later trouble her, she said, 'Don't bother. It's pointless.'

She was never convinced they could make it, so why go there again? She still slept in Enzo's old *Batman Forever* T-shirt sometimes, and she had claimed his brass Zippo lighter as her own, but she really liked David. Their connection was calm, carefree.

Enzo Morelli was teenage fiction, she told herself. He belonged in the past.

CHAPTER ELEVEN

Richard had no idea who Nate Petersen was, not until Ursula swooped in, jumping at the chance to work with an auteur, thoroughly impressed that Erika had his business card. Erika pitched the idea to Stable Denim, explaining that Nate was keen to collaborate in the name of iconic fashion. After Erika had sent the brief, along with Enzo's audio and profile, Nate had been all systems go, not remotely hindered by the lacklustre budget. William Torrence discovered that his youngest son was a fan and signed off on the campaign at his insistence, in return for a signed T-shirt from Nate's latest movie.

'I'm thinking The Great Outdoors!' Richard announced, splayed in his chair in the boardroom. 'The ultimate dream of the urban male. Escape from suburbia!'

'Escaping into Stable Denim instead?' Nate said, joining them over videocall, exuding his usual confidence, with a low-plunging T-shirt exposing his chest.

Richard's hands were casually laced behind his head as he gazed at Nate. 'Obviously, the jeans are our main focus, and I can't see it working on a sound stage in some studio. No green screen for us — what d'you say?'

'Completely agree, my man,' Nate said. 'I've taken a look at what we're trying to achieve here and I'm hoping that what I've got in mind will answer the call. Let me share my screen, folks.' He switched to an aerial shot of a mountainous range, yawning into green spaces. 'Connisdale National Park. This place has everything we need in terms of elemental draw, enduring drama, and sensory connection. My guys have the all-clear — free use of designated spaces, no payments necessary, should we commit.'

'Great, great,' Richard said. 'Get our guy, Mr Morelli, out there. Climbing, exploring the terrain, that kind of thing.'

'Not exactly, man,' Nate said, returning to occupy the screen. One leg was lazily hoisted over the arm of his chair, and his elbow rested on his knee, as if he were missing an acoustic guitar. 'To me, that's the obvious take. Too obvious.' He gazed off-screen, looking pensive. 'This is about a guy searching — not so much exploring the landscape, but seeking truth. A truth that can only be found within himself…'

'I love that,' Ursula said, and from the look on her face, she possibly loved Nate, too.

'Yeah,' Richard said, with a curious glance in Ursula's direction. 'My thoughts exactly.'

'What I do think,' Nate said, sitting forward, 'is that, in terms of social media content, Ursula — it is Ursula, isn't it?'

'Uh-um,' Ursula managed, looking dazed.

'Beautiful name. It means "bear", but I take it you know that?'

'I didn't know your name means "bare",' Richard said. 'As in, naked?'

'No,' she said, issuing a look that landed like a slap.

'There's a real need for us to be playful, here, Ursula,' Nate said, as a smile spread across her face. 'I think we've a chance to create a real dichotomy here. The Stable Denim Guy versus the Dad Jeans wearer.'

'Got it,' Richard said, attempting to interrupt Ursula's unrelenting gaze.

'The Stable Denim Guy,' Nate said, 'for me, is the embodiment of the emotive self.' He suddenly brought up his knees, limbs bent as if he'd landed from a tree. 'The Dad Jeans guy, he's our customer — that's who we'll address through social media, which is why your approach is absolutely vital to the success of this project, Ursula.'

'Thanks,' she grinned, turning pink.

'So, how about we split the existing script?' Erika said, attempting to sober proceedings before Ursula became a puddle of adoration. 'We'll keep the product details and design spec on social. And we'll place our core brand values centre-stage with you, Nate.'

'That's exactly it!' Nate said, balancing on his chair with both feet on his seat. 'Let the viewer connect on a deeper level, not as some overfed, bloated consumer. My team cited some territories for the client. I'll have them send details across. We're looking at a day's filming with our guy, and, if it makes your journey any easier, this incredible part of the country is in my neck of the woods. It's twenty minutes or so from my place, and you're very welcome to stay. Call it your base and be my guests.'

'Are you sure?' Ursula said, mouth gaping.

'I would like nothing more than to welcome your presence to my meagre lodgings,' Nate said, taking a small bow. 'We're collaborating, man, as long as we've the will and the passion.' He cupped his hands as if taking the world between them as Ursula almost shook with anticipation. 'We've the chance to make something truly special, here. That's exactly what I believe we're capable of.'

Erika had faked sleep after David returned home sometime after two. A meeting with his publisher that turned into dinner and drinks, apparently.

He fell into an almost instant sleep, breathing deeply and steadily, as she readjusted her pillow. Erika smoothed her hair away from the back of her neck, one leg outside the covers, wishing she could get up and do something useful without disturbing David. Instead, she drifted in and out of the pros and cons of the Stable Denim pitch, alongside a perpetual to-do list. This week's thrilling tasks included buying a replacement lightbulb for the utility room and speeding up the slides on an outreach presentation.

Welcome to a night of being in perimenopause. She lay on top of the covers, relieved she'd left the window on the latch, one hand wandering to the unfamiliar weight of her newly rounded C-cups. She hadn't taken her supplements. She wasn't sure if they worked, but felt better during times like these, when there was a good chance, she might feel worse without them. Polly tried to get her to subscribe to a HRT/perimenopause app which flagged every spoke in your cycle, but Erika wanted things to look forward to, not updates on the last rumblings of her eggs. It was bullshit, all this, and the worst part was, it made you feel old. When you felt old, you thought about death. When you thought about death, it made you want to do all the things you still wanted to do, before you were too dead to do them.

Erika had realised it wasn't just a saying, how the years crept up on you. From the front, there wasn't too much to complain about. Her bust had stayed pinned in roughly the same place. She'd been twenty-two when she had Matt, and her body had snapped back into place by the time he'd grown into a toddler. The tops of her arms and her thighs, fair enough, could use some of that regular exercise she'd been half-heartedly pledging to do for at least ten years, but overall, there was nothing to worry about, not until she got a rare glance at her rear. She'd swooped around when she'd first seen it, as if a semi-naked, much older woman was standing behind her in matching knickers. Having never appeared in a sex tape, Erika wasn't in the habit of assessing herself from behind, but thanks to the hall of mirrors in the ladies' changing room at the local department store, she got a full view.

She'd been naïve enough to think her bottom looked the same without the support of stretch denim, but it appeared she'd been secretly ageing rear-first. Her buttocks looked dehydrated, and her car didn't even have heated seats.

Some mornings she awoke with her sheets soaked through, like a Victorian with a high fever. She was emotional without warning and had been in tears watching an Animal Protection advert a few months back, prompting her to call and pledge a monthly donation. Now she got upset remembering orphaned gorillas when she got her period.

She turned back the duvet and pulled at her T-shirt for air as heat spread across her chest. An angry rash was forming along her legs, even though she'd applied her magnesium lotion. She was intrigued by the thought of other people's To Do lists. It was all in those tiny details, wasn't it? Life was boring for everyone, surely? Except, Erika wasn't feeling quite as bored lately, not at all, actually.

She was probably feeling restless because of the impending campaign shoot. She'd been thinking about Enzo, still reacclimatising to this smoke signal from her past. Erika had never fully understood what they were to each other. As strange as it sounded, as a writer, she needed a name for it, appreciated a noun. She wanted to put a label on him, maybe so she could neatly place whatever they were at the back of her mind.

Ex-boyfriend? They hadn't clocked in as a couple for very long, so did that really count? Now, he had become a friend, but he was already an old friend. And, technically, they had slept together, but no one was friends with their exes. And, as well as the lack of a noun, what about punctuation? Their relationship, friendship, whatever it was, it never seemed to carry a full stop. You'd think twenty years without contact might suggest one, but now, here he was, best described as an ellipsis.

Desire. There was a word. She immediately thought of Destruction and Fire. The perfect portmanteau. Christ, she sounded like David.

She wondered if Enzo was nervous about tomorrow, still awake, too? They both used to struggle with sleep. Although, that had its advantages back then. The novelty of sharing a bed, an absolute banquet when you're young and in love, had been reduced to picking at cold leftovers after a few years of David. She loved watching Enzo, fresh out of bed, putting on a CD, wandering around in his boxers. Maybe it was because he spent so much time at her old family house, but sharing a place never felt awkward. No clashes of routine, an understanding of each other's need for space, along with an instinct for closeness. Intimacy with him gave her a confidence she'd assumed was all hers, but discovered was very much something between them.

She was looking forward to seeing him in the morning, except, embarrassingly, she'd been having vivid dreams. For the first time in years, instead of being annoyed by waking up in sheets as damp as a terrible secret in an awful thriller due to her surging hormones, she felt a tiny bit excited.

Erika gave a slight jolt as David gave an abrupt snort, arms and legs lashing out, as if momentarily swimming against the tide. There was never any going with the flow for her husband, not even in his sleep. Him being nine years older, he used to joke, he would always keep her feeling young. Of late, quite the opposite was true: David's withering lack of enthusiasm was clocking up her mileage. He'd practically chaperoned her at Monica's dinner party, in the same way he used to supervise Matt in front of company. He'd seemed concerned she might embarrass him, while she was expected to behave like a mascot. She was tempted to hire a Mr Peanut costume the next time he wheeled her out as The Wife. *Mrs David D. Forde.* Erika knew all marriages, all relationships, hit occasional bumps in the road. Moving in together, having children — the normal ups and downs of any family. While anniversaries made it all seem pretty straightforward, the accumulated mileage in a marriage wasn't all that simple to calculate.

As her husband breathed low and steadily beside her, she felt grateful to him for being what she'd needed back then, but she was trying to figure out what she needed now. A friend, she thought. If David was more of a friend, would he be kinder? More enthusiastic? *Faithful?* These nightly interludes of introspection were becoming more frequent: remembering who she used to be, and thinking about how she much preferred that version of herself. She remembered simple things she never realised she'd been taking for granted, like how her husband used to love her, and now, during night times, the realisation became less daunting: he no longer did.

'Dear God, Erika.' David's voice cut through the darkness. 'Are you still awake?'

'Sorry…'

'Surely this isn't normal,' he flapped at the duvet with one foot. 'You're like this every night.'

She turned on her side, quite unsure of how to define normal, these days.

CHAPTER TWELVE

The next morning, Erika told David about the new developments with the Stable Demin campaign. She hadn't expected him to be thrilled about her working with Nate Petersen. She knew there'd be some kind of sulky response — hell hath no fury like the great author scorned — but as they reconvened for their usual kitchen small talk, his reaction was a revelation, even to her.

'My God, you simply can't resist an opportunity, can you?'

'What opportunity?' Erika placed her walking boots in the porch with her holdall, ready for the trip.

'To humiliate me.'

'*Humiliate you?* How am I humiliating you?' she demanded, surprising herself, entirely stoic. This was the man sloping out to fake-sounding meetings in his good aftershave and conducting an affair using a phone in their garage, and she was humiliating him? 'Don't be so ridiculous —'

'Do not *dare* patronise me!' David swiped the glasses from his face. 'Now I understand why you somehow thought it appropriate, *flirting* with that arrogant *shit*. Insulting *my* work, at a dinner in *my* honour!'

'In your *honour?*' Erika said. 'Nate expressed an interest in working with the agency, not the other way around, if you remember. *He* gave me *his* card.'

'And barely a moment passed before you reached out with the perfect client,' he snapped, refilling the kettle and toasting a reduced-price crumpet. 'How convenient.'

'It's convenient for the client,' she said as she sent Richard a text, letting him know she was about to set off. 'If you want to work with Nate Petersen, David, why don't you ask him directly, instead of taking it out on me?'

'Work with him?' He sneered, as if he had any choice. 'I've no intention of working with him.'

'Then why this reaction? Why was he even invited to a dinner *in your honour*? The invitation wasn't accidental, was it? Monica told me herself. How was I supposed to know how it would turn out?'

'Well, as long as it turned out well for you, darling…'

'Is that what you think?' she said, clicking onto Google Maps, glad for the excuse to escape. 'That I go to your dinners, your pretentious, *boring* events, to network? I go because I'm expected to. If you don't want me there in future, you'll hear no complaints from me. I'm not apologising because someone was interested in talking to me about what I do, for once. If you're that offended, go and ask Nate to apologise.'

'So, that's what all this is about? Erika wants her moment?' he said. 'Well, you enjoy it, sweetie.'

'Sweetie?' she said, throwing her bag over her shoulder. 'That's especially condescending from someone who claims equality's so close to his heart.'

'Give my regards to Nate,' he said, heading into the garage with his crumpet and a vacuum flask.

'It's work, David, not some holiday,' she said, mimicking his usual tone.

Setting off on a working road trip was everything Erika needed. She was glad to put her foot down and put some distance between herself and the suffocating presence of David, even in his self-imposed exile. She turned up the volume on the new birthday playlist Matt had compiled for her and shut the lid on self-pity. She couldn't wait to see the team and felt her excitement grow as she took the next exit, leaving the motorway. There they were, Lingua Franca, ditching office life to film a campaign with a lionised director.

As she turned into the carpark of the nature reserve, she saw Nate standing with the campaign crew. They were a huddle of waterproof jackets and insulated mugs, mapping areas where they were free to film. Finally, she noticed a dusty, red ute sweep into view, and felt wonderfully juvenile for a moment as she spotted Enzo behind the wheel.

The irony was, while David was furious at her working with Nate, Erika still hadn't said a single word to him about Enzo. Maybe she could admit that with David doing whatever he was doing, a part of her liked having her own secret, no matter how innocuous. Erika had no idea how to convince him, once the campaign came out, that casting Enzo was down to nothing more than coincidence.

'Here he is! Our Stable Denim Guy,' Nate said, giving Enzo the once-over. He was newly kitted out in a pair of bespoke Stable jeans and a denim shirt. 'Hello there, you handsome bastard!'

Nate let his wraparound shades hang around his tattooed neck, abandoning a spate of questions from a cluster of assistants and striding over to welcome his leading man.

'Good to see you.' Nate offered a fist bump. 'And look at this!' He gestured, scanning the panorama of blue sky. 'The heavens are on our side, man!'

Enzo looked up, seeming subdued. 'I guess so,' Enzo said, rubbing his hand along his chin.

'Come on!' Nate stood back, inviting enthusiasm. 'You look cool as fuck. Might get a pair of those bad boys myself.'

'You sure are one *fine-looking* Stable Denim Guy,' Erika said, delivering the words in her best Texan accent to make Enzo smile.

'And you sure are one fine-looking woman, Erika Karter.'

Erika Karter. There it was again. Her maiden name, from back when she was his girl.

'Who's this?' Nate said as Richard's arrival completed the team. He bounded out of his Range Rover sporting mirrored aviators, a leather jacket, and noticeably oversized, Hi Top trainers. 'Your stunt-double?'

'Not unless we're filming *Top Gun*,' Enzo said, and without thinking, Erika lightly touched his arm and laughed. He stroked the back of her head, caught out by that old familiarity as for a second, neither of them censored themselves.

'Traffic bad, was it?' Nate said, as Richard looked puzzled. 'Looks like you set off back in 1985.'

'Got these yesterday,' Richard said, ignoring the remark and digging his hands into his pockets. 'They're a gift from Stable Denim.'

'Bit tight on you, aren't they? Actually...' Nate said, raising a finger. 'Hold that thought. Ursula, can I run something past you, princess?' He wandered off in her direction.

'Hi Tops?' Erika said as Richard kept one nervous eye on Nate, dithering as the director threw his arm around Ursula's shoulders. 'Are they absolutely necessary? You look like you've had a disagreement with the Mafia and stepped into two blocks of concrete.'

'At least one of us made the effort,' Richard said sourly, reading the logo on Erika's sweatshirt. 'One Beautiful Bitch?'

'Birthday gift from Matt.'

'Didn't think David would've picked it out, somehow,' Richard said, noticing Enzo, taking an awkward step towards him and just as quickly rocking away. 'Looking good, Mr Morelli!'

Enzo didn't respond, still looking at Erika. His glance ended in a smile, which she shared. Aware of the affection between them and feeling it must be obvious, she made an excuse about needing to speak to the team.

'Right, everyone,' Nate said, s slapping his hands together. 'Richard here will be kindly playing the part of our Dad Jean wearer.' He took him by the shoulders. 'He's our consumer. This guy can only dream of inhabiting the same kind of physicality as our Stable Denim Guy. Ursula, down there, is heading up direction for our socials. She'll be working with Richard, creating a nice dichotomy between shots. All good?'

A succession of mumbled, nodded agreements were sparked among the small group.

'Remember, folks, Mr Morelli embodies the fantasy, okay? He's that guy, that *sexy bastard*, we all want to be,' he said with a big grin.

With his arms folded, Enzo gazed overhead at the mountains, as if he wasn't listening to a single word.

'So,' Nate said, as the crew began moving. 'Enzo? We're going to grab a few testers.' Nate squinted into his Mini Pro, a piece of kit he carried like a weapon and operated with one heavily tattooed arm. 'Let's dive into your fucking *soul* here, my friend! Underplay the fuck out of it, like we said, my man!'

Nate hollered instructions to assistants who were crouching low, a process that struck her as wonderfully old school. They were measuring light and angling reflectors, a hive of activity between the booming war cry of, 'Action!'

Nate gave soccer coach-style pep talks to Enzo in between shots, reiterating his intent. Erika could tell which shots were destined to make the final cut. She liked the cutaway shots of Enzo's long legs as he stood in a ravine, shading his face from the sun. *And what a face.* Nate caught the softness of his lips against day-old stubble and the naked sadness in his eyes. Thick, black eyelashes casting shadows along his cheekbones. His face was damp, as if from rainwater, which was actually bottled water, provided by one of the crew.

'Right, babe,' Ursula said, after Richard had removed his memory foam-looking footwear. 'Go the same way as Enzo, but we don't want you looking too confident.'

'What's that supposed to mean?'

'Well, he's cool, the Stable Denim Guy, and you're the normal one, aren't you? Maybe you could stumble around a bit?'

'Stumble around? Until I bloody kill myself or break a leg?'

'Don't worry.' Nate slapped his hand on Richard's shoulder. 'We've got you fully insured.' He laughed. 'I'm joking, I'm joking. You're the bloke on social media. There you are, scrolling on your phone. Here's our guy, Enzo. You can't possibly put yourself in his place. Then, the consumer sees *you*. Recognition makes Stable Denim attainable, reassuring enough for them to click through to that essential purchase, okay?'

Richard remained unconvinced as he took to the footpath, trying not to complain about the grit beneath his bare feet. He made it to the rocks, picking pebbles from his soles and rolling up his jeans, wincing at the spray-back from cascading waterfalls and almost slipping into the river.

'That's it!' Ursula shouted. 'Just try and have a laugh with it!'

As she waited around between takes, Erika checked her phone. She thought David might have texted, but there was not so much as a quick message to wish her a safe journey.

Maybe this was what she needed to get used to: independence, letting go of the safety net.

'Yes, mate!' Nate called to Enzo, sharing the latest playbacks with Erika. 'This is beautiful stuff!'

'I can't wait to present this back,' she said, peering at the screen. 'It looks incredible.'

'I've got something else. Forgive me for sounding sleazy here, man,' Nate said as Enzo perched on stepping-stones, the river running across his naked feet. 'But can we get you out of that shirt? I want to try something.'

'Well, I dunno…' Enzo said, shaking his head and then finally playing along. 'Will you still respect me, Nate?'

'Do we really need that?' Erika said. 'We don't want it getting too cheesy, do we?'

'Trust me,' Nate said, holding up his hands to share his visual. 'Enzo, could you stand with your back to us? We're not trying to exploit you with any cheap, six-pack shots here!'

'Good,' Enzo said, calling down, 'because I've got a two-pack, at best.'

'I want to create a sense of the world on his shoulders, y'know?' Nate said to Erika, adjusting his camera.

Erika watched Enzo remove his shirt, revealing those oversized shoulders, almost ready for combat. She remembered the other times she'd seen him take off his shirt, getting ready to climb into bed with her.

'Looks fucking great, man!' Nate called. 'Could you put your hands on the back of your head, like, yeah… That's it!'

Enzo's long, sleek body was exactly how she remembered, along with his expert hands, his mouth taking her breath —

'Got it!' Nate called. 'You can regain your dignity now, mate. And, I'd say,' he said, turning to address the crew, 'our work here is done.' He clapped appreciatively, the team returning the gesture.

As the crew broke into sub-groups, beginning to pack up, Erika noticed Enzo hunched over on the rocks. She went to him, bypassing Nate and Richard. The assistants looked concerned, offering water.

'I'm fine,' he said, taking a drink and wiping his mouth on the back of his arm.

'Can I get you anything?' Erika said.

'Nothing works,' he said, his expression clouded, face drawn in pain.

'Bloody hell,' Richard said, following Nate and joining them. 'You want to get some of this, Ursula? He looks worse than I do.' He unbuttoned his shirt, revealing a thatch of overgrown chest hair. 'I'm fine with a few testers, Nate. We can mix things up a bit, if you like.'

'No, no, mate. That's all good.' Nate zipped up his jacket with a good-natured laugh. 'We'll leave the nudity to the professionals, eh?' He gripped Enzo by the hand, helping him up. 'We don't want to completely take the piss out of you, now do we, Richard?'

CHAPTER THIRTEEN

As everyone packed away, strapping in and heading off, Enzo dialled down the fuss, insisting he was fine to drive. Erika joined the rest of the crew in an ant-like trail in the direction of Nate's place, flanked by chiselled landscape and stretches of untenanted terrain. The route levelled out as they passed through a village, nothing more than a stone tavern, a newsagent, and a post office.

Erika was beginning to consider that maybe Nate really did live the reclusive lifestyle he claimed to have converted to, opting out of his former, high-profile antics.

As traffic slowed to join a connecting road, she noticed the gate marked Private. The tight twists and turns eventually led to another set of imposing, black gates. A flawless expanse of manicured lawn surrounded the driveway, winding up towards a huge house. Striped, spiralled turrets topped the white façade, some parts resembling a church. Other aspects were unapologetically eccentric, like the topiary, which was shaped into mer-people bearing tridents.

In the entrance hall, where the crew was now dispatched, Erika's first instinct was to look up at the vaulted ceiling. To her left was an almost life-sized portrait of Nate. Rendered in oils and wearing nothing but a pair of riding boots and velvet jacket-tails, his basking cock presided over the cast-iron fireplace.

'That's a bit much, isn't it?' Richard said, lifting his shades to the top of his head.

'That's *a lot* much,' Ursula said, taking a picture on her phone.

'Lovely people!' Nate appeared on the mezzanine, standing behind an oak balcony. 'You'll find keys in the bowl on the table with your names and room numbers. Make yourselves at home.' He spread his arms in welcome. 'Drinks will be served … *now*!'

'I'm beginning to wish I'd booked a Travelodge,' Enzo said, sidling up to Erika as chatter rang out across the space. 'How about you?'

'Not exactly the low-key evening I was expecting.'

'Have you been outside?' Enzo said, handing Erika her key and rummaging to find his own. 'There's a marquee and a load of people out there having drinks.'

'Matt's going to love this,' Erika said. 'Here I am, at Nate Petersen's house, probably about to witness a live orgy.'

'I feel like I've already witnessed one.' Enzo gestured behind them. 'Did you see the artwork? I think Nate slipped the artist a few quid…' He grinned, waiting for her to go ahead upstairs. 'That's not drawn to scale.'

'Says Mr Stable Denim, clenching his butt in his jeans,' Erika said as he laughed, busted. 'Why do men do that? Your bums look perfectly fine at ease. No need to clench them into hotdog buns.'

'I was thinking more sourdough batard, actually. I'm incredibly sophisticated and cultured, I'll have you know,' he said, as they reached the first-floor corridor. A pretty young woman in a long, cotton dress with daisies in her hair gestured down the hallway, inviting them to find their rooms.

'Looks like this is me,' Enzo said, stopping in front of room two, on the left.

'Well, hello, neighbour,' Erika said. Her room, number three, was on the right.

'Don't be a stranger,' Enzo said, with a mischievous smile thrown over his shoulder.

Erika pulled a face, closing the door to find a mahogany four-poster, draped in heavy, navy velvet, and a fireplace with a blood-red rug in front of it.

She put her holdall on the tightly bound bed, noticing a fully stocked tantalus on the bedside table, as if they were expecting Princess Margaret. She walked towards the stone-encased windows, kneeling on the chaise-longue in the bay. The window was slightly open, and a breeze billowed through. The man had swings, croquet, and swans. *Actual swans!* She wandered back and sat on the bed, so high she could swing her legs. She was starting to like this, being away from things. Maybe Polly was right: this was exactly what she needed, some time to herself. She tied up her hair as she unzipped her case.

She felt lighter as she turned on the shower and caught a glimpse of the cloudless, pale blue sky through the skylight. When she was finished, she wrapped herself in an oversized towel and massaged her new geranium and orange lotion into her poor, sad bottom, then across her arms and along her legs.

Erika got to her feet as she heard people passing by her door, joining the party. She debated whether to call David as she changed into a jumpsuit. Should she reassure her husband she was still alive, in case he was wondering? As she checked her lipstick and spritzed perfume, she suddenly wondered if he wasn't alone. What if he was with the person at the other end of those texts? Planning to spend the night with them at their house, in their home? She imagined that woman sitting there, on her side of the couch, casting silent judgement on the wallpaper, noticing framed photographs of the family she'd infiltrated. Erika picked up her phone.

'Hello.' David sounded calm, and therefore she decided he must be alone.

'Thought I'd call to let you know we've just got to Nate's place.'

'Well, don't let me cramp your style.'

'David —'

'I'm in the middle of something.'

'Something or someone?'

'What?'

'Nothing. Best let you go, then.'

'All right, then.'

David ended the call without a goodbye. Every move felt either clumsy or strategic with her husband, Erika thought, making her way to the staircase, the vestibule now deserted.

She heard laughter and the pulse of music from somewhere in the distance. As she made her way to the bar, she caught sight of Enzo, in a corner cove against a backdrop of gleaming bottles. Enzo put his head on one side as their eyes met. There was no better feeling. When it came to physical attraction, he wrote her rulebook. She hadn't felt anything like it in years.

'I'd almost given up,' Enzo said, easing the smile from his face, as if silently chastising himself.

'I called David,' Erika said, as if issuing some kind of warning. 'My husband.'

'How is he?'

They looked at each other for a moment, then smiled, the tension breaking.

'So,' Enzo said, sipping his drink, dressed in combats, shirt and flipflops, like some kind of sexy tour guide. 'I see Richard's unbuttoned his shirt again.'

Richard was dancing with Ursula, looking like a teacher at a school leavers' disco.

'I don't think it's right,' she said. 'Having to stare at your boss's nipples.'

'No one said anything about his nipples, Erika. Or having to stare at them.'

'You're right. There I go again. Projecting.'

'What can I get you?' Enzo asked, slapping a firm hand on the bar and sliding behind it. 'It's self-serve. A free-for-all, basically, so at least that's some small comfort.'

'Gin and tonic, thanks, bar personage.'

'One gin and tonic, coming right up, for the lady.'

He grabbed a glass and some tongs, adding ice.

'Are you chopping a lemon?' she asked as she watched his arm moving behind the counter.

'No, I'm just pleased to see you.'

She pulled that face again — the disapproving one that said, *you idiot*, but, she realised, actually meant *I would very much like to fuck you*. She couldn't help it. Watching him on the shoot earlier, memories of them became fantasies of him.

'This is bad,' she said, as a few couples started making out around them. 'I feel like someone's mother.'

'You are someone's mother,' Enzo said, handing over her glass.

'Here's to being someone's mother,' she said, raising it as he joined her.

She took a sip, noticing the tapestries unfurled from exposed beams and sheets of music preserved in oversized frames. In each corner of the room, mannequin knights stood in armour, bearing shields, and sun-bleached rugs covered stone floors.

'Is it wrong that I've done this?' asked Enzo.

'Made me a drink?' said Erika, buoying the mood, remembering how prone Enzo was to introspection. 'The campaign? You're the perfect fit.'

'I mean, seeing you,' he said, and it felt rather wonderful, that rollercoaster swoop of elation as her stomach dropped. 'I could've walked away. Is that what I should've done?'

'If I were you, I'd be more worried about seeing your face plastered everywhere,' she said. 'Seeing me is the least of your worries.'

'You've got a point,' he said. 'Probably should've thought it through a bit more.'

'Having second thoughts?'

'Always.'

Well, didn't they both know that for a fact…?

'At the risk of sounding tarty,' he said, 'you look very nice.'

'Thanks,' Erika said, leading them outside before they were buried beneath an avalanche of conjoined couples.

'Nate's manning the decks,' said Enzo. 'He's what we used to call a Superstar DJ. Another one of his many, not so hidden talents.'

'You know, there's a good chance we're about to be mistaken for somebody's parents,' Erika said as they stepped into the marquee. 'Here to collect them too early.'

Lights and shapes hit the walls, music dense as a heatwave.

'Hey, there's our boy!' Nate said, standing behind a raised platform, wearing huge, red headphones and a mesh T-shirt. 'Enzo Morelli. The face of Stable Denim. What a fucking legend!'

Claps and whistles broke out from maybe fifty people in there, taking a closer look.

'And me,' Richard said, bouncing from the crowd, slightly breathless from the exertion of nonstop dad moves. 'I'm fronting it too!'

'And me!' Erika said, poking fun, deflecting attention from Enzo when she noticed how uncomfortable he looked. 'I'll be fronting it!'

'And me!' yelled a lone voice from the back of the marquee.

'No, I really am,' Richard said, indignant. 'I was filming *today*. Ask her.' He pointed at Ursula as bystanders began to lose interest. 'Anyway, who's getting in the hot tub?'

'Are we getting in the hot tub?' Erika asked, with no intention of doing so under any circumstances.

'We are not,' Enzo said as she followed him back outside. 'This wasn't quite what I signed up for.'

'Most things aren't. At least this is daft. If it's any consolation, I couldn't be happier with the shoot,' Erika said, as they wandered past small groups sitting cross-legged on the lawn, while a drunken game of boules was taking place up ahead. 'It's not entirely impossible, but it's a bit late for you to be backing out…'

'I'm not going to do that. I just…' Enzo came to a stop, folding his arms, his whiskey glass tucked under his bicep. 'When I turned up that day, Ursula mentioned I had a good shot. Then I saw you and got the feeling I'd be helping you out.'

'You did all this for me?' she said playfully, unconvinced.

'I don't think there's much I wouldn't do for you, Erika.'

Her smile dropped, but any response was cut off by a loud splash.

There were panicked shouts as the music stopped.

'Richard!' they said in unison.

CHAPTER FOURTEEN

The ambulance arrived within the hour. Ursula tried to keep Richard calm, his face horribly clammy and pale as he lay in a cold sweat on a picnic blanket. He was sucking on an ice cube, with one badly bruised leg propped up on a nest of silk cushions from Nate's countryside harem, refusing the various pipes and bongs being offered.

One empathetic partygoer wearing a patchwork waistcoat paired with a top hat, rather like a jubilant undertaker, told them that Richard had been demonstrating surf moves on the edge of the hot tub, when a swan had skimmed across the pond at high speed (most probably nesting, he explained, and Erika wouldn't have had him down as an ornithologist), spreading its wings in an undeniably elegant attack. Richard had keeled backwards, fully submerged, but leaving his leg on the side of the tub. It had snapped like a twig, the man said.

The atmosphere grew subdued as he was assessed by the paramedic. Richard was even less amused when he realised Ursula was filming the scene. 'For Dad Jeans,' she said. 'This is gold, babe.'

There was a ripple of applause as the ambulance drove away, followed by chants of 'Save our NHS!'

The arrival of dusk signalled low-level lighting and ambient music. Erika and Enzo had been sitting in two overstuffed wicker armchairs, like a couple of old-timers, on the edge of the grounds, after Enzo had fixed another couple of drinks. Although Erika had never been a festivalgoer, it felt like her own personal Glastonbury as they wandered towards a pullup projector, the house growing smaller in the distance. The music was quite pleasant from afar as they ruminated on Richard's injuries and watched the bizarre highlights from Nate's films as they played on a loop.

'I've never seen any of his stuff,' Erika said. 'Any good?'

'No idea,' Enzo said, 'but I think this is the one he reckons is like that Bowie movie — *The Man Who Fell to Earth*.' He took a swig of beer. 'It's his latest. It's about an intergalactic eco-agent who travels the universe. Looks like *Aquaman* for hipsters.'

'Is that what they are?' Erika asked. 'Hipsters?'

'Hola!'

Erika jolted slightly as Nate Petersen staggered out of the surrounding woodland, man-bun dishevelled, one heavily inked arm draped around Ingrid.

'You two!' He stood in front of them, almost tipping over, regaining his balance like a paper-chain figure cut-out by a child. 'There's something between you two…'

'Yeah.' Enzo pointed his bottle in the direction of the screen. 'You, and a big projector.'

'No, man,' Nate said. 'It's in the eyes, not the proximity. There's a *communion* between you! I saw it today. The camera lies, but the *eyes*? They're incapable of anything but truth! There's your narrative.' He turned to Erika. 'And your husband —David. Daniel. Forde. What's he all about? Godforsaken man…'

'He's my husband,' Erika said, as a well-honed instinct to defend David overtook her.

'Fair enough,' Nate said, raising his arms, no insult intended. 'But energy flows. It's magnetic, mercurial.' He grabbed Ingrid's bottom and she gave a playful screech. 'It's undeniable, life-affirming!' He placed a hearty kiss on her lips before the pair of them sauntered off in an almost zig-zag formation towards the house.

Erika and Enzo sat in silence, watching Nate and Ingrid disappear. Erika was self-conscious now, wondering if they looked inappropriate, sitting there. She was drinking with her ex, but it was all in the name of working together. They were nothing more than friends who'd known each other forever. It was nothing like Richard's hook-ups, or David's, for that matter. She wondered how many times her husband had done this, knowing there was nothing friendly or innocent about it. Did he give her feelings, their family, a second thought? Somehow, she doubted it.

'Are you upset over what he said about your husband?'

'No, it's fine.'

'How about what he said about you and me?'

Erika began to reply, but was unsure of what to say.

'Erika, it's just a drink. You don't have to be —'

'I'm not,' she said, quick to interrupt.

'Do you believe what he said about the eyes?' he asked, coaxing her response with a sceptical look.

'Yes,' she said, giving him her honest answer. 'I do.'

Enzo contemplated this for a moment, growing less amused and more mindful. He reached across the space between them, inviting her to take his hand. They stayed like that, holding hands across the distance as they finished their drinks, and watching scenes from Nate's movies: gazelle-like astronauts; bilingual babies; weeping centaurs; supernatural stowaways.

'You've had a shave,' Erika said, as the screen light washed across Enzo's face.

'I have.'

'How come?'

'Well, you know how it is,' he said. 'Women sometimes complain about the stubble.'

She gave a snort.

'Ah, there it is. That lovely laugh of yours.'

She snorted again.

'I shaved because,' he said, craning his neck towards her, 'if I hadn't done, I'd have had a full beard by the time you finished your first drink.'

'*Hot.*'

'Thanks,' he said, with a smirk. 'I think.'

'Hot's good,' she said. 'Matt tells me what to say. Cool, isn't cool, anymore. And never say trendy.'

'Damn,' he said, giving her arm a swing and letting it go. 'There go my hopes of being cool and trendy. What did Nate mean about your husband? He knows him, does he? Not that it's any of my business…'

She felt a familiar sinking feeling. It wasn't something she was proud of, not being enough for her husband. Did she want Enzo hearing that? More importantly, was she ready to admit that to herself?

'Everything's a bit *off* with David at the moment,' she said, aware she'd never mentioned his name until that night.

Enzo looked at her now, his ink blue gaze spilling across her face as though he read her feelings all too clearly.

'I broke into the garage. Kind of broke in,' she clarified, as he shot her a brief look of concern. 'My husband is always in there, you see, and it's weird, isn't it? Anyway, I found a phone. There were messages. He's having an affair.'

'Okay,' Enzo said, sounding measured. 'And you're sure about this? The affair?'

'It's all there. The proof.' Erika gave a rueful look. 'But what's the difference? That's what I'm thinking. He's doing whatever he's doing, and now I know, so at least I don't have to feel as stupid.'

'You're not stupid, Erika,' Enzo said. 'You're far from stupid.'

'Thanks,' she said, sipping her drink. 'You'll make me blush.'

'You know what I mean. You can't think of it that way. It's not about him wanting to make you feel stupid.'

'I do that all by myself,' she smiled. 'Sneaking around, stalking my own husband. Looking, well, hoping, actually, to find *evidence*. I was almost glad I'd found something at first. I felt less guilty about rummaging around. That's bad, isn't it?' She wondered what Enzo was making of it all, hoping he wasn't reacting the same way anyone else would react — somewhere between distaste and pity. 'Maybe I'm the problem. Maybe I should be investigating myself.' She tried to shrug it off. 'I never would've thought I'd end up the dull one in the fallout.'

'The dull one?'

'When Matt left for university, sometimes I'd pretend I needed petrol, just to break the monotony. I'd drive to the all-night garage and just sit there. I used that excuse twice in one night and David never even noticed, except, obviously, he did. Meanwhile, he's the man with no name, isn't he? Forbidden lovers. Secret phones. The exciting one…'

'Depends on your idea of exciting,' Enzo said as she noticed the soft, dark hair dusting his forearms as he rerolled his shirt sleeves. 'None of what he's doing makes you dull or stupid.'

'Ignore me. I'm being flippant. It makes it easier. Sort of.'

'Does your husband work with Nate or something?'

'It's a bit of a sore point, actually. I already told you,' she said. 'He's an arsehole.'

'Ah,' he said. 'He's gone professional?'

'He's a writer. A novelist.'

'Woah,' Enzo said, his tone begrudging the compliment. 'Impressive.'

'He thinks so,' Erika said, keen to change the subject. 'You said your dad passed away?'

'A while back, yeah.'

'Do you get out to Italy, to see your mum?'

'I've been a few times. She lives in Marina del Cantone. You'd love it.'

You'd love it. For a second, Erika let herself mentally elope with Enzo. He was right. She did love it.

'I'd like to go more often — maybe make a move out there. That's what Mum would like, anyway,' he said. 'So, are you going to leave him? Your husband?'

'I don't know,' Erika said, not prepared for the question. 'Everything feels too surreal to be making decisions right now. It's not as if he hasn't done it before.' Embarrassment weighed on her. 'Twice, that I know of.'

'That doesn't mean he gets to do it again, Erika.'

'No,' she said, nodding in agreement. 'Do you know what he said the last time? It was a few years ago now.' She smiled to cover her hurt. 'He said, would I rather he thought about her while he was with me, or just slept with her and got it out of his system.'

'Christ, Erika…'

'What can I say? He's very practical.'

'That's why you were glad you found the phone? Because you've put up with it before?'

'Maybe,' she said. 'He told me that he'd never do it again. He made all the right promises. So, when it happened again, we stopped talking properly.' She gave a resigned sigh. 'After that, maybe I didn't want him getting too close, but there was this terminal, unspoken dialogue going on between us the whole time. If you're with someone who has to make promises like that...'

'Why do people do this to each other?' Enzo put down his bottle, balancing it on the grass.

'For love?' Erika suggested, trying to deflate the brooding atmosphere. 'He's critical and uptight about everything these days, and I'm kind of ... homesick, I guess, is the best way to describe it. I've been living with this person for years, but without Matt I've no idea who he is or what we are.' Her thoughts landed back in the present. 'Sorry for offloading.'

'Don't be sorry. Friends talk,' Enzo said. 'This is good, by the way. Talking about it.'

'Telling you how miserable I am? Bet you're glad you waited this long to hear the enthralling account of my middle-aged existence.'

'So,' Enzo said, 'you have a son?'

'Yes,' she said, with the instant smile only Matt could bring. 'He's studying Entertainment and Events Management at LIPA. How great is that?' She took her phone from her bag and slipped on her glasses. 'Here, humour me,' she added, opening the gallery. 'That's Matty.'

'Good-looking kid,' Enzo said, leaning over. 'Looks like his mum. How is your husband with Matt?'

'Good,' she said. 'I mean, David's always encouraged him to work hard and be disciplined. Matt's happy, I hope. He had a great education.'

'Sounds like a hoot.'

'They get on,' she said. 'They're just very different, and always have been. David's a few years older and quite traditional. Matt's always been more creative. He's brilliantly unconventional.'

'You know, I never would've had you down for marriage.'

'Why?'

'Well, you were always brilliantly unconventional…'

'Marriage doesn't have to be conventional. It's what you make it, isn't it?' Erika said. 'At least, that's what I thought. You create your own little world, with your family, don't you? It's not about following convention.'

'That's exactly what marriage is. Otherwise, it would've been extinct long ago.'

'I miss my son,' Erika said, scrolling through her most recent pictures. 'I don't recognise myself without Matty. And David's a complete stranger these days. I don't think I can carry on doing this, can I?'

'Erika,' Enzo said, drawing one hand across his jawline. 'You know I can't answer that for you, but if you're asking for my opinion, you can have it, for what it's worth.' He talked into the encroaching darkness. 'You're in a situation you can't tolerate. The fact that we're having this conversation, and it's helpful to you…' He shook his head. 'Look, Erika. I don't know this guy, and right now, I'm glad that I don't, because he's not treating you right. I mean, you know this. He knows this. What else is it going to take?'

Erika said nothing, recalling the number of times she'd lain awake, thinking the exact same thing.

'The Erika I knew,' Enzo said, amused, 'wouldn't have stood for this…'

Wouldn't she? Erika felt a spark of recognition.

'That Erika would've kicked him to the kerb,' he smiled. 'Like you did with me…'

'What?' she said, open-mouthed in denial. 'I didn't kick you to the kerb. You'd do your usual: drift in, drift out, like the bloody tide. I got tired of holding my breath, waiting around until next time.'

'That's not how I remember it,' he said, his features softening. 'And here we are again. Next time.'

'No, not next time,' she said, snatching away any suggestion. 'Let's make this the last time we go all these years without speaking.'

CHAPTER FIFTEEN

Erika sat in her pyjamas, planning to demolish a tube of Pringles and the family bag of peanut M&Ms she'd packed for the journey. There was no sign of dinner arriving in Nate's non-stop universe of drinks and dancing. She was happy to be back in the Bridgerton room after her unplanned heart-to-heart with Enzo. She'd told him how tired she was and dashed up first, avoiding the awkwardness of saying goodnight at the door.

She glanced up at the mirrored canopy above her four-poster, feeling like Anita Pallenberg, wondering how much DNA was still traceable on Nate's guest-room sheets. She did need to do something about David. They had to face it and work on their marriage. Except, where was the motivation? The thought of working on it bored her. They were past that point, weren't they? But no matter how obvious it seemed, the thought of leaving remained somehow alien, equally as uninspiring as the thought of staying together.

Noticing her phone, she took out her charger. It was not a good time to be worrying about her marriage, right before going to sleep. A selfie of Richard in a hospital bed and a text from Ursula greeted her. He'd been X-rayed and was about to be fitted with a cast. They had no idea what time they'd be getting back. Erika also had a missed call from Monica, but nothing from David. It wasn't completely unheard of for Monica to get in touch, but at ten past eleven? She called her back.

'Is David okay?' she asked when Monica picked up. It felt so odd, having to ask someone else this question.

'There's a situation you need to be aware of. There's a bit of friction, shall we say, on social media. A few exchanges sent from Matt's account to David.'

'From Matt? What do you mean?'

'Matt posted an unfiltered reaction to David's book, and, well…' Monica paused. 'It's not exactly a glowing review.'

'Right,' Erika said, not entirely surprised that Matt didn't like the book — the kid read Nietzsche for kicks. But why he'd choose to post anything publicly, she had no idea. 'Well, it's his dad's book, so —'

'Erika,' Monica said, in professional mode, guarding her client's interests. 'You know I love Matt, but this tirade could be catastrophic. The allegations —'

'Allegations?' she said, wishing Monica would talk straight.

'Allegations of homophobia, Erika. What he's said is incredibly harmful. Matt's painted David as some kind of bigoted patriarch. It'd be pretty damning from any source, but from his own son…? I'm sorry to land this on you, but I thought it best to call.' She paused. 'Especially as David seems to think you gave Matt some sort of blessing.'

'What's he talking about?' she said, resenting the thought of him bitching about her with his agent. 'This is the first I've heard of any of this. Why would I be okay with it?'

'Matt mentions you and your work with Stix & Stones in some of the posts,' she said, with a disapproving sigh. 'He implies David plagiarised your work, jumping on the non-binary bandwagon.'

'Monica, Matt hasn't said a word to me, apart from admitting he hadn't got round to reading the book. I wouldn't expect him to air his opinions publicly, no matter how strongly he felt. Please let David know that I knew nothing about this,' she said, realising that they'd just hit an all-time low, going through his agent. 'I'll speak to Matt, but what else am I supposed to do?'

'It's one hot mess,' Monica said, sounding as tired as Erika felt. 'And this stuff's getting picked up. It's a hugely sensitive topic on just about every level. I'm preparing a response with David, but I'm expecting to field a lot of enquiries over the next few days. Where we go from here is anybody's guess.'

'Well, good luck. Thanks for letting me know,' Erika said. 'Any reason why David didn't pick up the phone himself?'

'He's pretty sore about the whole thing, as you can imagine.'

'Vividly.'

Once they'd hung up, Erika went online and read Matt's social media posts.

As a proud member of the LGBQT+ community I urge u NOT to buy this book. The work of cisgender male @DavidDForde exploiting lives in cheap & ignorant way.

Okay, so Matt wasn't holding back.

SPOILERS GUARANTEED! @DavidDForde has written these novels for years with a throwback ALPHA MALE character — who no longer IDs as male?! He doesn't have the ability or the right!

'Matt…' Erika shut her eyes for a second, contemplating the impact on his father.

In the end — phew! Hetero-boy, Finn Schuyler, isn't one of US at all! HUGE relief to guys like @DavidDForde, still confused by their feelings for Sean Connery in Dr No.

Erika put her hand over her mouth and let out a snort of nervous amusement. The posts continued to dredge up just about every dubious aspect and unsavoury nuance of David's work. The thing was, she couldn't entirely disagree.

Heteronormative fantasy? We get it. But to flip this dinosaur and have him carry a Pride flag? NO. @DavidDForde is last person who should write on this topic.

What he was saying was true. The first couple of books in the series had come to life as enjoyable spy thrillers but as time wore on, they became loaded with every tired cliché of the genre. In one, Finn identified his estranged son by his ability to nail a Brazilian airhostess. To make an about-turn, with sudden statements on gender identity, was a risky move by anyone's standards.

I don't ID as non-binary but I have relationships with PEOPLE. It took painful years to accept WHO I AM. @DavidDForde will cry creative freedom BUT this is SO calculated! #DoNotRead.

Erika winced at the hashtag.

Momma is an advocate. Her agency @LinguaFranca headed up @Stix&Stones #BornBeautiful+ — one of the 1st #malecosmetics brands. LOOK at @DavidDForde's jacket artwork! He's not AUTHENTIC but he could try ORIGINAL.

The next post was a photo of Matt wearing elaborate make-up, holding the *Code Name: They* paperback and giving it a thumb's down. The caption read:

Incognito … not-so. #InTheMix #AllShadesOfThePalette @Stix&Stones.

Great. This was all she needed. Stix & Stones had liked and shared, copying in @LinguaFrancaAgency and giving her a shoutout. Erika called Matt.

'So, I take it he told you?' he said when he picked up.

'No, Matt. Worse than that. He had Monica call me.'

'Ah, so you've been banished?'

'Looks that way. Your dad thinks we're in cahoots, apparently.'

'We are, always have been,' he said.

'Matt, what you've done,' she said, not sure quite where to start. 'This is his career, his reputation. Couldn't you have had a private conversation? Why post this stuff when you know it's going to hurt him?'

'And what about how I feel? What about all the people he's going to hurt? Belittling people's lives, trivialising what they've been through? It's pathetic. He's pathetic.'

'Matt, come on. I really don't think that was his intention. You know that's not what your dad's about. He's writing a character, a fantasy. It's not a manifesto.'

'Then what was his intention, apart from keeping his name out there? Selling more shitty books with literally no right to discuss this topic?'

'I think he was just trying to … you know how he is,' Erika said, with no real idea herself. She'd already circled this with David, only to be shunned as some kind of ignorant bystander to his great artistry. 'He's trying to be topical.'

'Well, hey, I've made him super topical.'

134

'Look, I agree, he's gone about it in a clumsy way. But, Matt, you shouldn't have posted those comments online. He's your dad. This affects everyone, the entire team. You, me.'

'His team don't even want to be part of it! I was contacted by Halo Jones — you know Halo?'

'Halo? Yes, I had dinner with them the other night.'

'*Them* — see, you get it,' Matt said, sounding elated. 'It's important to use correct pronouns. Anyway, Halo contacted me for a response. They're doing a podcast about Dad writing a non-binary character. I hadn't read it yet and declined to comment, but then Halo said that Dad's own social media people find the whole thing uncomfortable!'

Erika knew that was true, remembering the dinner table that night at Monica's as the conversation had soured.

'They're all dying, having to fake-support the cause,' he said. 'But if people expect me to have an opinion, with Dad wading in on this, I'm not putting on some united front like a politician's wife. It means too much to me, Mum.'

'I don't understand why Halo assumed you're part of the LGBTQ+ community?'

'Because when they contacted Dad, guess what the first thing he said was?'

'He played the my-son's-one-of-yours card?'

'Of course he did,' Matt said. 'And I'm sure he told them he has friends who are Black, too. Halo slipped into my DMs and asked if I'd be up for a chat. I know what you're saying, Mum, I do, but why didn't Dad mention any of this to me before publication?'

'I think he still sees you as a kid,' she said, trying to soften the impending fallout. 'You just need to explain this to him.'

'No way. He'll expect an apology, and that's not happening, so saddle up the horses and let's ride it out.'

Erika wished Matt had kept his opinions offline. The whole thing playing out across his social media channels implied David had some kind of issue with Matt, which had never been the case. Erika was the one who'd let Matt down at first. Her reaction to his coming out had not exactly been the cool response he'd hoped for, or even how she would've expected herself to react.

They'd always been close, so she was hurt that she and David were the last to know. David inadvertently initiated the conversation over dinner, talking about a possible stage adaptation of the TV drama *It's a Sin*. When Matt started with, 'Well, now seems just as good a time as any…' before trailing off, Erika thought he was joking. It was David who got to his feet and hugged their son.

'What about Soph?' Erika said, unsure what else to say. Sophia, Matt's first, and apparently last, girlfriend, sprang to mind. They'd been sixteen when they'd started seeing each other and were completely inseparable.

After the dinner table bombshell, she listened to Matt as he was completely candid, a change that was set to continue. She could already see how he felt more relaxed in himself. He gave his account of the panic and fear that had preceded his coming out — all the things you read about, none of it resonating until you heard it from your own child.

He told her how — despite her best efforts — he and Sophia had slept together. They'd had Sophia's house all to themselves for three days a week after college before her parents got home. But he knew that, no matter how much he tried to convince himself otherwise, it was more admiration than attraction that he felt for her. He'd always liked boys. He'd even fallen in love with a boy and had thought the boy loved him too. It hadn't lasted long, and it had broken his heart from what Erika could tell, but he said he'd felt more for him than he'd ever felt for Sophia.

Erika wanted Matt to fall madly in love with whoever he loved madly. She told him this, and she meant it. Only a few weeks later, she jumped into the Lingua Franca collaboration with Stix & Stones, campaigning for Matt and every other kid who felt they needed permission to be themselves.

CHAPTER SIXTEEN

As predicted, the posts from the previous night were only the start of the debate surrounding *Code Name: They*. Erika had texted David first thing, to let him know she'd spoken to Matt and to tell him she was right there if he needed her. She received no response. Clearly he was lying in wait to confront her face-to-face.

'There you go. Cancelled,' David said, appearing almost as soon as Erika pulled into the driveway. 'I've been cancelled. Happy now? They've cancelled me.'

'Who's cancelled you?' She grabbed her bag from the back seat. 'Cancelled what?'

'*Code Name: They*. It's no longer available in all good bookshops. Several interviews have been cancelled, including on BBC Radio. So, there you go. I've been cancelled. Matt's cancelled me.'

'David —'

'Don't David me. He knows full well what he's doing, make no mistake about that, Erika. He knew exactly what was at stake, and he went right ahead and did it anyway. This is the thanks I get.'

'I'm sure he didn't —'

'Of course, he did!' David followed Erika into the house, where she stuck on the kettle, although she wouldn't have refused something stronger. 'Don't try to defend him. His actions are wholly indefensible. He waded into a conversation of his own making, offering these cretins — trolls, bloody keyboard warriors — ripe feeding ground for a witch hunt, thanks to his character assassination.'

'That's not fair,' Erika said, knowing she was fighting a losing battle. 'He was asked to give his opinion. Halo approached him.'

'Ah, yes. Halo. Another dinner party guest who couldn't wait to stab me in the back. And now, here I am. You know, it really is incredible to me how Matthew could share his views with a digital audience without having the decency to discuss it with me first. He put it straight out there, as if he was giving a press conference.'

'I think he might've felt the same way,' Erika said, gesturing with a cup as David vehemently shook his head.

'So, he's discussed this with you, of course,' he said, 'while ignoring any correspondence from me. He struck the match, lit the fire and walked away. And I'm the one left to deal with the heat.'

'Nice analogy,' Erika said, taking a seat at the dining table, already exhausted.

'Are you even taking this seriously? Do you have any idea what's going on here?'

'I made it perfectly clear that he should have discussed how he felt with you, and kept his personal opinions between us.'

'Oh, come off it,' David said, opening the fridge and pouring himself a homemade smoothie. 'You've been filling his head with this nonsense since the day it suited you.'

'What nonsense?'

'You know exactly what nonsense. Ever since he came out, you've gone on about Matthew's right to have a voice and take a stand. The problem with that is, Matthew's the only one doing the talking. He gives his speeches without listening to other people express their opinions. All that Stix & Stones bullshit,' he said, silencing her with the grandiosity of a conductor. 'Don't even try saying otherwise. You paraded him round like a free pass.'

'I didn't parade him round! David, I know how upset you are,' Erika said, tilting her chin as he was about to retort, 'but I'm not responsible for this. The longer you speak, the more I think that maybe Matt's got a point.'

'Of course you do. Right behind him as usual, aren't you?'

'Maybe it's a good thing, your coverage being cancelled,' she said, getting up and deciding to leave him to it. 'I've got a feeling you might make things a hell of a lot worse, with the mood you're in.'

'Worse? You really think that's possible? So far, I've been labelled transphobic, homophobic, misogynist, bigoted, ignorant, and even racist — can you believe it? Me! This guy — represented by a French Ghanaian woman.'

'Do yourself a favour: don't start mentioning Monica's ethnicity.'

'No, of course not, God forbid. Why give the accused the opportunity to speak in his own defence? I'll tell you why not: because I'm using the wrong fucking pronoun, that's why.'

'Have you spoken to Nate?' Richard asked over the phone. He was working from home thanks to being issued with crutches that he could barely use and another prescription of potentially addictive painkillers. 'I'm in plaster up to my ball sack, and he's decided to further humiliate me by making it part of the launch. I mean, at what point did this campaign become the Nate Petersen show?'

'Yeah, he mentioned something,' Erika said, cringing. 'I mean, to be fair, it does fit with the footage.'

Nate had concocted the idea of hosting a live screening for the launch, confident that the campaign was strong enough to justify the flourish. The unveiling was set to take place the following week.

'He wants me to hobble out in the middle of Keys Court wearing the same pair of Stable Denim jeans A&E cut me out of, like some kind of crippled Hulk!'

'Can we talk about this later? I'm with Enzo,' Erika said, glancing over to where he sat, studiously unfolding a paperclip. 'We're running through the schedule.'

'Ah, the man himself,' Richard said, doing a pretty good imitation of Nate. 'Sure, I'll be here, popping some more codeine, if you need me. Catch you later.'

'Richard. Politely furious as usual,' she said, about to get back to work before her mobile rang again. 'Sorry, I need to get this.'

'Do you know Dad's set Monica on me?' Matt was already mid-rant as she answered. 'It's "imperative" I bow out of the conversation. Well, I just have. I've let everyone know he's had his "people" drown me out.'

'For God's sake, can you please stop posting all of this?' Erika pleaded.

'What?' Matt was aghast. 'You're actually taking his side?'

'I'm not taking sides, but where does this end?'

'It starts with freedom of speech and ends with authentic representation.'

'Brilliant,' she said. 'Huge weight off my mind.'

'Wow. Thanks for the support, Mum.'

'What do you expect? It's me who's got to live with him. Great,' she said, as Matt hung up. 'Sorry about that, Enzo. It's just life as I know it imploding.'

'Was that him? Your husband?' Enzo asked.

'No, that was Matt. He and David are at war.'

'I thought you said they got on?'

'They do, but...' She paused. 'You know what? Can we not talk about it right now?'

'Come on,' he said, picking up his keys. 'Fancy some lunch? I know a place.'

Twenty minutes later, Erika followed Enzo's truck down an incline as she saw a sign for The Ranch House up ahead.

'This is very rugged. You're really getting into the whole Stable Denim thing, aren't you?' she said, as they stepped up onto the deck. Enzo led the way across a bar filled with old-fashioned Americana, with Springsteen on the jukebox and exposed beams and floorboards.

'This place has the best burgers in the Wild West,' Enzo said as they slid into a booth, sitting opposite each other.

Erika remembered that once, years back, they'd gone to a '50s-style diner. Enzo had signed a menu for the waitress, who'd recognised from the Him & Hair ads. Erika had barely said two words to him all the way home.

'So, what's your story?' she said, after their order was delivered by a guy dressed as a cowboy. 'Kids? Wife? Partner?' She cut into her burger as Enzo bit into his. 'Inside leg measurement?' she added, realising she sounded like a questionnaire.

'Thirty-four inches. No partner. No marriage. No kids.'

'Okay,' she said. 'Well, that sounds very neat and tidy.'

'Not exactly.' He thumbed a dollop of ketchup from the corner of his mouth. 'Women want those things. I never did.'

'Any particular reason?'

'It didn't work out all that well for my folks,' he said. 'It doesn't seem like the right fit for most people, in my opinion. I've never heard much to convince me otherwise. Rob, my brother, is married with three kids. He's happy enough, being unhappy.'

'How come you ended up working with him?' Erika asked. 'What happened to the photography?'

'Well, the thing about photography is it's hard to make an actual living, taking pictures.' Enzo grabbed a few fries and smiled. 'It's an old story, isn't it? Old dreams being put aside. I didn't have the ability for it and found it frustrating. I did a bit more stuff and worked with Christian — remember him?' He looked at Erika and she nodded. 'Then I met someone who wanted me to get a *real* job. So, I ended up selling top-of-the-range *refrigerating systems*, including the ones they've got back there.' He gestured towards the kitchen. 'We had our moments, but one day I took a good look at myself. I was a bloke in a suit, filling out order forms and hoarding receipts in my company car. I think that what she thought she wanted…' He trailed off. 'You try, both of you, but as long as you both feel like you're trying, you start to resent it. Rob was looking to expand the business and asked if I wanted in.'

'So what happened with your parents?'

'My dad went back to Italy first,' he said. 'Mum went over after he got ill and ending up staying to manage the restaurant. The family helped her get rid of him when things weren't working out. He was never the fatherly type, my dad, at least not with me. He sucked the air out of that house. He said something about Josh and I playing fighting games when we didn't have a pair of balls between us. Can you imagine a grown man saying that to a couple of fifteen-year-old boys? He gave me a crack on the head on the way out, but that was him being friendly. He liked keeping me on my toes.'

'Was he like that with your mum?' Erika asked. She didn't remember Enzo's dad, only Val, Enzo's mum. Enzo looked like her, with the same soft features.

'I'm sure they had their moments,' he said, easing his shirt along his forearms. 'They argued. Money, work. The usual stuff. He took it out on me, I think. No idea why. Maybe because I was the oldest? Him and Rob seemed to manage fine. I'd only have to look at him the wrong way and he'd be incensed. I remember literally being scared of his shadow as a little kid. I'd carry on playing as if it wasn't there until, you know...' He cast his eyes downwards. 'You can't ignore a shadow when it knocks you off your feet. I used to imagine knocking the fucker to his knees. Remember me and Josh getting into training?' He grinned, flexing his arms like a conjurer, before taking another bite of his burger. 'Your mum fed us up on omelettes.'

'Did she know, your mum?' Erika couldn't begin to think how she'd react if David ever made Matthew feel that way, let alone laid a hand on her son. 'Did she try and stop him?'

'Mum used to ... I don't know.' He leaned back, dabbing his mouth. 'She took it as playful. He'd say it wasn't fighting, because it wasn't how men fight, it was how little girls fight.' He gave a sour smile. 'I knew exactly how it would go down one day. I took a swing at him. A few weeks later, Mum said he was going back to the coast. She was quite matter-of-fact about it. I never saw the man again.'

'You never saw him?'

'There were no big goodbyes. I landed him a high and mighty, looking him dead in the eye,' Enzo said, still with a trace of satisfaction. 'He took a look at the blood on his fingertips and finally had a reason. He laid me out flat — dislocated my shoulder. He sent my teeth straight through my lip. I told Josh I came off my bike, but he knew. And now, here I am.' He looked at his bottle, taking a swig. 'Making you feel sorry for me.'

'I never knew that, about your dad,' Erika said, thinking back and searching for clues. She thought of the way Enzo used to walk, lost in thought, maybe living in fear of what his dad would do next time.

'Good,' he said. 'I wouldn't have wanted you to. So,' he said, lips damp with beer, 'presumably, things were good at some point, between you and your husband?'

'David was charming, determined and kind,' she said, happy to oblige by changing the subject. '*Compelling*, I suppose, when I was still young enough to be compelled. He was ambitious about everything he did. He still is.' She paused. 'He's just not so captivated by me.'

'And how about you, with him?'

'How do I feel?' Erika sat back, mulling it over. 'Disappointed, I suppose? It's hard to remember how we used to be happy and somehow got to this, two completely different people. Maybe without adding Matt to the mix, we wouldn't have ended up together at all.'

'Is that why you married him? Because of Matt?'

'We wanted to be a family.'

'You would've still been a family. You didn't need to marry him.'

'Do you have to say it that way?'

'I'm just slightly suspicious of people so determined to get married,' Enzo said. 'What's the expectation? The bottom line is, if you sign up to an archaic institution, you can't be surprised by archaic behaviour. Him having affairs, you ignoring it — isn't that part and parcel? Upholding the myth of happily ever after?'

Erika grew tense, pride wounded even though part of her agreed with him. 'Couples fall apart whether they're married, living together, or not.'

'Exactly,' he said. 'So why tie yourself to something that makes it ten times harder to walk away?'

'Because no one sets out to walk away.'

'Well, isn't that quaint?'

'Maybe we're not all as impressed by the mystique of the eternal bachelor, Enzo,' she said, thinking of Richard. 'That's far more of a cliché, if you ask me. Making a commitment to someone might be quaint, but it still means something to some people.'

'I'm not saying it doesn't,' he said, 'but it obviously doesn't mean much to your husband.'

'Clearly,' she said, hurt by the glib summary. 'Pretty self-righteous, aren't we?'

'Not at all,' he said. 'It's just that I care about you and question people who stay in monogamous relationships with no plans to stay faithful.'

'You've never been unfaithful?'

'I haven't, no,' he said. 'And it's kind of disappointing, the way you ask that question, sounding so convinced of the answer.'

'You've never been tempted? Not once?'

'I've met women I've been attracted to when I've been with someone else, of course I have, but I've never acted on it. I don't need to be married to know that's not acceptable,' he said. 'Men pretend they can't help themselves to absolve themselves of blame. Instead, their partners think it's their fault. Try to be the ones to cure them, make them good guys. And it's interesting how you don't ask me whether someone's ever cheated on me.'

'Have they?' Erika asked, agreeing with every word he'd said. That was how she'd got through some of the previous years, working towards David's redemption.

'I know it's hard to believe, Erika, with my good looks and natural charisma,' he said, smiling as she rolled her eyes, 'but yes, I've also been made to feel incredibly stupid.'

'By who?'

'The same woman who convinced me to sell fridges for a living. I owe Brian, her "friend" who got me the job, a great deal of thanks for providing me with the perfect excuse to quit. But it still hurt the old ego.'

'That's how I feel. I don't appreciate being made into the stony-faced wife.'

'You're not stony-faced, Erika.'

'You know what I mean. The martyr, then. The reject. I used to tell myself I was putting up with it for Matt's sake, but now...' She shook her head. 'I don't want to be that woman. Mind you, I don't want to be the middle-aged divorcee, either — pretending I'm having the time of my life, sitting at home every night with a bottle of rosé, buying revealing dresses, taking up salsa.'

'How revealing?' Enzo asked, looking interested, and they both laughed. 'It'd be more of a cliché, surely, if you stayed married to him. You might enjoy salsa, anyway. I've heard it can be very erotic.' They laughed again. 'There you go, then. If you think all you've got going for you is salsa lessons, stay with him. Maybe this whole thing will end, and you can get on with ignoring it, like you've done in the past.'

'This is as good as I get at ignoring it, these days,' Erika said. She couldn't go back to putting up with it, not without reason. 'I just can't help wondering what this other person is like. The glamorous mistress...'

'Glamorous?' Enzo said, looking sceptical. 'I can't imagine being all that interested in the dashing good looks of any man who was sleeping with my wife.'

'Well, I can't help it. I'm curious about who she is and how they met.'

'Then find out.'

'How?'

'If he's having an affair, they must meet up?'

'Presumably,' she said. 'He seems to be going to a lot of business things recently. I've never known him have so many late meetings.'

'There you go then. Tail him.'

CHAPTER SEVENTEEN

Erika never thought she'd be the type to get into podcasts, but once Matt got her into substituting radio junk for her own choice of guest and topic, she was hooked.

She was currently sitting in her office, tuned into Halo Jones's show. This week, David was a guest. After all the gloating Erika had had to listen to following the announcement of his initial sales figures, she couldn't say she was feeling supportive.

'It's the highest point I've reached in years,' he'd told her, bounding around like an untrained puppy. 'Controversy certainly pays well.'

'Hello, all you good people! Thanks for joining me, Halo Jones, for the Saints & Sinners podcast. First up, we'll be bringing you an exclusive chat as we welcome award-winning author, David Daniel Forde,' Halo said, just as Richard hobbled into the office. Erika shushed him, trying to listen.

'I think it's fair to say that the release of David's latest novel, Code Name: They served up a fair share of controversy, with the author's own son, Matthew Forde, leading the debate surrounding David's decision as a cis male writer, to introduce a non-binary character into his work. David, many thanks for joining us.'

'I still say, good on Matt,' Richard said, as Erika helped him pull the chair from his desk, propping up his crutches. 'It's about time someone told David where to shove it.'

Predictably, David wasn't a fan of Richard, not only because Richard insisted on telling him how lucky he was to have Erika every time they met, but also because Richard side-stepped every attempt David made to mention his books.

'*My pleasure, Halo,*' David said, sounding relaxed and pleasant — almost unrecognisable, in fact. '*Thanks for the opportunity to clear up some of the misconceptions surrounding the novel.*'

'A captive audience,' Richard said, putting on his glasses. 'He'll be in his element.'

'*For many years, as a writer of spy thrillers, I received criticism for rather stereotypical representations of gender, along with various other tropes of the genre,*' David said, as Richard groaned and threw back his head. '*I felt the time was right to explore new ground.*'

'*But don't you think, David, there's some truth in the adage: write what you know?*'

'What *does* he know?' Richard said. 'That he's far too talented for this cruel world?'

'Richard, please,' Erika said, typing away as she listened. 'Can you button it?'

'*Halo, if every author wrote within those guidelines, we'd lose so many of our best loved characters, entire works of fiction, in fact.*'

'*Let's not forget,*' Halo said, '*a considerable amount of gay fiction has been written by straight, female authors. And I'm stating the obvious here, but if artists followed those rules, where does that take them? Writing memoir as fiction? Depicting only their own gender and ethnicity, reflecting only their own experience within their work?*'

'*Exactly, but still,*' David said, '*you can bet, at this very moment, someone's going to be offended.*'

'I know I am,' Richard muttered. 'Pretentious oaf.'

'*What I do believe, Halo, is that writers have a basic responsibility to do the work and bring as much accuracy as possible to readers. On that note, I can assure your listeners that I've only ever fired a handgun in the presence of a fully trained instructor.*'

As far as Erika knew, the only gun he'd ever handled was a water pistol during the school holidays.

'*It was important for me to make a change, cover new ground.*'

'*And, by new ground, you're referring to the decision to replace Finn Schuyler's identity?*'

'*Exactly,*' he said. '*Although, this has been misinterpreted as Finn identifying as non-binary.*'

'*A misconception which you feel was perpetuated by the jacket artwork.*'

'Oh, come off it!' Richard said. 'They knew exactly what they were doing.'

'*Richard! Can I please listen?*'

'*The artwork was a bold choice meant to ignite readers' expectations. In the last instalment, Destination Danger, we were left unsure as to whether Schuyler had survived. The hope was to emphasise that cliff-hanger, leave things a little ambiguous with Code Name: They.*'

'*I have to admit, David, having the novel depict what we assume to be Finn Schuyler's jawline, with a lipsticked mouth?*' Halo said, sounding sceptical. '*And the title, using the inclusive pronoun? That can't have been a misstep, surely?*'

'*Absolutely correct, Halo, but the title wasn't chosen as a direct reference to Schuyler's gender identity. I've never made any claim to be writing LGBTQ+ fiction.*'

'Bullshit!' Richard said, cupping his hand around his mouth like a megaphone.

'You know what?' Erika said. 'This is like irritation in stereo. Him in one ear. You in the other…'

'Okay, okay…'

'*So, why, David, did you decide to move away from Schuyler? He's been there right from the start, the protagonist of an incredibly successful series of novels.*'

'*I felt Finn deserved the right to hand over his badge, and, after doing my sums, his retirement was imminent,*' David said, a horribly rehearsed smile in his voice. '*I felt it was time to develop a new world. What I didn't want to do, was walk away from the genre. I've written several books outside of the Schuyler series, and readers have begged me to return.'*

Erika almost laughed at the exaggeration. Richard mimed zipping his mouth shut.

'As long as I'm still excited to let my imagination loose in the world of espionage, and my readers remain entertained, a new lead character can only pave the way to further adventures.'

'…said Ian Fleming,' Richard sighed. 'Sorry, couldn't resist.'

'And it's this latest inclusion, the mysterious, new, leading role, which has courted controversy, most notably, from your son, Matt's very public response.'

'That's right, Halo,' David said, prompting Erika to turn up the volume. *'Very public, very painful, but entirely Matt's right to voice his opinion. I'm incredibly proud of the great sense of responsibility my son has as a member of the LGBTQ+ community.'*

'Quick recap for our listeners,' Halo said. *'Matt, your son, believes non-binary representation shouldn't be written by a non-binary author.'*

'That's correct, Halo,' David said, sounding humbly wounded. *'I can't speak for Matthew, but I think it's frustrating for him and the wider community to witness the lack of representation, the lack of prominent LGBTQ+ authors — and characters, for that matter. I wholeheartedly agree that it's a problem.'*

'To be clear,' Halo said, *'I reached out to Matthew Forde following initial reviews of the novel, but Matt declined to comment prior to posting his personal response.'*

'Matt's been singled out because he's my son, but his comments echoed initial criticism of the novel. I do feel the follow-up, due to be released at the end of the year, will put a lot of these misgivings into context.'

'Nice plug,' Richard said, avoiding Erika's eye.

'Could you give us any hint as to what that context could be, David?'

'I've been as captivated as everyone else by the emergence of more female-led action roles — the proposal of a female Bond, for example, which

caused near-outrage. I'm keen to facilitate the shaping of character identity with the reader's own ideals to a greater extent,' he said. '*As a novelist, I've far more scope to leave overall assignment to them.*'

'Hedging his bets,' Erika said, shaking her head. 'This turnaround is all down to Matt's comments and coaching from Monica. Before that, it was just a bad book.'

'That Monica's a smart lady,' Richard said. 'Behind every successful man…'

'*An interesting concept,*' Halo said. '*And, I wanted to say, David, as a fan of your work, I very much enjoyed the novel. Listeners can find my five-star review on the Halo Jones website.*'

'*Thank you, Halo. That means a great deal to me. Ultimately, after far more years than I care to remember, I want to continue telling damn good stories,*' he said, sounding like a politician at a press conference. '*Espionage has the capacity to confine us to less obvious definitions, where identity is not only irrelevant, but classified information…*'

'Oh, please,' Erika said, having heard enough of David prattling on. It was bad enough at home. 'He probably spent as long concocting that soundbite as he did outlining the novel.'

'Smug, isn't he, your husband?' Richard said. 'I can speak now, can't I?'

'If you must,' Erika said, closing down the site. 'At least the whole shit-fest with Matt's been turned into compost.'

'Would you marry him again?' Richard asked. 'I'm serious. If he asked to renew your vows, or you could travel back in time, would you still say yes?'

Erika remembered her conversation with Enzo, surprised by how wounded she still felt by admitting defeat.

'It's almost a dare, isn't it? Marriage…'

'That'd make the vows more exciting. "We dare you to take this woman to be your lawful, wedded wife." I like it,' he said, grinning broadly. 'I'm thinking of asking Ursula to marry me.

What?' He paused as Erika put her head in her hands. 'I've never felt this way, not since my deranged ex-wife. I love Ursula. I don't want to lose her.'

'You don't want to lose her? Well, there we go, then. Get married. Again.'

'Erika, I'm serious,' he said. 'You're the closest person I've got to a best man.'

'No, no, no,' she said. 'Not getting involved. Your life, not mine.'

'I thought you liked Ursula?'

'I do like Ursula, it's not about me not liking her,' she said. 'It's about *you* not liking her as soon as the honeymoon's over, and me having to listen to the whole debacle on a daily basis like last time. And to add more complication, she works here, so we may as well start recruiting now.'

'Don't be like that.'

'Like what?' she said. 'Honest? Rational? Look, to be fair, I'm probably not the best person to ask about this at the moment.'

'Yeah, I'm picking up on that. It wouldn't have anything to do with having your *friend* Mr Morelli around, would it?'

'No. It wouldn't.'

'Oh, come on,' said Richard. 'It's me you're talking to. The guy obviously thinks a lot of you.'

'Why? What makes you say that?'

'I could see it straight away. You were almost going up in smoke when he walked into the studio, and you were picking at your food over lunch. And now you're asking me why I think he likes you, as if you're still at school...'

'I know he likes me, Richard. We've been *friends* for a long time.'

'Just friends?' He held her gaze.

'More than that, on occasion.'

'On occasion, eh?' He smirked. 'Well, there we go.'

'You can wipe that look off your face. I'm married. The fact you still think that counts for nothing is exactly my point.'

'You haven't been happy with David for years.'

'For better, for worse,' she said. 'You never quite mastered the part about forsaking all others. You said getting married was the biggest mistake of your life, and I agreed wholeheartedly. You're not the type, Richard. Usually, you don't need reminding of that fact.'

'It was a mistake marrying *her*. The first one. Not Ursula.'

'Because Ursula's going to change you, is she?'

'She already has if we're having this conversation, right?'

'But it's not her responsibility to change you. Marrying Ursula because you want to keep hold of her — you think that's a good reason? What happens afterwards? Once you know she's going nowhere and the boredom sets in?'

'I need to grow up and make a commitment. That's what I'm telling you.'

'Ursula probably wouldn't thank me for saying this, Richard, but you're doing exactly what you did with Jenny. You and Ursula want completely different things. She wants a family someday, and you've made it quite clear you'd prefer a vasectomy. How's that going to work?'

'Because I love her.'

'I'm going to be very honest with you.'

'Not too honest, please,' he said, adjusting his leg. 'I'm still in a lot of discomfort.'

'You're a great guy. Great to work with, a great friend, but an absolute fucking moron when it comes to relationships.'

'Tad harsh.'

'How do you end up dating these women who want to get married?'

'Catholics,' he said. 'Can't work it out. I'm like Midnight Mass — I just seem to attract them. They're cool at first, then they fall in love. I meet a lovely, sexy woman, then she changes and wants to plan the next few decades together, from now until death. It's depressing.'

'Depressing? Richard, do you think you might've uncovered the flaw in your plan? You'll string Ursula along and you'll both end up hating each other — the same way it went the first time, with Jenny.'

'I don't *hate* Jenny. It's just, we'd be sat in front of the TV, her asking what I fancied for dinner. I'd be flicking through channels, thinking, this is it. This is the rest of our lives. Why isn't she clawing at the windows? Because the only thing keeping me here is gravity.'

'So, how's this going to be any different?'

'I love Ursula, Erika. I swear, I've never felt this way.'

'Christ…' She sighed. 'And do you not think that might wear off? Like, straight after the vows, maybe? Or it might trigger you, the moment you find yourself discussing dinner?'

'You're right. I can't predict the outcome. No one can.'

'Well, I'd hedge a wild bet…'

'Look, I don't know if it'll last two years or two weeks, but I can say I will absolutely give it my best shot. I want her to be happy. I want both of us to be happy, and I think we can be. While we're being honest, maybe you're right. You aren't the best person to talk to about this, because *daring* yourself to stay married, when you're completely miserable, seems to defeat the entire purpose.'

'Tell you what, Richard, show us how it's done. I'll be surprised if you get through the first month of matrimony without complaint.'

'You mightn't complain, Erika, but you're going to end up a very bitter woman if you're not careful.'

'*Bitter?* Well, do you know why?' Erika snapped. 'Because I married someone like *you*. Someone who made promises he couldn't keep. I know exactly how it feels. The lies, the cheating — because *you're* not happy, as if only *your happiness* matters. You just lope off, get whatever you need from wherever you can find it, and we're not supposed to have any feelings about it, unless it's to blame ourselves.'

Fear gripped Richard's face. He seized his crutches as if to escape or defend himself.

Erika hadn't finished. 'Maybe you're right. We shouldn't stay married to people like *you*, because men like you seem to do everything in your power to make it otherwise. And you're the ones who propose in the first place! So, if I end up *bitter*, Richard, don't forget: my relationship started with the sweetest of intentions, just like yours.'

CHAPTER EIGHTEEN

When things were out of her control, Erika usually waited them out. But here she was, standing in a phone box, waiting for her ex-boyfriend to pick her up so they could follow her husband and discover the identity of his mistress.

'Hi,' she said, getting into Enzo's truck as if this was their regular thing. 'Thanks so much for doing this.'

'Where're we going?'

'Just take a left at the end of the road,' she said, pulling down the sun-visor. 'No mirror?'

'Barely any engine. What do you need a mirror for?'

'You'll have to tell me.' She paused, tipping her head forward. 'How's this?'

'You're wearing a wig?'

'I can't follow him around in plain sight, can I? May as well have driven my own car otherwise. You're wearing a baseball cap…'

'Yeah, it's not a disguise, though, is it?'

'Sort of is. I could've brought you something. A fake moustache.'

'I'm glad to see you're taking this seriously.'

'Oh, I am. Lighten up,' she said. 'It's a shit show, but I've been married a long time. This is the most exciting thing that's happened in years.' She adjusted the blonde bob. 'What do you think? Cute?'

'Fucking mental,' Enzo said, indicating left, scoping the road up ahead. 'You look like a young Debbie Harry, after a terrible haircut.'

'I like the truck.'

'The *ute*.'

'What's the difference?'

'Ute sounds cooler.'

'Fair enough. That's him,' Erika said, jumping to attention. She pointed out David, who was approaching the roundabout. 'Silver Golf!'

'Okay, Erika, I see him.' Enzo said. 'Do you want to stop drawing attention to yourself with the waving and pointing?'

'Oh yeah, I suppose,' she said, settling back against the seat. 'Do you know what he said when I left this morning? See you later!' She huffed. 'The lying shit…'

'But he will see you later.'

'Oh, you know what I mean!' she said, sneaking another look at herself in the side mirror. She was quite enjoying being a nylon blonde. 'He's never that chipper. It was a dead giveaway. A fatal glitch in the system.'

'Any idea where we're headed?'

'He says he's going to see a play.'

'Oh, yeah,' he said, vaguely recalling instructions. 'Theatre-goer, is he?'

'Never this often. Twice in one month. He was in the garage for thirty-five minutes, whitening his teeth, shaving his —' She was thankfully distracted by the road up ahead. 'Look, there, now! The theatre's coming up…'

As traffic slowed, she watched as David drove straight past the turn-off.

'*Yes*!' she said, with a clap. 'I knew it!'

'Excited?'

'Sorry,' she said, settling back. 'But yes, I am! It feels so good to be right…' She adopted a country and western accent. 'When my man's been doing me so wrong…'

'Were you always this weird?'

'I don't think so,' she said. 'Not until recently…'

Enzo turned the radio on. "*You're listening to Tower Radio. I'm Simon Greening, and this is Kenny Rogers…*"

Enzo nodded along as an old song came on. 'What can I say, I'm just an old boy with a bad taste in music.'

'I like this song,' Erika said, making herself comfortable.

'You always used to do that,' he said. 'Sit on your hands like a kid in assembly.'

'All these years,' she said, noticing her hands pushed flat beneath her thighs, 'and that's what you remember?'

'That's not all I remember, Erika, no.'

There was an awkward silence. Did he recall the kind of details she had stored?

'Did you ever think about me?' he asked.

'Yes,' she said, caught off-guard. 'Did you?'

'Every day. Whenever I was naked. I'm joking. Of course, I thought about you.'

'And the one thing you didn't think,' Erika said, 'was how, one day, we'd be in your ute tailing my cheating husband.'

'No, funnily enough. I didn't. I hoped you'd be happy.'

'Well, happy is a lot to expect, isn't it?' she said, warming to her theme. 'When I was younger, I thought I'd have it all figured out by now.' She paused. 'What was I like, when I was younger?'

'You were, well…' he said, turning onto the coast road. David was a few cars ahead. 'Interesting, I suppose. Nice. Different.'

'Oh.'

'Do you have to vet every compliment?'

'I don't vet compliments. I don't get compliments. I'm married, remember?'

'In that case, I'd say you weren't like anyone else. You still aren't,' he said. 'You were always very gorgeous, very lovely.' He glanced at her. 'Stop pulling that face. That's how I remember you. You always had something about you. I was lucky you gave me the time of day.'

'Wow. Glad I asked.' Erika tried to distract herself from the sweetness of his compliments by winding down the window.

'It doesn't work your side,' Enzo said.

'I hate to ask, but is this thing even safe?'

'Safe? Of course it's safe. It's falling to pieces and rusted in places, but I wouldn't trade it. It's a very simple thing, this ute, and maybe that makes me a very simple man, but I'm right at home the minute I get behind the wheel. At least the radio's still going strong.' He looked up ahead, keeping tabs on David. 'Music and a full tank. That's all you need.'

Erika gave a snort. 'How about a dog and a few lonesome nights, camped out in the back of this thing?'

'You love this, don't you? Taking the piss,' Enzo said, trying to keep the smile from his face. 'Would you rather I'd done the same as you? Got married, had kids, and bought a nice house in the suburbs?'

'No, I'm glad you haven't. At least one of us veered off track. I imagined you might still be in the city,' she said. 'Running some cool London gallery.'

'You could've been there with me if things had worked out.'

'Enzo!' Erika had almost forgotten they were tailing her husband. 'He's indicating…'

'Looks like we're going to dinner,' Enzo said as he swung into the carpark. 'That'll be nice for us.'

'We got Thai to celebrate Matt's A-levels,' Erika said, wondering if David was going to the same place. 'David had a dispute over the bill. Roti bread should be complimentary, apparently.'

'Don't look at me,' Enzo said. 'You married him.'

They slowed down, turned into a lay-by, and watched David fix his hair and pull on his jacket. It was his good one, she noticed. Enzo started the truck again and found a bay near the front.

'That's him? He's not what I expected.' Enzo gazed out from beneath his cap. 'Not even close.'

'What did you expect?' Erika asked as David stood outside the foyer, put on his glasses, and checked his phone — his usual one. 'Is he a catfish?'

'I don't know,' he said. 'Did he just smell his own armpit?'

'Obviously eager to impress.' Erika slid further down in her seat. 'Shit...'

A woman with curly hair in a long, green dress made her way towards David.

'Her?' Enzo said. 'Do you think he's with her?'

'I think that's Anya.'

As David and the woman embraced, Erika felt queasy.

'Do you know her?'

'She's his ex-wife.'

They watched as David placed his hands either side of Anya's waist. She pecked him on the cheek and pulled back to take a look at him, removing lipstick from the side of his mouth.

'She's a dental hygienist.'

'Good to know.'

'I found dental stuff,' she explained. 'In the garage. Gum trays, all that paraphernalia. Why would he be seeing his ex-wife?'

162

They watched as the pair made their way into the restaurant. David opened the door, insisting that Anya go ahead.

'It's not all that unusual, is it? Exes meeting up,' Enzo said. 'Like us, for example? Maybe he didn't want to tell you in case you thought something of it. They might have things to talk about.'

'What would he need to talk to her about? How she kept all the good albums? Early signs of tooth decay?'

'Okay, then,' Enzo said, flexing his hand with the same pained look he'd had on the shoot. For some reason, Erika knew not to question it. 'Maybe they're having a red-hot affair. So, now what?'

They drove away and parked up in Fernleigh, right on the coast. Erika hadn't thought beyond the point when she found out who David was meeting. She'd been fully prepared to confront them, but when the moment came she didn't think her legs could've carried her.

She'd felt entirely numb, silenced by the chaos of her reaction. Enzo had filled the silence on the drive down, telling her about the lobster rolls from this great place he knew.

They entered the small shop.

'Hey, Billy!' Enzo said to the guy behind the counter, who was short and stocky, with a friendly face. 'You've lost weight!'

'Eleven pounds!' Billy said, smoothing the sides of his apron and giving his tummy a pat. 'Wife can't keep her hands off me!'

'There's always a downside, Bill!'

Billy's laughter reverberated as they paid for their food and said their goodbyes, taking a seat on a bench out on the promenade. They sat side by side, watching the sunlight glistening on the water. Erika steadied her thoughts, her mind somewhere off in the distance. Her tears began to flow. She'd never had any inkling there was something still there between David and Anya. He'd not so much as mentioned her in years.

'I know the food's good,' Enzo said, holding up his lobster roll, 'but I didn't expect you to get so emotional about it.'

'I can't believe I'm sitting here while my husband is down the road, on a date.'

'Could be worse,' he said. 'You could be on a date with him.'

'Don't worry, I already thought of that,' she said, trying to smile as she took up his offer of a napkin.

'And this,' Enzo said, taking in the view as she blotted her eyes. 'This isn't so bad. Sitting here with me, getting a bite to eat during our intrepid Friday night. I mean, your husband mightn't like the sound of it...'

'It's lovely,' she said, 'but it's hardly a date.'

But was it a date? Erika enjoyed Enzo's company a little too much. She found herself thinking of him even when he wasn't around.

'I know,' he said. 'And instead of making wisecracks, maybe someone needs to put their arm around you.' He set his food on the bench. 'And I'm afraid it's going to have to be me.'

He pulled her towards him, and she allowed her head to rest against his shoulder.

'How did someone like you end up with a man like him?' he asked.

'Someone like me? I bet you say that to all the married women,' she said, straightening back up. 'He wasn't always like that. Actually...' She sighed, resigned. 'He *was* always like this, but I thought he'd grow past it. And I know how that sounds, me going along with it, but we could be good together at times. The truth is, I wasn't exactly a catch. I was the one who got pregnant.'

'I think the bloke plays a fair part in getting a woman pregnant.'

'Sometimes, apart from Matt, I think I only stayed because David never ended it,' Erika said. 'Bad, isn't it? Then I'd panic, thinking how humiliated I'd feel if he ever left me for someone else. I don't know.' She took a breath. 'I could've made more of an effort.'

'I think it's safe to say that most people would go off someone who's been cheating on them.'

'Good point,' she said, tired of thinking.

'Listen, I wanted to know that things had turned out okay for you, at least better than they had for me,' Enzo said. 'You know I care about you, so it's difficult to sit on the fence, but whatever you decide, I'm here.' He looked at her. 'All I'm going to say is, I know you're scared, but you seem more upset talking about spending the rest of your life with this guy. People make mistakes, but from what you've said about your husband…' He trailed off. 'Anyway, I'm glad I can be around.'

'Thank you for saying that.' Erika briefly leaned against his arm. 'It's still so strange, the thought of us not being together, especially now Matt's gone, too. Although I'm sure David would disagree. He'll have a new lease of life, I suppose. He'll be free to do whatever he chooses. I haven't got a clue. It seems so boring, the thought of being alone.'

'Erika, everything's going to seem boring, compared to living with someone who's leading a double-life, breaking into his garage, and finding out he's having an affair with a dental hygienist.'

'True. Very true.' She smiled as he laughed. 'I wish I could be like that, like her,' she said, gazing up and noticing a woman standing alone on one of the balconies overlooking the bay.

'Look at her — perfect blow-dry, just the right amount of cleavage. Do you think she's divorced?'

'Sorry to disappoint you, but no. That's Ginny. She lives with her husband, Amara. Don't get too excited,' Enzo said, as she frowned, wondering how he knew the details. 'See the place second from the top?' He pointed to a glass-wrapped balcony. 'That's where I'm staying. Our company built them. Come on, I'll show you around.'

CHAPTER NINETEEN

Erika followed Enzo along a wonderfully light and airy corridor. 'Well, this is rather nice,' she said, pleasantly surprised as he showed her into his spacious apartment. 'Very contemporary.'

The place was impeccably decorated and incredibly tidy. Almost too pristine, in fact — not exactly what you'd call lived-in. The kitchen had walnut-topped surfaces and was equipped with a coffee machine and a matching family of ridiculously expensive-looking appliances.

'Now, the coffee machine, I can see you using,' Erika said. 'But the juicer? And is that a diffuser?'

'Not down to me, I admit,' he said, opening the balcony doors and flooding the space with sea air and sunset. 'They're from Rob's wife, Della. She likes to keep things civilised. We've been using the place as a bit of a showroom for the rest of the units.'

'*Units*? Ah, I thought it looked well-kept,' Erika said, admiring a console table where two brass figures, sculptured hares, sat alongside an egg-shaped glass ornament.

'I run a tight ship, for your information. It's the married guys who expect housekeeping. Here you go,' Enzo said, inviting her to join him outside. 'You're now the glamorous woman on the balcony.'

'Well, I'm a woman standing on a balcony…'

Erika took a breath of sea air. Her eyes followed the water beneath the citrus sun. She didn't know if there was such a thing as vacation living, but Enzo's apartment had to be it.

'Small pleasures,' he said, surveying the view beside her. 'Got to steer the ship the best you can, take life's small pleasures where you find them.'

'Did you get that off a beer mat?'

'Probably.' He smiled. 'Or maybe I'm incredibly wise and philosophical, Erika. Wait until I show you the lounge.'

Erika followed him back inside and took in the gleaming walnut floors. She hadn't quite noticed before, but a couple of large, carpeted steps ran around the perimeter of a sunken space, where an industrial-looking coffee table sat at the centre, neighboured by two softly worn, butterscotch sofas. As Enzo pressed a button on a remote control, a slender screen gradually revealed itself from inside a slim cabinet.

'Press the button on the side,' he instructed as Erika took a seat.

She began to laugh as her chair elevated. 'This place is a bit of a bachelor lair, isn't it?'

'*Lair*? Do you mean a bachelor pad?'

'No, I mean, a lair, like a Bond villain. I'm expecting Roger Moore to cartwheel down in a safari suit, grab a drink, and regale us with anecdotes long into the night.'

'I'm quite happy, hanging out here in my bachelor lair, if you don't mind.'

'This place is incredible. Honestly,' Erika said, as he gave her a suspicious look. 'The location's unreal. I mean, if you'd have asked me, I'd have pictured you living somewhere low maintenance and drinking warm beer at a pockmarked table. One plate, one pan. That old mattress you used to have on the floor.'

The moment she said it, she wished she hadn't. She'd been spending so much time trying to convince herself they were just old friends, that any reminder of their past felt uncomfortable.

'So, do the ladies like this place?' she asked, moving on.

'Well, I'm flattered you ask,' Enzo said, making his way into the kitchen, 'but you're the first one I've managed to *lure* up here. Apart from my brother's wife and my nieces, that is — but I'm guessing you were asking with something far less platonic in mind.'

'None of my business,' she said. 'Far be it from me to pry into a gentleman's affairs.'

'Weren't we just doing exactly that to your husband?' Enzo said, opening the fridge as she smiled at the absurdity. 'Anyway, now I've got you here in my lair, would you care to join me for a drink?'

'Oh, go on then,' Erika said, walking back outside to scan the coastline.

'Beer okay?'

'Beer's great, thanks,' she said. She couldn't remember the last time she'd had a beer on a summer evening, especially in such a perfect setting. 'Wow, you're even using coasters. Who knew you could be so domesticated?'

'Okay, Erika. I think we've established you're disappointed I'm not living like some comic book antihero.' He took a swig of beer. 'So, are you going to do it? Are you going to leave him?'

She didn't especially want to talk about it. She was still resisting the pull of sadness, the reality of things with David. Anya was attractive and successful. What the hell could she possibly see in David that was lacking in his younger days, except for gum disease? Although, to be honest, she couldn't figure out how someone who spoke at length about tooth enamel could give her husband an erection.

169

'I don't have much choice, do I?' Erika said. 'I can't change how things are. I wish I felt wonderfully empowered, saying that, but quite honestly I don't.'

'But you like the look of this place? Minus the sunken lounge, obviously.'

'Including the sunken lounge,' she said. 'I love it. It's fun.'

'Then you should look at some of our apartments.' Enzo sat back. 'And, if they're not the right fit, we'll figure it out. Find you a place.'

She glanced back through the apartment, imagining something similar becoming her home. Somewhere a few floors up, like this, with something decent to look at and not a tweed hat or a miserable old bookshelf in sight. Matt might visit more often. How much would he love seeing her living someplace like this?

'The main thing is, I don't want you worrying,' Enzo said, placing his bottle on the table. 'We'll make it work.'

'You don't have to look out for me,' Erika said, but it did feel good to be less alone. 'I appreciate the offer, and thanks for tonight. I know it's not the greatest way to spend an evening, stuck in the middle of my drama, so thank you.' She reached into her bag. 'Look what I found.'

She held out the Zippo lighter and watched Enzo's smile as he took it. She wondered what he was thinking as her own thoughts took her back to old times. He'd felt so comfortable, putting his arm around her.

'You keep it,' he said, as cries of soaring seagulls brought their attention back to the present. Enzo took a quick drink, standing up. 'There's something I wanted to show you.' He disappeared inside.

Erika sat for a few moments and closed her eyes, unable to resist the interlude of evening sun, the warmth on her skin that felt like a blessing.

'I thought you might like to see these.' Enzo offered a tattered, A4 envelope.

Erika peered inside, saw the black and white prints, and guessed straight away what they were. She slid out half a dozen photographs, the ones Enzo had taken that morning, over twenty years ago. The first four showed her lying against pillows, softly dishevelled. The last two shots showed her looking up into the lens as Enzo captured them both lying together. In the final photograph, Enzo was kissing her neck as she smiled into the camera held overhead.

She didn't speak for a moment. Neither of them did, not only because they were naked in the shots, but also because those photographs reminded her of how it felt to be together. It was there, in the way he looked at her, in the way she'd allowed him to capture her. No shame, no censure. There she was: Erika Karter.

She looked so perfectly content in his presence, and, from the way she looked into the camera, there was no doubt about how deeply she'd fallen. That realisation brought a sense of loss so sharp that she caught her breath.

'I hope I haven't embarrassed you?' said Enzo.

'Well,' she said, warm with emotion, 'very nearly, but no. You haven't. I love these.'

'I almost sent them to you a few times but decided against it. It seemed a bit creepy. You might have thought I was trying to blackmail you,' he said, as they shared subdued smiles. 'These two are my favourites.' He selected the first shot of her. 'Whenever I think about us, that's exactly how I remember you.'

Erika watched him studying the photographs, and had to stop herself from telling him how happy she was to spend time together again.

Enzo selected the next picture, the one of him kissing her neck. 'And this one, because whenever I see it, I remember exactly how I felt. How we were. Young love, eh?'

'I'm glad you've still got these.' Erika was still slightly taken aback and aware of those old feelings not so far from the surface, 'but they make me feel a bit sad, too.'

'Yep,' he said. 'There is that…'

'It's good to see you again,' she said, briefly squeezing his wrist. 'And I still say you were a really talented photographer.'

'You give me far too much credit, Erika. Those photos are only good, better than good, because you're in them. That's what I couldn't do in a studio. Capture sincerity, get past the lens. You always had this absolute belief I could be good at anything. It always made me want to prove you right.'

'And you did,' she said. 'You have.'

'Well, I wouldn't go that far, but I never forgot you, Erika.' Enzo slid the photographs back into the envelope. 'It messed with my head for a while, after what happened in Dublin. The way we left things.'

'Yeah, I know. I'm sorry. I shouldn't have cut you off like that. I was still very —'

'I get it. You don't need to explain.'

'I said a lot of things, but I don't feel that way. I want you to know, I never blamed you.'

'You had every right to be angry,' Enzo said. 'But there's no point. It's not helpful to either of us, agonising it into some tragedy. We were kids, but I do regret hurting you.'

'Well, that took two of us, and like you said, we were kids,' she said. 'All in the past.'

'Hey, at least we've got a past, and we were very good at it.'

'We were,' she said, unable to resist placing a kiss on his softly stubbled cheek, her face against his for a moment too long. There was no need to say another word.

CHAPTER TWENTY

After her evening with Enzo, Erika cast her mind back to that minibreak in Dublin, it was the last time she'd seen Enzo Morelli, back when she'd been an enthusiastic member of her friend Claire's hen party.

The squealing, giggling, chattering brood were determined to give Claire her dream send-off ahead of her meticulously planned wedding to Joe, her childhood sweetheart. Joe and his friends were also celebrating his stag do in Dublin, and had flown out a day earlier.

Having ended things with David after finding the letter from Chloe only a fortnight before, the hen do was the perfect opportunity for Erika to take a break from her broken heart. She just hadn't expected the other women, all five of them, to have boyfriends. She had no issue, in theory, with being single, but she couldn't escape the question of why she was the only one left on the shelf. Enzo had disappeared from her life. Then David had cheated. Unable to shake the thought that there was something wrong with her, she drank eagerly, partly to celebrate with the others, but mostly to commiserate with herself.

'NO!' Erika shouted, sometime after someone ordered takeout chicken buckets that were mostly skin and bone, and after she had accompanied one of Claire's friends back to the hotel and Enzo Morelli appeared like an apparition.

'This is like that film,' she said, peering up at him and adjusting her Horniest Bridesmaid sash. 'That Jack Nicholson movie. The hotel one…'

'*The Shining*,' Enzo said, taking a seat next to her. 'Nice hat.'

'It's a *crown*!'

'It's…' He studied the top of her head. 'It's a ring of cocks.'

'Is it?' Erika took the crown from her head. 'Oh, yes. Little penises. *ENZO!*'

'Will you please stop shouting? I'm right here.'

'Aren't you surprised, though?' She grinned. 'We're in Dublin. You're in Dublin! We're *both here* in Dublin,' she said, jumping up and down in her seat.

'I'm not surprised, no.' Enzo took his wallet from his pocket. 'As riveting as this conversation is, would you like a drink?'

'What have you done with my *fiancé*?' Claire called, weaving her way through the bar with an inflatable, naked man under her arm.

'Last time I saw him,' Enzo said, 'he was in a basque and stockings on the Hal'penny Bridge, complaining he had the shits.'

'You're here for Joe!' Erika said, suddenly struck by the realisation. 'Oh yeah…'

'Oh yeah,' Enzo said. 'Josh and I went to school with him.'

'And I,' she said, full of conviction, as if solving one of life's great mysteries, 'went to school with Claire!' Erika rested her head against the back of her seat and closed her eyes. When she opened them, she went on, 'Don't tell her, but I really don't think I can drink anything else.'

'Claire left half an hour ago,' Enzo said, sipping a pint of Guinness. 'You fell asleep and she left.'

'Have you been here the whole time?'

'Just in time for you to fall asleep,' he said. 'I mean, I know I'm not the most interesting of conversationalists, Erika, but it still hurts. Here.' He edged her glass nearer as she gave a snort of laughter. 'Have your drink. Lime and soda, remember?'

'Why aren't you with the blokes, being a stag?'

'Not in the mood. I checked out as soon as I laddered my stockings.'

Her eyes darted to his legs, dressed perfectly respectably in jeans. 'Oh. You're joking.'

'You really are wasted, aren't you?'

'Not really,' Erika lied, stifling a yawn. 'Not as bad as I was after we had those horrible blue shots after breakfast. I can't walk to another pub. I don't want to sing, or drink, or hear about Joe. I'm done. Not one more minute.'

'Do you want to go somewhere else?'

'Straight to bed?' she suggested, emptying her glass in one go.

'That's very forward of you, Erika. Ah, that lovely, snorty laugh of yours,' Enzo said. 'How I've missed that sound…'

She snorted again, leaning her head against him, suddenly bashful. They exchanged a smile, Enzo stroking the back of her head, the way he always did.

'I mean, do you want to go somewhere else?' he said, studying his empty glass. 'Would you like a traditional Irish coffee, in the much quieter hotel down the way?'

'How far?' Erika asked, her bare arms horribly cold.

'Two minutes away. I'm not staying in the same place as the lads. I booked late. I wasn't sure if I fancied tonight. It turns out I didn't.'

Erika nodded, and Enzo hoisted his jacket around her shoulders as she stood, checking her bag for her phone, room key, and purse.

'I see you lost the quiff,' she said, as they reached the foyer. 'Your hair's gone curly again.'

'It's not a conscious style choice,' he said, opening the door. 'I just haven't had it cut.'

Enzo sunk his hands into his jeans pockets as they met the night air, and he offered her the crook of his arm as they took to the street.

'How are you this sober on a stag do?' Erika asked, concentrating on balancing her heels across the cobblestones.

'Stamina,' he smirked, as she caught a look at him under the streetlight. That face of his, her favourite face. 'That, and antidepressants.'

They continued on their way and said nothing. She was happy staying quiet, the walk reviving her as city lights drew her attention to alternating stacks of buildings.

'It's not because of Angie,' he said, catching her eye.

'She's doing okay?'

'She's still having treatment,' he said, 'but it's not looking good, if I'm honest.'

'I'm sorry.' Erika squeezed his arm. She wondered how bad the depression was, because she could sense it. He seemed cordoned off from everything, everyone. 'So, why are you taking antidepressants?'

'I guess some of us are pressed,' he said with a shrug. 'And some of us are de-pressed.'

'You'll be pressed again,' she said, placing a firm kiss on his bicep. 'I know it.'

'Yeah, well,' he said, taking hold of the brass door handle as they reached the dimly lit bar. Green velvet seats the only reminder they were in Dublin. The air was sour with beer, but there were only a few quietly occupied tables, and thankfully, not a hen or stag to be found. Enzo ordered a Guinness for himself, and an Irish coffee for Erika.

'It's nicer in here,' she said. 'The lights were too bright at that last place.'

'How are you coping, Erika?' Enzo unbuttoned the cuffs of his shirt, rolling up the sleeves to reveal his slender forearms, dusted with dark hair. 'What have you been up to?'

'Drinking. Talking about sex. Wearing plastic dicks. Usual hen do stuff. How about you?'

'Drinking,' he said. 'Refusing to wear lingerie.'

'Not like you.'

'What have you been up to *generally?*' Erika tried not to think it, but he looked so sexy as he asked, with his lips wet and lazy. 'Seeing anyone special?' He tried to turn it into a joke, but the casual enquiry stung.

'No.' It was almost a lie. Her sheets barely cold from David: her supposedly safe rebound relationship. 'The last bloke I dated was a right idiot. Put me off,' she said. 'What about you?'

'Yeah? I heard that last bloke you dated was seriously handsome, witty and charming, just terribly misunderstood. And no,' he said. 'There's no one.' He paused. 'It's good to see you.'

'Is it?'

'I was a bit bothered about that, to be honest. Seeing you,' he said. 'I wasn't sure whether it would be a good idea, running into each other.'

'What do you mean? I'm happy you're here. It's been the best part of the day. I mean, that's not exactly saying much, but still…'

'You weren't so thrilled last time we spoke, as I remember.'

'You mean after you left? Hmm, no, I can't think why,' she said, pretending to mull it over. 'What did you expect? Whistles and applause?'

'No, but I obviously expected too much.'

'Oh, come on.' She slouched. 'Don't put it on me. You packed up and never got in touch.'

'You told me not to bother, and I did get in touch.'

'Months later, and I never said that.'

'It was *one* month. I know, because I'd been waiting for a text, maybe even a call, before I decided it was getting ridiculous. I called, and you told me it was pointless, not to bother. So I didn't get in touch again after that, and neither did you.'

'You pissed off to live at your friend's place. What was I meant to think?'

'My friend has cancer,' he said. 'That wasn't good enough for you?'

'You packed a case, jumped on a train, and said you didn't know when you'd be back.'

'That's right. And I still don't, but that didn't mean we were finished.'

'And you thought that by not contacting me, it would make it obvious we were still together in the meantime?'

'I thought you needed to cool off, and you'd call when you realised you were in the wrong. Why didn't you?'

'I thought about it,' she said, remembering several times when she'd been tempted to do exactly that. 'But I don't know… Maybe I'd been waiting for it. The end. Confirmation I wasn't important enough to you.'

'Erika.' Enzo shook his head. 'You have these conversations with yourself. Angie and Christian have been great to me. When they split up, I tried to be there for both of them. Angie's never been more than a good person in my life. That's what she does: takes in waifs and strays. They couldn't have kids, her and Christian.' He took a drink. 'Me, and some of the crew, they treat us like family.'

'Why didn't you just say that?'

'I did!' He almost laughed. 'How many times? You didn't want to hear it. You made up your mind based on … God knows what. You just presumed something must've happened with Angie.'

'I never thought anything for definite. I just knew you wouldn't be coming back. I was trying to make sense of how disposable you made me feel.'

'Really? Well, in that case, you knew more than I did. I'm there because I'm needed. What was I supposed to say? Sorry, Christian, I wish I could help keep your studio afloat, but my girlfriend thinks this whole thing stinks, so give us a call for the funeral.'

'That's not what I meant.'

'I'm not staying forever,' he said. 'I thought we were good?'

'Yes.' She found it easier to assess things now, outside the relationship. It felt less daunting, looking back. 'I think we were.'

'I've known you, how many years? I still don't understand why you think I'd suddenly disappear.' He leaned closer. 'Me going to help a friend doesn't mean I ended things with us. You'd practically moved in — that's not a complaint, but I thought it was obvious that things were good. Anyway, you haven't missed anything. I wasn't good to be around for the first couple of months. I'm still not.'

'You are,' she said, taking his hand. 'I've missed you.'

Erika woke, swaddled in a hotel robe she only vaguely remembered putting on. She felt eggshell-delicate from twelve hours of drinking, shouted exchanges, distorted soundtracks and horribly high heels.

Enzo was beside her. 'It lives,' he said, one arm behind his head. 'You okay?'

'Uh-huh.' She found the bathroom, approximately one noxious breath away from the single bed. 'Please tell me this is your toothbrush,' she said, her mouth already clamped around it.

'It is,' he said. 'Think you can manage not to melt it?'

She scrubbed her teeth and washed her face, then needed to lie down again.

Enzo was opening the window as she climbed back onto the bed. She repositioned herself beside him without a word, laying her head on his chest.

'Hungry?'

Erika nodded and curled up tighter. She had no intention of leaving his bed yet. He kissed her forehead. She moved towards the smooth contour of his neck, traced her fingers along his jaw, wanting to ease that look of unrest. Enzo's kiss was hesitant, then suddenly confident, with the understanding of a shared destination. The heaviness of his body against her eased any doubt as she kissed away his sadness and he kissed away her confusion. She slipped free from her robe, her arms around his neck and her legs around his waist.

The breakfast room was all frilly doilies and tied-back curtains. Erika was newly ravenous, after her rather marvellous wake-up call. 'I wonder where everyone got to last night. Do you know, not one of those bitches sent a text. Anything could've happened to me.'

'Anything just did,' Enzo said, wearing a conspiratorial smile. 'Joe will be feeling rough. Mind you, if he's brave enough to be marrying Claire…'

'Don't be so horrible.'

'Oh, come on,' he said. 'She doesn't let him out of her sight.'

'She never did,' Erika said, 'but they've been together all this time. Joe's had long enough to change his mind. He asked her to marry him. He didn't have to propose.'

'Maybe you're right. What do I know? I don't know Claire that well,' he said, leaning back. 'Joe was saying Josh gave him a few pointers before he asked her out — it might not have happened otherwise. So, Josh has got a lot to answer for...'

'I didn't know that,' she said, thinking of her brother. 'That's sweet.'

They were both silent for a moment.

'Four years since Josh died,' Enzo said, turning the salt jar between his fingers. 'It doesn't feel that long.'

'I think it feels longer,' Erika said, remembering the dream she sometimes had about her brother. 'I still expect him to walk in like none of it ever happened.'

'I know I should've been there.' Enzo took her hand across the table. 'I should've gone to the funeral.'

'Yes. You should have.' She pulled back her hand. 'At least your mum was there. I still don't get it. You said you felt *too close* to him. Wasn't that the point?'

'Not too close to him. Too close to what happened,' he said. 'I hadn't seen him in a while.' He looked at her. 'I got a text from him that night.'

9.53 a.m. on 3rd July was the last time Erika heard from her brother. She congratulated him on his degree results: a 2:1 in Graphic Design. Erika texted later on, asking when he was planning on getting back to their mum's that summer so they could coordinate their visit, but she never got a reply.

'He was out, everyone was, for the results,' Enzo said. 'We couldn't get a cab to the club for ages.'

'You saw him?'

'Yeah, but by the time we got there, he was smashed. We all were. And then he saw her. Dani — that girl he'd been seeing.'

The waitress arrived with their food, muting the discussion, neither of them remotely hungry anymore.

'He started having a go at the lad she was with,' Enzo went on. 'He completely lost it. They threw the lot of us out.'

Erika had never seen her brother behave that way and could barely imagine it. Josh was always so easy-going — not the kind of kid who got into trouble.

'We got into the next place and got a couple of rounds in. When I'd had enough, I couldn't find Josh. Instead of making sure I found him, I left.'

Josh had died at 3.13 a.m. from a seizure brought on by a cardiac arrest, triggered by an amphetamine overdose. He died alone on a pavement on a cold, wet night. A stranger called the ambulance. Josh was gone by the time the paramedics got to him.

'I felt —'

'Responsible?'

'No, not responsible. He was with his mates. I was with mine. I spoke with the police. I didn't want to go through it again with you. Look, Erika ... everyone took stuff, dabbled. I did, Josh did —'

'No. Josh didn't, not until Dani. That's why,' she said.

'Okay.'

'No, not okay,' she said. 'I kept looking for you at the church, convinced you'd show up. Your mum was embarrassed.'

'Yeah, I'm more than aware of that.'

'Had you taken anything that night?'

'Yeah, I think we probably all had.'

'So, you knew Josh had?'

'He never mentioned it and neither did I. Erika, kids do that,' he said. 'They'll be doing it in ten years' time. They were doing it ten years before us. We didn't invent it. If it wasn't for Josh, you'd have been doing the exact same thing.'

'Don't tell me what I'd have been doing if my brother…' She left the sentence unfinished. 'All the time we were together, you never mentioned this?'

'I didn't want to have this conversation any more than you did, no. And then, there I was, shacked up with his sister. I've always carried guilt about that.'

'You couldn't turn up to the funeral for one hour for Josh, *for me*, but when you found out about Angie, you rushed to her side. Do you know how that looks? How that made me feel?'

'Your mum didn't want me near the funeral — that's why I made sure I was there for Angie,' he admitted. 'I'll never know if staying with Josh would've made a difference. That's something I have to live with. Do I regret being there for Angie? No, of course not.'

'Good for you. At least my brother's death wasn't completely pointless.'

'His death was completely fucking pointless.'

'You haven't got a clue. The looks. The gossip… That's how people remember him: the boy who died from an overdose. That's all anybody ever remembers about my brother.'

'That's not how I remember him. That's not how the people who knew Josh remember him.'

Soon after Josh died, her mother and Ewan packed up the house, got married, and moved to a different city. The truth was, Lynda couldn't face what had happened, and neither could Erika. They'd drifted apart, found comfort building new, unrecognisable lives. Erika plunged straight back into her studies. Their mum, who she once was, ended when Josh died.

She started over again as Ewan's wife. Their family, her childhood, stored away, perhaps easier to reconcile than Josh's death. The only photograph of Josh, her mum kept in her purse. Erika felt like a reminder of everything missing. Her brother's existence became like some old favourite toy, sought only in memory.

'Where are you going?' asked Enzo as Erika stood up.

'Back to my hotel.'

'Erika…'

'I'm not here for you. I'm here for Claire.'

CHAPTER TWENTY-ONE

After a week spent finalising the live Stable Denim campaign launch and chasing William Torrence for his sign-off, Erika was more than happy to take some time out and go on the planned retreat with Polly, even if that included a lot of strange activities, not enough food and zero alcohol.

However strict the regime, it was a far better option than shoving David's secret phone under his nose and demanding answers about Anya. She'd been playing out that exact scenario almost continuously, though her anger had finally cooled to an icy calmness.

Polly spotted Erika almost immediately. The pair of them burst into laughter as they greeted each other. Erika was relieved to find the place as impressive as the photo gallery promised. They wheeled their cases across imposing marble floors, the air con deliciously cool and beautifully scented.

Astral, Divinity Wellbeing's programme coordinator, according to her pin, explained that the air con was bestowing the scientifically proven benefits of aromatherapy, courtesy of essential oils and plant extracts. Erika was happy to go along with whatever was allegedly happening for her benefit, until Astral added: 'Scents are essential to our wellbeing. That's why they're called essential oils.' Erika said nothing, biting her tongue as she and Polly then made their way to their first lesson: Introduction to Aura Greatness, a session that would free negative energy stored deep within. As it turned out, aura greatness was located between the legs.

'As women, we store negative energy deep within the divine sanctity of the vagina,' said Skylar, their instructor, squatting before them with a radiant expression. 'This is why it's *so important* to *really ease* that pelvic floor as low as we can.' She got up and patrolled the perimeters of the large conservatory where they had gathered, overlooking the sumptuous gardens. 'Nice work, Fiona.' Skylar approached a grey-haired, sparkly-eyed lady who wore a wide smile, as recommended in the Here Comes Happiness leaflet issued by Astral on arrival. Apparently, being forced to smile tricked your brain into believing you were actually happy. So far, to Erika's eye at least, all the collective grinning manically reflected in the windows looked slightly terrifying.

Skylar placed her hands on Fiona's shoulders, lowering the woman's body into a squat to quite a worrying degree. 'Allow your vagina,' she said, 'known as the precious *yoni* to the enlightened, to *deeply* breathe *in* the air of abundant positivity that flows freely at Divinity Wellbeing.' Skylar inhaled as Erika tried to comply, not entirely convinced her vagina had lungs.

'Then *out*,' Skylar said as she exhaled. 'Really relax those lower energies,' she said, bouncing elegantly on tiptoe. You'd never have guessed she was working anything more than her hamstrings. 'Experience clarity from your most sacred chakra.'

Erika checked to see if Polly was finding this as bizarre as she was. Her friend wore a ponytail and headband, along with yoga socks, mitts, and a tasteful two-piece in pale grey and lemon. She somehow managed to make all this seem simultaneously graceful and energetic as she got into the pelvic swing of things. Erika wondered what underwear Polly was wearing, because her sports thong really wasn't being all that supportive of her most precious chakra.

'And *slowly*,' Skylar emphasised, clearly cautious about being sued for personal injury, 'let's *straighten* our knees. *Good*. Spine, spine, spine. Very good, ladies. Let's send those *feelings* a *message.* We're sending thoughts of divine gratitude deep inside the vagina before we lift our necks and raise our arms.' Skylar stretched. 'Allow your breasts to *rise to the Heavens* ... and *relax...*'

Erika ached already. It was exhausting, all this stretching, especially while wearing very tight clothes. Her chest horribly flattened, forcing her nipples south, leaving visible imprints of miserable-looking tits through her dry-weave running top. But when she looked around, everyone else seemed quite pleased with themselves.

'And finally, as we warm down,' Skylar instructed, taking to her yoga mat, 'let's keep our backs nice and straight as we concentrate on restoring our breathing, and silently say a few words —'

Let me guess, Erika thought.

'...to our vaginas.'

Erika closed her eyes, breathing deeply as Skylar continued talking through her arse.

'Let that sacred chakra feel your gratitude. Let her know she is cleansed, a vibrant space, as you gift your vagina with the divine light of spiritual intention.'

Cheers, vagina. Erika thought, trying her best to cooperate with Skylar's instructions. *I probably don't say this often enough, but really, big thanks from me. Thanks for the memories, which we'll keep between ourselves, but mostly for Matthew. He'd feel bad if he knew what he put us through, but he was more than worth it. Great kid. Oh, and please let my vulva know that I'm sorry about the thong.*

After they dined on a lunch of moonlight-infused water and a single handful of dried fruit, at what Erika decided must be ironically known as the Sustenance Station, the women were invited to their next session: Motherhood to Meditation. The group were now situated in a small studio and ushered into perfecting the lotus position, which was quite relaxing. Although, after smiling non-stop for almost two hours, Erika's face ached, as if she'd paid a prolonged visit to the dentist. This only reminded her of Anya, whose vagina had a lot of explaining to do.

'Please recline on your mat,' instructed their guide, a woman with pink highlights called Celeste. 'Make yourselves comfortable. Hands by your sides. Palms flat. *Inhale deeply*, *exhale deeply…*' Celeste almost sang.

Before Erika knew it, she was on the verge of a wonderfully deep sleep, her smile thankfully slipping from her face as she felt herself drifting away…

'As we recline into subconscious embrace,' Celeste suddenly eulogised as Erika's eyes snapped open, her mouth as dry as lunch, 'we restore our innermost senses by harnessing breathing to our minds, also known as the crown chakra. *Focus*, *focus*, *focus*. Picture each breath as an infinite ray of light, working along the spine, from the *top* of the head to the *tip* of the toes…'

That part was quite nice, especially compared to the first class. But when Erika opened her eyes, she saw that the blinds had been lowered and the room was engulfed in unnerving darkness.

'Let thoughts and images drift by. Allow truth to rise and meet you. Let all worry, responsibility and concern be free, as you invite providence!' Celeste said. 'Silence brings the message…'

Erika lay for a few minutes, remembering those photographs Enzo had showed her, happily distracted by thoughts of what might've been. She still hadn't breathed a word about Enzo to Polly, afraid that she'd judge. She also wondered if he was right, and there was nothing going on between Anya and David except a bit of off-the-record tooth whitening.

She slowly became aware of her surroundings, unsure whether she had invited providence, or if she was still supposed to have a grin plastered on her face. It was too dark to check whether everyone else was still holding theirs in place. She held her breath but couldn't concentrate on her infinite light, not with Celeste prattling on. She felt herself growing uneasy in the darkness, miles from home ...

'*OMMM!*'

Celeste's sudden hum sent a chill through Erika's heart. She had no idea what her inability to relax in a darkened room full of strangers said about the state of her crown chakra, but after dining on slivers of melon and spinach leaves, Erika tried to be open-minded about joining the group for Moon Bathing.

'For centuries,' said Skylar, who returned that evening in a long, hooded robe, as if about to head off to Stonehenge on a broomstick, 'our sisters have worshipped the cycles of the moon.'

Fuck worshipping the moon, Erika thought. She'd have preferred to be worshipping a plate of food, preferably while holding a wine glass.

'By "sisters", do you think she means witches?' she whispered to Polly, who sat beside her in the gardens, as instructed. 'If this involves an altar, I'm leaving.'

'We dedicate this altar —'

'Shit,' Polly said, stifling laughter as they watched Skylar pick up a pair of poles, about a metre long, stabbing each one into the ground. 'I think we're about to be sacrificed.'

'You might be,' Erika said, as Skylar balanced a third pole on top. 'I've still got my trainers on...'

'Sister Moon!' Skylar crooned, raising her arms and looking up. 'The embodiment of the female spirit! Divine in her turning of the tide, the guardian of our wombs.'

'Not more of this,' Erika said. 'I never knew pagans were amateur gynaecologists…'

'I think I'm starting to ovulate,' Polly said. They covered their mouths as they snorted.

'We gather to thank you,' Skylar called to the skies, arms outstretched. 'Ladies, let us stand, gathered together, as I anoint this most sacred altar. For tonight, our dreams shall be our guide!'

They watched in alarm as Skylar hitched up her heavy robe.

'We're not going to limbo, are we?'

'That's what it looks like,' Polly said as Skylar bent backwards, approaching the poles while somehow reclining at ninety degrees.

'Bloody hell,' Erika said. 'Good for her. I haven't been at that angle since my youth…'

'Take each other's hands, ladies.' Skylar slowly draped herself under the pole. '*AARRHHH*!' She let out a furious roar, shaking demonically. 'That's right.' She stood to smile inanely at the group, who smiled inanely back, mostly looking horrified.

'We shall, this night, take command of our energies with a *ROAR*!'

'This is one way to spend a Friday,' Polly said, as they got to their feet.

'Hands, under, and *roar*!' Skylar demonstrated, limboing under the pole again as if her spine was made from butter — not that dairy was permitted — while her hands splashed at invisible waters. 'Raise your pelvis to Sister Moon!' she cried, giving a thrust. 'Let us reconnect through our dream divinity as sisters!'

The ladies started clapping now, more out of fear than enthusiasm, Erika thought, avoiding closer proximity to Skylar the same way you might navigate an unattended bonfire. The rhythm of the clapping picked up its pace as they mimicked Skylar's disturbing dance. They each attempted the limbo, some ducking under, others surprisingly flexible, including Fiona, a classical pianist, who travelled far better in a state of recline, than she managed on two feet.

'Come on, ladies!' Skylar was positively manic. 'Make it your own!'

Erika clapped along, cheering the ladies. They wore genuine smiles now, with not a grimace in sight. After stretching away stress, talking to your vagina, and whatever other waffle they peddled at the place, was this all it really took to seek yourself out?

'Sister Erika!' Skylar called. 'Give praise to pleasure!'

'Get up there, Sister Erika,' Polly nudged her to attention as Skylar beckoned.

Sister Erika hadn't realised she was holding up proceedings, so in the spirit of entertaining the ladies, she gyrated towards the poles, determined to put on a show. Polly went limp with laughter as Erika rolled her hips as slowly and provocatively as possible, feeding herself to the limbo with her eyes on Sister Moon. She was astounded to find she'd cleared the bar as she straightened her spine.

'*YES!*' she squawked, open-mouthed. 'Did you see that?'

'Let the moon be your witness!' Skylar grinned, giving Erika an affectionate tap on the shoulder before resuming clapping and encouraging Polly, who merely ran under the thing while sticking out her tongue at Erika.

'May dreams bestow wisdom on all of us this night,' Skylar said, commanding the skies. 'Darkness becomes light! The call of our hearts answered in the skyline of the soul!'

Polly handed Erika another supposedly cleansing concoction from Celeste, who was offering blankets and purified water, which tasted suspiciously like regular water, while congratulating the ladies on their efforts as if they'd just completed the London Marathon.

'Let us continue in silence, please, ladies,' Skylar instructed. 'Clear your minds, focus on what troubles you, open your heart, and face those feelings as Sister Moon inspires your sleep.'

Erika checked her phone. No word from David since she'd left, not that she expected friendly concern. The atmosphere back home had descended further. His social engagements were more frequent, and already aware of the answers, she'd stopped asking questions.

Erika wasn't sure if it was down to limboing for Sister Moon, but as a soundtrack of strangely reassuring aquatic sounds flooded her room, she forgot about things back home and drifted off to sleep.

New Years' 1999 was everything she'd been living for during those last few weeks of the university semester. She was determined to seize one last interval before being forced to atone for the last twelve weeks of doing little more than showing up. There'd been mention of celebrating at their aunty's place until Josh saved Erika from sobriety, persuading their mum that she shouldn't be guilt-tripped into seeing in the next one thousand years with a gaggle of elderly relatives balancing paper plates on their knees. Instead, he invited his little sister to the amazing party his girlfriend, Dani, was throwing.

Erika painted her nails a sparkly blue and opted for a rather daring turquoise halter-neck dress and mules. She backed up her coursework on a floppy disc ahead of the Y2K bug and got ready to leave with her university bestie, Sonal Shah.

'The house is in Notting Hill?' Sonal asked, peeling the back off a stick-on bhindi.

'Just like the movie,' Erika said. 'Dani's sister is a stylist. Josh said the house is unreal. *Kate Moss* is meant to be going…'

'Really?' Sonal said, more than a little dubious as she clipped a waist chain around her exposed midriff.

When they arrived, the door was opened by a beautiful, waif-like girl. Erika mentioned Josh as instructed and was invited upstairs, bypassing passionate, impromptu embraces. She took in the coloured lights swirling across the walls, the tinfoil-covered chandeliers and the strange arcade sounds, until finally they reached a plateau. Ahead of midnight, there was a truly terrible live set from a band who were apparently massive with the kind of people who adored undiscovered talent. They were called Holier Than Thou and featured Dani's brother on bass.

'It turns out that one of Josh's mates shot the album cover,' said Dani, Josh's Kylie-sized girlfriend, a mass of blonde hair with a glossy pout. She was handing out free copies of the EP.

'Was it Enzo?' Erika said, the only friend of Josh's she knew who'd got into photography.

'Think so.'

'Is he here?'

'Not sure. Best ask Josh.'

What if Enzo was there? And what if she got to snog him on New Year's Eve? It would be her first kiss of the millennium! Erika scanned the crowd as she ladled another glass of murky punch, her watch marking 11.47 p.m. Sonal gave her arm a squeeze of happiness, exchanging a mischievous look, before swanning off with a guy she introduced as Taylor.

Erika joined a decade-long queue to the bathroom as Josh ambled past.

'Is Enzo here?'

'Two minutes,' he said, busy on his phone.

He jostled away, and she followed him into the kitchen, where he stood with a group of girls.

'Josh!'

Erika noticed one of them hand over cash. Josh counted the notes, then delved into his pocket.

'Is Enzo here?' Erika asked, erasing what she'd seen. 'Is he coming?'

'What?' Josh said, preoccupied. He wore an expression of brooding tranquillity that she had never seen before. 'Why are you always asking about Enzo, anyway?'

'*Ten!*'

'No, mate,' he said, answering his phone. 'You need to get here.'

'*Nine!*'

Dani sidled up and reached into Josh's pocket, asking, 'One?'

'*Eight!*'

'Plenty,' he said, shaking his head at Dani.

'*Seven!*'

'How much you thinking?'

'*Six!*'

He shook Dani off, fished for something in his jeans, and bit it in half.

'*Five!*'

He wiggled the pill on the tip of his tongue. Dani giggled before sucking it free.

'*Four!*'

'Can't do, mate,' he said, ending the call.

'*Three!*'

'Enzo's not here, Erika, no,' he said. 'Probably for the best, eh?'

'*Two!*'

'*HAPPY NEW YEAR!*'

Erika left Josh to snog Dani, making her way outside as a car pulled up.

'Oh my God,' Sonal said, sitting on the low wall and having a smoke as the car door opened. 'It's *Kate fucking MOSS!*'

CHAPTER TWENTY-TWO

Erika was surprised to sleep deeply until morning. She woke to the memory of Kate Moss at that New Year's Eve party and remembered her brother.

Josh had straight blonde hair, so thick, that as a kid Erika nick-named him He-Man. Erika always wished she'd got his hair and eyelashes, so much fuller and longer than hers. He was tall and slim, about five foot eleven, and, she knew, secretly gutted he hadn't reached the full 6ft mark. He was crazy about trainers and always wore a good jacket. Minor details, but when people found out he was her brother, she always felt quietly proud, and he never put her down by shirking her at school.

Josh studied without any big fuss, unlike Erika, who was practically ordered to finish her homework. Also, unlike her, he was super tidy. She was a bit jealous when Enzo started coming over, monopolising Josh's attention, until she gradually took back shared ownership of the games console. That's what they did, mainly: endless computer games and movies.

Erika always thought Josh would have kids. When she had Matt, Matthew *Joshua* Forde, she thought about how amused her brother would have been at the thought of her becoming someone's mum. She saw a lot of her brother in Matt, but knew that was mostly down to wishful thinking. Really, it was a similar closeness she'd felt with her brother which she now shared with her son. They'd generally got on; the only occasional downsides were the things Josh decided she didn't need to know.

Josh started dealing at university for some lad in the year above. By the time the older kid graduated, Josh had taken the reins and worked out the finer details of where to get his hands on the stuff. Dani was pointed in Josh's direction as the go-to guy on campus. Before long, he was joining her and her friends in partaking of his profits. All of this only came to light after the funeral, when Erika was desperate to fill in the gaps between the Josh she knew and the version she'd glimpsed at the New Year's Eve party.

She sat up and yawned away maudlin thoughts as sleepiness left her, distracted from dreams by the hollow growl in her stomach. She was ravenous and light-headed as she sipped a glass of 'Angel' water and a lymphatic detox supplement that she wasn't prepared to take, not quite sure it was legal. She didn't think she could cope with any more detoxing, but she pulled on her leggings, zipped up her hoodie, and opened the curtains to a pleasant-looking morning.

After a spinach and honey smoothie almost moved her to tears of gratitude, followed by a Unicorn Facial involving the massaging of her third eye —Astral tapping at the centre of her forehead like a deranged woodpecker before dousing her face in glycolic acid — Mind Swim was top of the day's agenda.

An experience which supposedly united the mind and body, Mind Swim offered the chance to reflect on the knowledge gained during your stay, which for Erika revolved around the necessity of regular meals, not treating her vagina like some kind of pen pal, and making more of an effort to have a laugh with Polly without having to worship the moon.

'Polly?'

Her friend made her way towards her, handkerchief pressed against her nose, with the results from her Unicorn Facial washed away by tears.

'Are you okay?' Erika whispered so as not to alert the staff. 'What's wrong? Are you hungry?'

Polly shook her head. 'Well, maybe a bit, but the Mind Swim,' she said, barely able to look at her. 'Awful.'

'This isn't right.' Erika placed a comforting hand on Polly's arm, hoping to make her see sense. 'Let's get out of here. We'll get a refund, go for a Maccies…'

'No, it's not that,' Polly said, blowing her nose. 'I mean, awful in a good way. The session was incredible, but very demanding. Luna's waiting for you.'

Erika wondered what could possibly have reduced Polly to tears. She continued down the corridor, shuffling past twin rows of identical doors. She searched her recesses for what could possibly trigger her own emotional response during the forthcoming interrogation. You had to guard against weakness with these people. Would Luna comment on the lack of body in her layers, desperately in need of a decent blow-dry? Observe her inability to refer to complete strangers as her sisters, as if she'd absconded to a convent?

'Erika Forde.' Luna stood to greet her, wearing a blue kimono and matching wide-leg pants. She took both her hands, looking deeply into her eyes. 'To meet you is a blessing to all.'

'Wow. Well, first time anyone's ever said that,' Erika said, taking a seat next to a small table bearing flowers, tissues and a carafe. Her armchair was noticeably lower than Luna's, enabling her to literally talk down to her, she guessed.

'Erika,' Luna whispered, 'welcome to Mind Swim, where your thoughts, as the ocean, will carry us on our journey. What is it that troubles you?'

'Well, where do we start?' Erika said, determined to keep her head above water, no matter how turbulent the Mind Swim. 'I mean, the whole world's in a mess. Politically, we haven't learned our lessons; we're still warring at extremes. The economy's —'

'Putting collective issues aside, Erika, let's focus on you,' Luna suggested. 'What is it that causes you to feel so removed from others, Erika?'

'Do I?'

'Part of the process here at Divinity Wellbeing is the observation of our guests,' Luna said, tapping her iPad, as if scouring files. 'You, Erika, have very much existed on the outskirts of the group — never fully connecting, not attempting to become one with your sisters.'

'Well, maybe it looks that way…'

'It does, it does,' Luna said, with a complacent smile. 'Why do you think that is?'

'I think, maybe, I'm observing, too,' Erika said, deciding to give Luna something to nibble on before escaping. 'I mean, I'm interested in the people around me, even if I don't feel the need to throw myself into things.'

'Ah, but you do,' Luna said, staring into her eyes, willing Erika to participate. 'Man is not an island.'

Erika nodded, looking past Luna's almost menacing gaze to yet another calming landscape on the wall. This one showed an ocean vista at night, or maybe at sunrise, she thought, spotting the emergence of a subtle yellow cuticle at the corner.

'How interesting, you being drawn to that image,' Luna said, updating her iPad.

'Well, I'm not really drawn to it. There's nothing else to look at, so —'

'Day Dawns on the Soul, that's the title.' Luna turned to the painting. 'We're only ever attracted to those things that mirror our experience. Those things which already exist within us.'

That's not true, Erika thought, drawn to the idea of poached egg on toast way more than an amateur-looking oil painting.

'A time of transition for you, Erika,' Luna announced. 'A new self, reborn.'

'Who knows?' Erika said, keeping it polite. 'Fingers crossed, hey…'

She'd only gone along with this rubbish to make her friend happy, but Polly was anything but. The staff were intrusive, possibly exploiting people who were particularly vulnerable. Luna might believe she was doing good, but to Erika, this style of therapy seemed to focus on pushing people to emotional breaking point. She doubted the woman held any kind of licence apart from for driving.

'Erika, there's a reason you came here to us this weekend.'

'Yes,' Erika said, 'it was a birthday present.'

'From Polly?'

'Polly's very upset. I saw her —'

'There's a reason why you chose to be here with Polly.'

'Yes, like I said, it was a birthday present,' Erika said, hearing the growing impatience in her own voice. 'I didn't have much choice.'

'More than that, Erika,' Luna said, closing her eyes, as if praying for a breakthrough. 'Come on, let's do the work. Let's swim this ocean together.'

Erika inhaled and sighed through her nose, not sure she had the stamina to play along. It was like discussing the quarterly gas bill with David.

'Okay.' Luna changed strategy. 'Do you think there's a reason Polly granted you this particular experience as a gift?'

Granted? She made Polly sound like a genie. She might rub her belly and make three wishes: coffee, eggs and toast.

'Well, if I didn't know any better, I'd say it was because she didn't like me very much.'

There it was: she'd said it. How was that for not fully engaging with the group?

'On the contrary,' Luna said, keeping her poise, 'Polly's very concerned with how you perceive her. She very much values your friendship.'

'Well, yes. I very much value our friendship, too,' Erika said. 'I was only joking, by the way, about her not liking me, in case you're making any more notes.'

Notes which Erika had every right to see, she reminded herself, so Luna could get right off her magic carpet, analysing everyone's every move.

'Do you feel your energies, yours and Polly's, are spiritually aligned?'

'I'm not sure what you mean, Luna. This all seems a little intense to me,' Erika said, 'but we obviously get on. We're good friends. We just have different ideas about what an enjoyable weekend looks like.'

'Some of our guests do need to work that bit harder, delve a little deeper, Erika. Enjoyable isn't something we actively claim to offer, but we do expect our guests to contribute the necessary application if they're to fully benefit from our approach.'

'Well, I have,' Erika said, standing up now. 'Thanks for your time. This was interesting.'

'Erika,' Luna said, taking her hands once again as Erika resisted the urge to shake free, 'you're withdrawing against the pain of sense memory. Tender, unhealed wounds harden into scars. You're unwilling to experience these growing pains, and that is the exact point where resilience is no better than self-harm.'

'Luna,' Erika said, on the verge of outrage, 'I'm not about to self-harm.'

'Sometimes, guests find it difficult to communicate openly. If you wish to end the Mind Swim, of course, you are free to do so, but I do feel Polly could use your support right now, and you may seem out of reach…'

Erika gave a nod, determined not to spend another second with these people. She walked out and made her way to Polly's room. The chamber staff with their inane, compulsory grins, vows of silence, everything about the place striking her as eery now. Enough was enough.

'Polly?' Erika knocked gently at the door, worried that some orderlies would come and give her a sedative. 'It's me. Are you okay?'

The door opened. Polly looked exhausted as she dragged herself back to bed.

'Listen,' Erika said, 'I don't know what that crackpot said to you, but really, it's nothing more than a fortune cookie. If you've paid all this money to lie on a bed and cry, you could've just stayed home with Steve.'

She was relieved when Polly laughed, unfolding a tissue before seizing up again.

'What the hell did Luna say?' Erika asked. 'Have you noticed that all their names are fake? Astral, Skylar, Celeste, Luna. It's like spending a weekend at a space station.'

Erika wasn't getting into it, not with Polly so distraught, but the place was unethical. They needed to report it to someone, some governing body, besides Sister Moon or their uteruses.

'Luna said,' Polly managed, 'that I need to find the courage to tell you.' Her face crumpled again. 'I didn't want to betray anyone's trust, but Matt…'

'Matt?' Erika said, attention caught. 'My Matt?'

'Tyler's not coming home, either,' Polly said. 'Because of me. Because of Steve.'

Erika didn't say a word, searching for the link to Matt in her friend's rambling.

'Matt and Tyler,' Polly said. 'They're spending the summer together, avoiding me and not telling you.'

'Not telling me? Why?'

'They're seeing each other. Well, technically, they're back together. They started going out while they were still at college.'

'Tyler and Matt? But I didn't even know Tyler was —'

'No, me neither. I walked in on them and reacted *really* badly. I started going on about how it could've been his father. How did he think Steve was going to react? I couldn't have been much worse about it. I told Tyler I didn't want them seeing each other.'

'*Matt and Tyler?*' Erika said, wondering how the hell she hadn't realised. Tyler was the boy Matt had fallen in love with?

'It was a lot to process,' Polly went on. 'I wanted to tell you at the time, but Tyler was adamant that it was over. Matt stopped visiting. We never spoke another word about it, and now this.'

'I never would've guessed Matt had feelings for Tyler. He'd been going out with Sophia. I was sort of relieved when he broke up with her and could fully concentrate on his exams.'

'Matt's been staying in Manchester. I agreed to keep it from you.'

'Polly,' Erika said. 'Look, I'm not exactly thrilled, but I get it. Dealing with Matt's been like herding cats, recently. Wow. Matt and Tyler...'

'I'm so sorry. This involved your son. I should've told you.'

'Look, I can't say I'd have reacted any differently, and to tell you the truth,' Erika glanced at Polly's bedside table, 'right now I'm way more annoyed about those Lindt wrappers. Please tell me you saved some for me?'

CHAPTER TWENTY-THREE

Erika managed to leave the retreat with surprisingly little fuss. All she got was a few disapproving glances, and the only enquiry was from Fiona, the champion limbo participant. Didn't Erika know they were about to do Fountain of Life? It was a meditative session created to lubricate the, well, you know.

'Fiona?' Erika said, pausing in the foyer. 'If that's what's troubling you, get yourself out of here, pour yourself a gin and settle down in front of *John Wick*. If that doesn't kick-start your fountain of life, believe me, nothing will.'

She drove off and stopped at the nearest service station, where she ordered a large burger, a full fat soda and a side of salty fries. She then sat in her car and called Matt.

'Namaste,' Matt said when he answered. 'Are we feeling enlightened, oh wise one?'

'I am, actually,' Erika said, folding up her empty wrappers and cartons (David would be proud) and putting her son on speaker.

'That sounds promising,' he said. 'You'll be swimming in open water next, Mum.'

'That's dangerous,' Erika said. 'A cry for help, in my opinion. One step away from living on a barge or drowning yourself, in which case, I'd opt for the latter.'

'So, come on then,' he said. 'How was it?'

'I had a nice time with Polly,' she said, which was at least partially true, 'and apparently, we're not to worry, because the moon's taking care of the rest.'

'Brilliant,' Matt said. 'The moon, hey? How smashing.'

'Exactly, but that's not why I called. I know why you're not coming home this summer, Matthew.'

'Oh, full title,' he said in a tone of warm mischief. 'Duly noted.'

'It's pretty hurtful that you thought you couldn't tell me. No matter what, your father and I love you, Matt, you know that.'

'What's with all the self-help talk? They really got to you this weekend, didn't they?'

'Not half as much as they intended to, and stop trying to change the subject. I'd rather ask you face-to-face, but that's a bit difficult when I never get to see you.'

'You see me all the time.'

'Only on my computer, and not nearly as much as usual. It might work for your dad, but it's not for me.'

'You're finally getting divorced, aren't you?'

'*What*? No!' she said, although the small voice in her head had been asking the exact same question for weeks. 'And *finally*? What does that mean?'

'Oh, please, Mum. Your mum this, your dad that. You and dad talk about each other like you're already in court. You may as well start referring to each other as the plaintiff and the defendant.'

'Stop being so dramatic. No one's mentioned divorce.'

'Look, in my opinion, I think you deserve a divorce.'

'Why don't you put that on one of your mugs?'

'Great idea. I'll send you both a matching set once the paperwork's finalised.'

'It's not an achievement, Matt.'

'It is if you deserve to be happy,' he said. 'I wish you'd just get it over with and move on. Both of you.'

Erika rarely dealt with this condescending, all-knowing version of Matt. He usually reserved that for David and other deserving causes. 'You're being obnoxious.'

'Of course I am. I'm allowed to be,' he said. 'I'm the one who's had to live in the shit sandwich between you and him my whole life.'

'Don't use that language — and your whole life? It hasn't been that bad,' she said, a blissful montage of childhood highlights playing out as she spoke. 'You were happy, weren't you?'

'Mum, I'm not talking about you as parents, growing up. You were both fine, and some of it was great. But I know who you are, and I see none of that when you're around Dad. I never have. He has that effect on people; he reduces everyone to a silhouette. He has to be at the centre of everything — no amount of praise is ever going to be enough. I think that's why he needs the surplus attention. I honestly think that's why he does the things he does.'

'What things he does?'

'You know what things. Mum, I know he's hurt you. I get it. I get why things have ended up like this.'

'I'm not hurt,' Erika said. 'I stayed. My choice. That's why it's like this.'

'The minute another book comes out, off he goes, sticking on his hats. He thinks he's him, doesn't he? *Finn Schuyler*. Authors — they're like rockstars for women in flat shoes. I'm sick of pandering. It felt so good, putting my feelings out there. My opinions never counted for much in our house, and I wish you'd spoken up. But I'm not keeping my mouth shut anymore, Mum. I'm not.'

'So, it's my fault?' she said. 'Of course, as usual.'

'It's absolutely not your fault, no, but maybe he needs to be with his adoring cardigan-wearers, and you need to not be around him, expecting anything different. We both need to do that. I don't need either of you sitting me down, announcing some split and expecting me to be devastated. I'd be relieved more than anything. We could finally all be ourselves.'

'There's nothing to announce, not yet,' Erika protested. 'But yes, it's a possibility.'

'Okay,' Matt said. 'So, what's been going on?'

'Your dad's been under a lot of stress, which you've not helped in the slightest.'

'You do know he thinks you're sleeping with Nate Petersen?'

'He said that to you? When did he say that?'

'Monica said you were away with Nate and told me not to mention it, because Dad's been pretty cut up.'

'There's nothing to be cut up about. I'm working with Nate, you know that,' she said. 'And please, credit me with some taste, if not a little more intelligence. The man dates teenagers, not middle-aged women, for God's sake.'

'So, you haven't met anyone else?'

'Of course I haven't. *As if!*' she said, Enzo Morelli crossing her mind as she denied all possibility. 'Why are you even asking me that? Why am I the adulterer?'

'Because it's still feasible, men finding you attractive, you know?'

'And if a man found me attractive?' she said, words clumsy as marbles. The fact was, Enzo *did* find her attractive. It was plain as day. 'You think I'd do that to your dad? You think I'd act on it?'

'Who knows?' Matt said. 'It's nothing *he* hasn't already done.'

'Well, I'm not doing that,' she said. 'And no, I haven't met anyone.'

'Has he?'

'Why don't you ask him? Sorry,' she said. 'I didn't mean that.'

'So, come on. I haven't got a load of half-siblings I need to know about, have I?'

'No, you haven't, not as far as I know, and this isn't funny! Anyway, we're your parents,' she said. 'How much do you really need to know?'

'It's not about how much I *need* to know. I want to know what's going on. Just be honest!'

'You're a fine one to talk.'

'We'll get to that in a moment. Hit me.'

'Okay,' she said. 'I found a phone hidden in the garage. Full of texts.'

'What kind of texts?'

'What kind do you think?'

'The phone was in the garage? A flip-phone with a cracked screen?'

'An old-fashioned thing with a cracked screen, yes. Didn't look like any of our old ones.'

'It's mine. Me and Tyler got a couple of second-hand ones when we were at college. He was worried about anything being downloaded onto perfect Polly's iPad. She practically managed his social media.'

'Don't go telling your dad that. It'll give him ideas,' she said, wondering if David and Matt shared a genetic predisposition to clandestine affairs. 'So it's yours? That makes sense. The texts sounded far too romantic to be your father's.'

'How much did you read?'

'All of it.'

'Sorry. Tyler chucked his away. Some of us,' he said, speaking away from the receiver, obviously aiming the comment at Tyler, 'are more sentimental than others.'

'Why didn't you just tell me you're staying with Tyler? What's the big secret?'

'Firstly, Steve's a neanderthal. Polly's a control freak, and you would've made it all about you.'

'What's that supposed to mean?'

'You remember Sophia? The constant monitoring, offering tea and biscuits every time you thought I might be exposing my boner.'

'Matthew!'

'You know what I mean,' he said. 'Then it'd be all the stuff about Polly being your friend, and how that could make things awkward, and next thing, it *would* be awkward. Joint family meals to prove how cool everyone is with it — just the thought of all that was enough.'

'Thanks. Nice to know we can't win, but you could've still come home.'

'Could we? I didn't see how that was going to work out. Sneaking around, dodging parents. It'd be like being back in college,' he said. 'Look, it's nothing personal.'

'Really? Sounds like it.'

'We don't get much time together, Mum, not with uni. We didn't need any drama erupting in suburbia. Anyway, the secret's out. We thought Polly might tell you while you were away.'

'I'd wish you'd told me yourself. So, the job, the placement, is that happening?'

'So,' Matt said, '*bit* of an exaggeration there. I've signed up freelance with an events company, but it's mostly been the side-hustle: Drink Up Coffee Cups. It's our baby.'

'Well, I'll leave you to tell your dad.'

'You're joking, aren't you? I'm not telling him anything. In the last text I got, he was thanking me for his sales figures.

There's another reason I'm happy staying put. He's been decking himself out in the old Harris tweed, has he?'

'I hate you arguing with your father.'

'Hypocrite.'

'We're not arguing, not as such,' she said. 'And please don't mention any of this to him. He doesn't know I'm thinking about leaving him yet.'

'Don't worry, I'll try not to spoil the surprise,' he said. 'So, you're still going to leave, even though the phone thing wasn't him?'

'He's been seeing someone else,' she said. 'I caught him out one night. He said he had a meeting, but he went on a date.'

'How do you know?'

'About the date? I followed him.'

'You followed him?'

Matt already sounded judgemental, so there was no way Erika could add in the part about Enzo.

'Please don't say anything, okay? You asked me to tell you, and I've told you.'

'Did you wear a disguise?'

'Very funny,' she said, her mind darting back to the blonde wig. 'Will you at least think about coming home for a week or so, maybe? Or I could come to you and take you both shopping? Stick some home-cooking in the freezer?'

'Yes, I'd like that,' Matt said. 'We'll sort something out.'

'You sound wonderfully noncommittal.'

'Not at all.'

'But you're happy?'

'The happiest.'

She could hear it in his voice. 'I'm so happy for you, Matt, honey.'

CHAPTER TWENTY-FOUR

It was barely two months since Lingua Franca had pitched the Stable Denim concept, and the big day had finally arrived. Erika was straight onto social media, checking visuals of Dad Jeans going live across the accounts of major retailers and influencers. Ursula had found the influencers, and while Erika was shocked by the fee that some of them charged, it seemed people trusted their judgement, attempting to dodge the perforated promises of advertisers.

At 12.45 p.m., clusters of weekend shoppers meandered, gazing into the gleaming retail windows of Keys Court. Music suddenly blared out, marking the appearance of Nate Petersen.

He stood at the top of the steps, which had now become home to the newly erected launch stage, pointing and waving. He was flanked by a security team Erika wasn't entirely convinced was justified, but if shoppers that afternoon had no clue who the guy was, they soon knew to stop and take notice.

The one thing he wasn't doing was wearing a pair of Stable Denim jeans, Erika noted as she watched from the top storey window of John Lewis's offices, overseeing corporate hospitality with William Torrence and Stable Denim's board of directors, along with assorted staff. No introduction was necessary as *Award-winning Director, Nate Petersen* appeared in neon scrawl across the screen behind Nate. He strode about in a pair of loose-fitting jogging bottoms, not exactly on brand, as he took the mic from Ursula, who was assisting from the side of the stage.

'Good afternoon, discerning high street shoppers!' Nate boomed, the audio whining for a moment. 'I want to talk to fathers, all the fathers here today. Dads, and all the people who love them.'

Erika wondered if that wasn't a little confusing. As people started filming, she became concerned they might think this was a stunt on behalf of Fathers for Justice.

'I've something important to share with you, because in just a moment's time, the world premiere of my new short film will be yours to tell your friends about — so keep your phones on, down there! We could have taken this to Sundance! But we've brought it here, exclusively for you guys, today! So, folks, are you ready to become part of retail history?'

Talking of retail history, there was no sign of Enzo. Erika, disappointed by his indifference, doubted her own excitement for a moment as the screen blinked awake, announcing the campaign:

Stable Denim vs Dad Jeans.
An original concept by Nate Petersen.

'I must warn you,' he said, stepping out of his sliders, 'being a Stable Denim guy is not for the faint-hearted!'

Erika froze as Nate pulled at his waistband, revealing white boxers. He freed himself from his joggers as if unveiling a monument, which thankfully he wasn't.

'Is this part of the script?' William whipped off his glasses with a look of distaste as Nate continued seducing the crowd.

'Thank you, kind person, whoever that was,' Nate said, grinning as a solitary wolf-whistle rang out. 'I'd like you to ask yourselves, what's a man without his favourite pair of jeans? Fellas, and the women who love you, I want you to remember the first pair of jeans that became real *game-changers* — made you feel like *the man* you truly are! The man you *wanted* to be, because that guy looked great! *YOU* looked great!'

He stood in his underpants, passers-by exchanging glances and showing reluctant interest.

'We all have the right to feel good about *who we are*! There's none of us here who haven't shared a moment of jean-wearing *greatness*! And that greatness,' he said, pausing briefly as Ursula handed him a pair of Stable Denim jeans and he pulled them on, 'is right here — a *FREE* pair of *Stable Denim jeans*. Good people, enjoy! I ask you to stop for a second, take a look, and follow the #DadJeans hashtag.' He dropped the mic, making a particularly dramatic exit as the screen blinked back to life.

Unbeknownst to Erika, Nate had made the executive decision to present the whole thing in black and white. Their room and the courtyard below stood in silent anticipation as Enzo Morelli appeared on screen, canvas holdall slung over his shoulder, towering above mountains and handsome as hell in a beautifully shot film.

'*Dad jeans*,' he boomed from the screen. '*There's a dark horse in town.*'

Hearing his voice and watching him onscreen, Erika had the same feeling as when he'd walked into the studio. He was the only guy for the job. Her heart jumped as shoppers stood, equally gripped by the footage.

'*Calling all medium-rise guys…*'

Enzo took to the terrain. There were close-ups of the jeans: seams and studs blended into the skyline and denim imprints appeared along the rockface. Erika was blown away by how Nate had edited the footage.

'*Remember those days, in your favourite blue jeans?*'

There was Enzo on the screen, with water dripping down his face. Blue sky, clouds shifting, birds in sudden flight.

'*That straight-talking, slim fit, button-fly…*'

Enzo was removing his shirt, barefoot, cupping his hands in water.

'*We're older, wiser…*'

He was as bleak and brooding as the mountainous skyline around him.

'*Denim designed to go along for the ride.*'

He sat now, looking over his shoulder, and Erika swore her oestrogen levels peaked.

'*Stable Denim.*'

There was a close-up of the label on Enzo's hip as he wiped the water from his face with the back of his arm. The camera panned the location, pulling back, running along his long legs and reaching his denim-clad butt.

'*We're back in the saddle.*'

The screen went blank as William and the board members broke into ardent claps. Erika scanned the room, receiving congratulations on a job well done.

Meanwhile, back on the street, the screen flickered to life once more with the Dad Jeans version of the ad, featuring Richard in glorious technicolour. He clambered about, even funnier now the shots were edited together. The footage ended with Richard on a stretcher sucking ice, quickly followed by promotional candid shots: before-and-after pictures of middle-aged men decked out in Stable Denim. Meanwhile, on stage, music blasted, announcing a troupe of Stable Denim-wearing models. They poured down the steps in jeans and T-shirts, sprawling out among a still respectably sized crowd, taking people's measurements ahead of the 100 free pairs of jeans on offer.

'Ursula?' a lone voice called over the mic. 'I've been a fool!'

Richard certainly looked like one. Erika's attention returned to the stage. William was looking at her from across the room, where he was loading his plate with a complimentary burrito, but what could she say? She nodded, as if everything was going according to plan.

'I'm the Dad Jean wearer up there, by the way,' he said, addressing the crowd while leaning on a solitary crutch. He beckoned Ursula from the side of the stage and she walked hesitantly into view, clearly not expecting the performance.

'Ursula?' Richard returned to his purpose, getting down on one knee, which was as awkward-looking as it sounded with one leg still in plaster. 'Please would you do me the great honour,' he said, presenting a small box, 'of becoming my wife?'

'*For fuck's sake…*' Erika growled.

'You always were a romantic at heart,' Enzo said, late to meet the investors.

'You missed the bloody launch,' Erika said, trying to keep her voice down, one accusatory finger pressed against his chest.

'What? I'm here, aren't I?'

She gave him an unimpressed look, then turned back to watch the proposal.

'Richard,' Ursula said, taking the mic. 'I promise, I won't marry you.'

Erika and Enzo exchanged looks.

'What?' Richard said, almost tipping over.

Ursula helped to prop him back up. 'I *never* want to marry you, Richard.'

Some of the crowd, presumably the married ones, began clapping.

'Maybe we should talk about this privately…'

'Oh, now he wants privacy...' Ursula said, gaining confidence and turning to the crowd. 'Richard, I never want to change the man you are, because that's the man I wanted to marry. But a very wise man once told me, it's impossible to desire what you already have.'

'Yeah, I did, that's true, but —'

'It was Nate Petersen, actually, Richard. But what I'm trying to say is, we make each other happy, don't we? I don't need proof — not the kind of proof that would change how we are.'

Richard looked confused, sticking the ring box back in his jacket.

'I love you, Richard, and I know you love me too. I do,' she said. 'So, please, if it's okay, can we stay *choosing* to be together? Will you never marry me, please?'

'I ... yes!' Richard said, loving the endorsement. 'I do! I mean, I will!'

'Who said romance is dead?' Enzo said, applauding along with the rest of the room, who seemed convinced this was part of the event.

Outside, the crowd began to disperse. The Enzo version of the ad played out again as William went back to chatting with colleagues and tucking into lunch.

'The ad,' Erika said, pecking Enzo's cheek, 'is better than good.' She turned to address the room. 'He looks incredible in the campaign, doesn't he? Everyone, I'd like to introduce Enzo Morelli, your Stable Denim Guy. The gathered party balanced plates and glasses on tables, offering haphazard applause.

'So, you can at least bloody watch it.' Erika lowered her voice, directing Enzo's attention back to the screen as a commotion broke out at the office door.

'Mum!'

'Matthew?'

'The one and only,' he said, inching past a PA who looked to Erika for confirmation.

'My son!' she explained, as he made his way over, decked out in the Stable Denim promotional kit of brand T-shirt and jeans. 'Matt?'

'Yup,' he said. 'Dreamt it all up myself! Been on the floor, down there with Joe Public, taking sign-ups while dressed in Stable Denim,' he said, striking a pose.

'You were down there? You were one of the models?' Erika grabbed his arms, holding him close. 'I've missed you so much.' She was unable to resist standing back to assess him. 'This is my son.' She looked at Enzo. 'This is my boy.'

Local press became national press. Social media engagement was skyrocketing, according to Ursula, the only one who really understood the tracking and translated the figures. Richard was delirious with his contribution and dads all over the place were already sharing GIFs. Nate Petersen led the procession of campaign collaborators into some club Erika had never heard of, but according to Matt, it was very exclusive and a very big deal.

William Torrence started popping some moves in a pair of Stable Denim jeans that, with his shape and stature, made him look prematurely incontinent, the waistband was so high. Ursula and Richard, celebrating their romantic truce, flooded their table with shots of Grey Goose. Matt and a few of the models hit the dancefloor, and shortly before she called it a night, Erika was merry enough to join in. She remembered the ladies of Divinity Wellbeing and the moon-bathing night, when they threw caution and dignity to the wind. Life was too short not to dance how and when you felt like dancing. She noticed

Enzo, arms folded, beer bottle tucked beneath his bicep, trying to keep the smile from his face and shaking his head.

'I'm having *THE BEST TIME*!' Erika yelled over the music as she joined him at the bar.

'Yeah, I can see that.'

'I've just realised, I've never seen you dance.'

'Are you forgetting how incredibly cool I am, Erika? Cool guys don't dance.'

'That's not true,' Erika said, noticing Matt, who was watching them. 'Look at my son.'

'Okay, I'll rephrase that: I can't dance.'

'Yeah, I can't imagine you'd be a good dancer. You're too uptight.'

'Exactly. Someone's got to look uptight on the edge of the dancefloor to make everyone else look good,' he said.

Erika nudged him playfully. 'We couldn't have done any of this without you, you know. The whole campaign. It's all down to you.'

'Well, you know what?' Enzo said, as if finally reaching a conclusion. 'I've loved it. I have, honestly. I was worried, but sod it. You only live once, don't you?'

'I suppose so,' Erika said, feeling giddy. 'You looked hot in the film.'

'Not too uptight?'

'Yes, but in a hot way.'

'So, you!' Matt interrupted to accost Enzo. 'You were my Uncle Josh's best mate.'

'I was,' Enzo said. 'Josh was a top guy.'

'The ad looks amazing,' Matt said, as Erika wrapped her arm around his waist.

'I'm so happy you're here,' she said, pulling Matt closer for a moment. 'You two are two of my favourite people in the whole world, do you know that?'

'She's so *extra* when she's had a drink,' Matt said, talking over the top of her head, almost as tall as Enzo. 'She used to come into my room after lights out, talking about you and Josh. Between you and me, I think she fancied you.'

'Girl code, Matt,' Erika said, giving him a silencing look. 'On that note, could you please order your mother a taxi on your app thing?'

'It's barely eleven, Mum. Oh God,' Matt said as a new song came on. 'Come on!' He gripped her arm. 'You can't sit this one out — *dance*floor, now!'

'Oh, Matt, I can't,' Erika said. 'I'm far too eager, which means it's time to call it a night.'

'Matt, brilliant to meet you,' Enzo said, offering his hand, before offering Erika his arm. 'Come on, Cinders. I'll sort the taxi. Let's get you home.'

CHAPTER TWENTY-FIVE

Erika spent the entire journey telling Enzo about Matt and Tyler. She explained how the phone in the garage was Matt's, not David's, and how Polly had spilt the beans at their weekend break, after the space station weirdos had tried to starve them and make them talk to their vaginas.

'Could've been worse,' Enzo said. 'At least you didn't have to mingle and make conversation with everyone else's.'

'It was for menopause, the retreat. That's why we went,' she said. 'Well, actually, I'm perimenopausal — only on the brink of extinction. Polly's a couple of years older, so she says she's like the torchlight, telling me what's ahead. She's brilliant, Polly. I love her. She's my best friend. Do I sound childish, calling her that?'

Enzo shook his head.

'There's no help, no information. This secret society of women are all going through it, not knowing what's happening, except that it's another *woman thing*, not worth listening to,' she said. 'I have mood swings, with my hormones, but you don't know you're having one until after you've had one, if you see what I mean? I mean, it's bad. I saw a World Wildlife Fund ad, and now I get really upset thinking about orphaned gorillas when I get my period. I've got restless legs, which is a horrible thing, even though it sounds daft. See? They make it sound daft. Daft names, probably because some *male* doctor thinks it's a joke. Same with hot flashes, though everyone knows about those, but it's as if it's *oh it's nothing* getting a bit hot, but no, it's not nothing. It's horrendous. I mean, I only get mine at night, but Polly has a hard time. Sometimes, she'll have a client booked in, and she's trying to get in the mood, but it's like she's got heatstroke. It's like she's going to faint or be sick, her clothes sticking to her. But she can't just ask them to wait, not while they're paying, so she can go off and shower in between clients. She's a counsellor, by the way. I'm making her sound like a hooker, but she's a very good counsellor, except with herself — that's why she got so intense, finding out about Matt and Tyler. You'd think she'd know exactly what to do, wouldn't you? But when it comes to your own family…' Erika pulled a face. 'Weird, isn't it?' She closed her eyes.

'Erika?'

'Yes,' she said, opening her eyes after her rant.

'You're home.'

'Oh,' she said. 'That was quick.'

'You've been talking about perimenopause for the last five minutes,' Enzo said, as she realised the light was on in the front of the taxi. The driver looked very cross. 'Sorry to interrupt, but any longer and I'll be having perimenopause myself.'

'I don't think you *have it*,' she said, straightening up. 'I think you're *in* perimenopause or starting perimenopause, but that's only a guess. See? We don't even have the language for it. Sorry,' she added, as Enzo leaned over, sliding open the door. 'Thanks for a lovely night, a lovely campaign.' She banged her head on the way out, playing down how much it hurt.

The street was dark and empty, except for the headlights and rasp of the taxi, which was hovering to make sure she got safely inside. She turned the key in the lock and then gave Enzo a wave before letting herself into the house. As she shut the door, she winced as her handbag slipped from her shoulder, dropping to the floor with a thump. She realised she'd shut her eyes again as she gripped the banister to step out of her heels with an exaggerated movement, as if her feet were somehow prone to sudden outbursts, aware of making the slightest sound.

'Don't worry,' David called from the lounge, 'I'm awake.'

Erika put her hand to her chest in fright. She hadn't noticed any lights on as she walked down the drive. When she stepped into the lounge, she found David sitting in pitch darkness.

'If this is another attempt to lower the electricity bill, David,' she said, settling against the sofa, 'I think you're taking things way too far.'

He switched on the lamp. 'Have fun, did we?'

'I did,' she said, squinting at the sudden light, with the distinct feeling that admitting to having fun was the wrong answer. 'Matt's home!' she went on, trying to sow something pleasant. 'He smuggled himself into the launch!' She gave a giggle of delight, curling her feet up on the settee. 'He organised the whole thing with Richard to surprise me. He's still out, having a ball — it turned into a bit of a double-whammy. Richard proposed to Ursula and Ursula turned him down, saying she never wanted to marry him, and they both seem pretty happy about it.' She paused for a response, but there was none. 'You?'

Erika noticed David was holding one of his good whiskey glasses. It was a heavy, crystal tumbler, usually reserved for celebrations, but he didn't look as if he'd been celebrating.

'I kept getting these notifications from your place. *Stable Denim*. Why didn't you tell me your old acquaintance, Mr Morelli, was back on the scene in quite spectacular fashion?' he asked, gazing at his phone before turning it towards her. 'Fucking him, are you?'

The question was crude and unexpected, as if he'd spat at the stars.

'No, David,' she said, every drop of alcohol metabolising into a premature hangover. 'I'm not.'

'No, no, of course not. Right-o, my mistake,' he said, sipping his drink. 'So, humour me, if you would. Let me paint a picture. There you are, working away as usual. I don't know, maybe it's been a particularly taxing day, putting your little one-liners together. Maybe you're trying to think of something that rhymes with denim, something vastly draining like that, when suddenly … Erika, good for her, has a rare brainwave! What if I ask my ex-boyfriend if he fancies grabbing a nice, fat, pay-check, and maybe, if I'm lucky, he might throw in a belated fuck for old times' sake?' he said. 'How's that?'

'Venom.'

'What was that?'

'Venom, almost rhymes with denim. Thought it was appropriate,' Erika said, determined not to let him turn her very good day into something bad. Had David ever liked her enjoying herself, having a few drinks, becoming a bit merry? Not especially, not since way back when they were dating. Despite his protests to the contrary, she always believed, deep down, he didn't like to think she was having a better time than he was, and even seemed to feel it was inappropriate for married ladies with children to have fun. Fun and foolishness was presumably for the boys, like having other women. 'I didn't ask Enzo to try out. I hadn't heard from him in years, not for the whole time we've been together,' Erika said as David sneered in disbelief. 'Ursula put him forward. He was the best candidate.'

'I'll bet,' he said. 'Fancied a quick lie down on the old casting couch, eh? I thought you might say that, funnily enough. Okay, then.' He settled back in his chair, lacing his hands across his middle. 'Go right ahead, then. Set the record straight, Erika. I'm all ears.'

'I've already told you.' She pinched at her temples, which were beginning to ache. Bolstered by the fact she knew her husband was a liar and a cheat, she wouldn't allow him to feel he had the upper-hand. Matt was right, and without fear of breaking up their family, or ruining his childhood, it was about time she spoke up for herself. 'If you choose not to believe me, there's not much I can do about that, is there?'

'Well, what a small world,' he said, looking amused. 'Full of wonderful coincidences.'

'It certainly is,' Erika said. 'Well, you should know. How's Anya Lasagne?'

'She's doing very well, thanks,' David said, picking up his glass. 'Some people just evolve with the seasons. She looks even better these days.'

'Yes, lovely dress, too,' Erika replied, feeling a childish thrill as she noticed a jitter of surprise unsettling David's self-satisfied expression. 'Any particular reason why you took your ex-wife for dinner? Apart from the obvious?' She removed her earrings, aware that she was shaking. 'You were cheating on me from day one. Do you know how humiliating that was? When I called in at the theatre, I saw the way they used to look at me, assuming I was some simpering idiot, willing to ignore it.'

'Everything I told you about Chloe was true. Nothing happened. She was just a sweet, silly girl, who sent a sweet, silly note.'

'And what about all the others? I'm not an idiot, David. We've stuck to the same script for years,' she said. 'Do you know how repulsive it felt, sharing a bed, knowing what you'd been doing?'

'But we were good together, weren't we?' he said, going over to the window. 'I mean, marriage, it's an escape, isn't it? Or at least ours was, wouldn't you agree?' He took a drink. 'As for Anya, it's not that obvious, would you believe. Quite interesting, in fact,' he said. 'Anya contacted me after everything with Matt became so public.'

'Really? Well, that was nice of her. Taking an interest.'

'She was very interested, yes — curious to know if Matt was my biological child. I have to admit, Erika, I'm understandably quite curious myself.'

'David,' she said, admitting defeat, because if he'd wanted to ruin her evening, talking this nonsense, he'd won. 'It's been a long day. I'm tired. Could we continue this charming conversation in the morning, when neither of us has had quite so much to drink?'

'I'm absolutely fine,' David said, raising his glass. 'You see, it's a particularly painful topic for her — or it was, for both of us, back when we were married and trying to conceive. Well, you know the drill only too well, don't you, love? The upshot of it was that Anya was fully fertile. But after the kind of rigorous examinations you tried to insist on me having, the results weren't quite as reassuring for me, I'm afraid. I already knew what a second round of those things would confirm — a very slim chance of me fathering a child, unfortunately. Almost impossible, in fact.'

It took a few seconds for Erika to understand his meaning.

'I won't bore you with the finer details, Erika. Hardly matters to you, not now anyway, but varicocele caused the issue. Low numbers, low quality. Anya practically had my balls sitting on ice by the bedside. She was devastated, and in the end, as you know, we decided it was best to part ways.' He pondered his glass. 'I was rather more upset than her, I'd guess. I felt rather sorry for myself, being stuck with the problem. But all's well that ends well. Anya's got two daughters now; she went and got herself a thoroughbred stud. And, by the looks of Mr Morelli, it appears you've gone and done the same.'

The information slowly unfurled across Erika's understanding, taking a few seconds to resonate. 'You're telling me you can't have children?'

'Highly unlikely, sweetie,' he said, perfectly calmly. 'Highly unlikely.'

'You don't think you're —'

'Matt's biological father? No, Erika. I have to say I don't, all things considered.' He broke into a yawn. 'Do you? I convinced myself, I suppose. There was still a chance, however miniscule, and there you were, pregnant. I couldn't face going through all that again. I decided, at least you'd have the baby that you'd inevitably decide you wanted, which I knew, I couldn't give you. I thought it was the perfect solution, at the time.' He saw the look on her face. 'I wanted to marry you, Erika, I did. I wanted you to be happy, and after everything that went on with Anya, I thought I could finally make a go of it and be happy again, too. No blame or disappointment lurking on the horizon.'

Erika had so much to say that she didn't know where to start.

'Now, with Matt gone,' he said, 'you're left with what you're left with, aren't you? I can hardly stand being in this house with you any longer. I'm far happier next door, out in the garage with space to myself, but you can't even let me have that, can you? I won't be sticking around. I take it you've already gathered that?'

'You left this marriage years ago,' she said, resigned to the betrayal. 'I should've done the same. You always chased the next thing that came along, then came snivelling back with promises and excuses. I did what I thought was best for Matt. I thought we actually meant something to you.'

'You did mean something to me. I was always last on your list — understudy to everything you actually cared about.'

'This isn't some play you wrote, David. You're not anyone's *understudy*, and I'm not some character you created, trying to live up to these warped expectations you have of a wife. *I exist!* I want to know who I am when I'm not *reacting* to *you*. I was your wife, not your priest, hearing your confessions and absolving you of guilt.'

And what about her guilt? No one had absolved her of that. *Dublin*. After that night with Enzo, she'd gone back to David, reasoning with herself that it was only one night.

'In that case, can you begin to imagine how I felt, watching my wife *doting* on another man's son? Do you know what it takes, putting that thought to the back of your mind? Loving and caring for a child as if he were my own?' he demanded, growing more furious. 'Do you know how many people could stomach that? And you, still brooding over your ex.'

'That's not true. I wasn't brooding over anything except your lies, and who are you to call me out? Matt's been the only consistent man in my life. I gave up on what ifs a long time ago.'

'I want you to leave.'

'What?'

'I want you out, Erika,' David repeated. 'Now. I don't want you here tonight. I'll be leaving as soon as possible. I'd appreciate it if you kept your distance until then.'

CHAPTER TWENTY-SIX

Should she have left? Erika couldn't think straight. She felt as if she'd been submerged in ice water, with segments of conversation still rising to the surface.

Matt would be coming home. She'd almost texted, but what could she do? With any luck, he'd stay out late enough for his head to hit the pillow, oblivious to her absence and David's demeanour. Everything would seem clearer in the morning, she told herself. Not knowing where else to go, she called Enzo and got a taxi to his place.

'Could I please have a drink?' Erika said as he answered the door, still dressed in his jeans.

'Already made you one.'

'You're probably going to need one too,' she said, realising how cold she felt.

'You spoke to your husband?'

She nodded and followed him down to the sunken lounge, taking the small glass. 'That's strong,' she said, eyes watering at the acidic aroma of lemon.

'Limoncello.'

They sat in silence for a moment, Erika shivering slightly as the shock began to thaw.

'Here, get this round you.' Enzo reached behind the settee and draped a blanket over her shoulders.

'Fake fur?' Erika said. 'Gone a little soft around the edges, haven't you, in your later years?'

'Got myself a pair of slippers, too.' He refilled her glass and topped up his own. 'Moccasins.'

She gave a snort and tucked up her feet, body heavy with a growing sense of relief. Then she picked up her glass, delaying what she was about to say. 'David said Anya, the ex-wife, contacted him to find out if Matt was his biological son,' she said. 'I got pregnant after Dublin.'

'Yes…'

'I didn't think there was a chance…' Erika went on. 'But with David, there's a fertility issue.'

They looked at each other for a moment, then each looked at their glasses.

'You think Matt could be mine? You think he could be ours?'

Ours. She nodded, the thought entirely disorientating.

'Why did you never tell me this, Erika?'

'I don't know.'

'You do.'

'Because it was one time,' she said, feeling like the same idiot who'd been surprised by her own pregnancy. 'We'd split up, me and David, a couple of weeks before. When I got back from Dublin, I got back to my life, and you weren't part of it. You never were, not for long. You never wanted to be. I'd been seeing David for a while. I ran into him again and gave it another shot. The odds of it being you —'

'You wanted it to be him.'

'I didn't want it to be anybody. I didn't want it to be happening at all. I got sick of you evaporating every time things got too close. That's why, in my mind, there was a ninety-nine per cent chance it was David's, rather than down to one night with you.'

They were silent for a few moments.

'Erika, it's not a coincidence, me showing up,' Enzo said, almost business-like. 'Someone contacted me. I got an email asking about you.'

'*What?* An email from who?'

'I spoke to a woman. No names,' he said. 'She called and told me about Matt and your husband.'

'Wait. You knew about this?'

'She said Matt could be mine and gave me your details at the office. This person, she knew what she was talking about. I had no reason to doubt what she was saying. I called your place a few times but hung up. I mean, I don't know, instead of calling you out of the blue, asking questions, maybe I thought I'd leave it to chance, Erika. That's why I agreed to do the campaign. I've been waiting for the right moment. I thought it would give us some time.'

'Who was it? Who was the woman?'

'I don't know. She was kind of apologetic. There was no reason to think she was lying. I thought maybe I'd get to know what was going on with you. Maybe you were going through something, a divorce? I didn't know, but by the time I realised you didn't have a clue, you had me decked out in denim, following your husband.'

'Was it Anya who spoke to you?' Erika asked. 'It has to be Anya, don't you think?'

David had said Anya had only contacted him after she'd seen Matt's comments online. But perhaps David was lying? That would hardly surprise her.

'She said she was a friend of your husband.'

'Well, he's had plenty of those.'

'She said it wasn't easy for her and she had no bad intentions — she was adamant about that. But she thought I had a right to know.'

'I agree, you did,' Erika said. 'But it might've been nice for someone to run it past me, first. I suppose I should be grateful she didn't just dump this on Matt.'

'Look, me wanting to know, it's not just about that,' Enzo said. 'There are implications.'

'Just a few…'

'I don't even know if I would've done this to you — turned up like this, I mean — but I'm sick,' he said. 'You've noticed — you've seen me when I get those cramps. My arms and legs, seizing up out of nowhere. It's Kennedy's disease. Degenerative. A parting gift from my old man. This thing, it only affects males. They don't know why. Women carry the gene without symptoms. My dad had it. My brother got the all-clear. I got first prize.'

'So, what does that mean?'

'They don't know too much. What they do know is, chances are, physically, I'm not going to be much use. I'm going to need assistance one day. *Adapted living.* Hopefully that's a long way off, but they can't predict these things. Basically, Matt's going to need to get tested.'

'Fuck…'

'Yeah.'

'Will you…' she began. 'Does it…'

'No,' Enzo said, anticipating what she guessed were the standard questions. 'It's not going to kill me off, which in some ways…' He trailed off. 'You okay?'

'Who cares if I'm okay? Fuck if I'm okay.'

'Have your drink.'

'Enzo?'

'I know, but we can't go back, Erika. I didn't want to show up in the middle of your life like this, and if it hadn't been for this thing…' He looked at his hands as if his body wasn't his own. 'Like I said, maybe I wouldn't have done this, but I couldn't have you not knowing, not when it could affect Matt.'

'I loved everything about today. It reminded me how much I love my job, and how much I love having you around. Then Matty came home…'

'Erika, I know for some reason you think I wouldn't have been there for you and Matt, but I would've been,' he said, taking a seat next to her. 'I wanted to sort things out. I wanted to do that in Dublin. I tried. I called. I called a few times. It was the same after all that stuff over Angie. And, yes, I should've explained things better. Everything with Josh was a lot. But you decided to end things.'

She knew she'd cut him off. Maybe losing Josh somehow made turning away easier, especially from people who reminded her of her brother's death. Her mum had reacted the same way, keeping her distance.

'Your mum made it quite clear to me that she didn't want me at Josh's funeral,' Enzo said. 'I understood that. The woman lost her son. I chose to respect her wishes. The things I told you, about my old man…' He paused. 'I quit on Josh that night because he started on me; trying to get a reaction, bringing all that stuff up. He wasn't the same lad. Neither of us could've changed that.'

'Enzo, I was done blaming you a long time ago. You loved Josh, I know that, and I've loved you for as long as I can remember. That's never going to change.'

'No, it never has,' he said.

'Don't say it like that.'

'Like what?'

'Like you don't want it to be that way.'

'What am I supposed to say? It doesn't help either of us, Erika, it never did.'

'You don't have to say anything,' she said, taking his hand.

'You know, I didn't expect things to be the same. The stuff with Matt — that's all I was trying to get my head around. I didn't expect to feel like this, but I'm glad.'

I'm glad. It took her straight back to when they were teenagers. She smiled as he placed his hand on her cheek, enjoying the certainty of the man who'd co-existed in her thoughts for so long.

'You asked me the other day, what you were like,' he said quietly. 'There was always something magical about you, Erika.'

She placed a single kiss on his lips. Her need was stark and unapologetic. Enzo kissed her back, sudden life on still water, and the years fell away like Autumn. As their kisses became insistent and their hands sought warmth, neither of them questioned it. Erika pulled at his shirt, her hands along his back, as he unzipped her dress and lay her down.

Enzo slackened his belt, dragging first his shirt, then his T-shirt over his head and sliding free from his jeans. Erika felt the urgency in every move. He took her, her own sounds surrounding her. A breath-taking coldness sighed across her skin as his teeth grazed her shoulder, holding her down as she inched her hips higher, unravelling.

'Well,' Enzo said, lying on his back afterwards. 'That was … loud…'

They both began laughing, half deranged, half delighted.

Erika attempted to sit up, already full of dull aches in muscles she hadn't used since that January offer at the gym. 'Why's there always a commentary with you?' she asked. 'I always get a one-word assessment. You called it "good" once, like something forgettable off the telly.'

'Well, maybe it was,' Enzo said, laughing hard as she glared at him. 'I think, given the circumstances, here in the *lair*, we can officially refer to you as a Bond girl.'

'You can, if you *never* want to sleep with me again, which I'd like to think isn't the case,' Erika said, trying and failing to get comfortable. 'Sorry, but as wild and spontaneous as that was, do you have a bed?'

'Come on,' Enzo said, sitting up. It still made her smile, the sheer novelty of his nakedness. 'I come complete with a memory foam mattress.'

'Do you now? Well, aren't you a bargain,' Erika said, as he found his shorts and she wrapped the throw around herself.

CHAPTER TWENTY-SEVEN

Matt was the first thought on Erika's mind the next morning. That, and the fact she and Enzo hadn't thought to use a condom, not until they'd made it to the bedroom. No wonder she'd ended up pregnant. She remembered finding condoms stashed in David's walking books once and wondering where exactly he was planning on walking to.

Erika stared at the back of Enzo's head, wishing she could stay there, brushing her hand against the velvet contour and leaving a kiss as she got up. She needed to get home and talk to her son. She got dressed, retrieving discarded clothing from the floor.

'What if he won't let you back in?' Enzo asked.

'Hi,' she said. 'I didn't realise you were awake.'

'Do you want me to come with you?'

'No, no,' she said, quickly zipping her dress. 'It's fine. I've got my key.'

'What if he's bolted the door?'

'I'll call Matt. He can let me in.'

'You're sure you don't want me to come with you?' Enzo stood with his jeans half-unbuttoned. 'Does he know you stayed here?'

'David? I don't know. I don't think he cares.'

'Well, we'll tell him.'

'No!'

'Okay.'

'Not because I don't want this,' she said, noticing his expression. 'I mean, just not now. I need to see Matt.'

Enzo insisted on dropping her off. David's car was missing from the drive, but Matt's jacket was on the banister. A handful of receipts and a packet of Camel Lights were left on the hallway table.

Erika changed into a sweatshirt and jeans. Her mobile rattled to life on the dresser. *Polly*. She almost didn't answer, but these days, especially with Matt and Tyler, her friend felt closer to family.

'Hello, darling!' Polly said, a broad smile in her voice. 'I'm just calling to ask how the launch went. Were you surprised to see Matthew?'

'Oh,' Erika said. 'I see…'

'Don't blame me,' she said. 'The boys swore me to secrecy, yet again. I'm in Manchester with Tyler. Thought I'd actually get him to tidy the place up a bit while Matty's away. Listen, can you talk? Don't take this the wrong way, but I've a strange question to ask. Steve says he thought he saw you this morning. I don't suppose you were kissing a man in a red truck?'

Erika looked at her hand, almost surprised to find a cigarette slotted between her fingers. She'd been sitting in the bathroom for the last half an hour, gazing out across rows of houses.

She slowly inhaled, looking out across the driveway. When David found her back at the house, he barely looked at her as he announced he was moving out. She hadn't expected him to take all his worldly belongings with him in one swoop, armed with newly purchased storage boxes, being very practical about it, but of course he was: the boring bastard. The man could barely walk from one end of the garden to the next without polishing the geraniums, so what did she expect? He spent the best part of an hour locating various gadgets, including a pocket-sized bicycle repair kit. He then bothered to ask her about an inhaler he claimed he never needed. But maybe he needed it for sex now with Anya? Maybe he liked dentists because he was into weird, oral sex games? It wasn't as if Erika knew what did it for him these days, and she was thankful for that. They could inject each other's arses with novocaine and go at it for hours, spread-eagled in Anya's hydraulic chair, for all she cared.

Erika exhaled steadily, sticking her arm out of the window, stubbing out the cigarette on the wall, and letting it drop.

'Are you *smoking*?'

David stared up from the driveway. Erika took a good look at him. Aside from his facial hair, he held all the appeal of a boiled egg. She started to laugh. How the hell had she ended up living with this boiled egg of a man? She laughed harder. She felt like now was the time to tell him how much she disliked the home dye job and that ratty-looking goatee he'd grown. It looked like something long dead, hanging from his face. More hysterical laughter.

'Yes, David,' she said, lighting up another for effect with Enzo's Zippo.

Enzo's Zippo. She looked at it, as if caught red-handed. The past squarely embedded into the present.

'So,' he said, picking up the discarded filter and examining it. He wore baggy shorts with too many pockets and not enough trouser. 'You smoke now…'

Either Erika was on a severe nicotine high or this was the exact moment she finally lost the plot, because it felt strangely … *great*. Then she realised it was Erika Karter who felt great: the Erika she was before she married David and became Erika Forde. Years ago, she'd shared the occasional, sex-fatigued cigarette with Enzo. They'd spent entire afternoons lying around, newly exhausted. In fact, if she remembered correctly, they'd done quite a lot of smoking back then.

'Yes, *I smoke!*' Erika Karter called down from the window. 'Like a chimney!' She exhaled in the general direction of her husband. 'I'm smoking in the en suite, because some of us are still young enough to be irresponsible about our health, and I'm pretty sure it's linked to gum disease. So run and tell Anya about that!'

'Don't bring her into this...'

'I'll tell you what she's good at extracting,' Erika called, taking another drag as she heard the slam of the garage door. 'Husbands! Oh, hello, neighbours!' The couple from next door slowed their pace as they walked their dog, bemused by the spectacle. 'Just so you know, it wasn't me who wanted to cut down your tree!'

'*ERIKA!*' David appeared again, holding a set of golf clubs she hadn't seen since he had a thirty-two-inch waistband.

'*DAVID!*' she said, mimicking him, about to shut the window. 'And take your bloody paperbacks with you!'

'Mum?' Matt said, standing in the doorway. 'Sorry to swear, but what the fuck's going on?'

Erika decided it was easier to work backwards. Yes, they were splitting up. No, she hadn't spoken to his father, because David had got there first. Yes, the whole thing was completely toxic.

'Oh, for Christ's sake,' she said, hovering at the window as a car pulled up. 'He's got Monica here.'

'It's too early for this. I need coffee,' Matt said, with a yawn. 'Want one?'

'I'd love one.'

'What are you doing?'

'Putting on my lipstick.'

'Now?'

'Monica always looks so … you know,' she said. 'Just because everything's gone to shit doesn't mean I have to look like it.'

'Hello, Erika,' Monica said, looking as effortless as an M&S billboard, with her hair clipped up in a chignon. 'I don't want this to be awkward, but I wanted to say, I'm sorry.'

'Ah, right,' Erika said, marvelling slightly at Monica's ever-present insistence on decorum.

'The thing is, Erika,' Monica said, frequently the bearer of bad news these days, 'I thought David might've mentioned that he's going to be staying with me.'

'That's very kind of you,' Erika said, as David walked in. 'It's going to be a little cramped at Monica's apartment, isn't it, if you're taking all your stuff?'

'I'm no longer living at the apartment,' Monica said. 'It only happened quite recently. What we mean is…' She turned to David, who looked like a man who couldn't admit he'd taken the wrong turn-off. 'David and I, we're moving in together.'

'Did you just say you're moving in together?' Matt said, carrying cups into the hall and offering one to his mother. He took a seat at the bottom of the stairs. 'As in, you and my dad?'

'Hello Matthew,' Monica said, with an unmistakeable edge to her voice. 'Haven't heard from you since all that hateful nonsense, almost destroying David's career.'

'Hateful?' Erika said. 'He's not hateful.'

'Did your sales figures a favour, though, didn't I?' Matt said, casually taking a sip. 'Dad's not complaining.'

'You're moving in?' Erika said, hoping for some response from David, who seemed to have lost his swagger. 'You've been seeing each other?'

'We have, yes,' Monica said, bracing herself for Erika's reaction. 'For quite a while now.'

'You do know he's been seeing his ex-wife?'

'She means the night we met Anya,' David explained. 'Monica joined us, Erika. All perfectly above board.'

'Perfectly above board? We're still married, you arsehole.'

'*Ha!*' Matt said, all eyes turning to him.

'How's Mr Morelli doing?' David asked. 'I take it that's where you stayed last night?'

'You stayed out last night?' Matt said. 'You stayed out with Enzo?'

'*With*,' David said. 'Not out.'

'Don't make this about me! You've been having an affair!'

'Really?' David sneered. 'Slept on the settee, did he? The perfect gentleman?'

'Erika, David and I…' Monica began, taking his hand. It was pathetic, Erika thought, how the man seemed incapable of speaking up for himself. 'We're in love. I know this must be a horrible shock. I'm not proud of myself. I never wanted to be that woman.'

'Well, you are, and you've given up that beautiful apartment for him?' Erika almost laughed. 'I do hope you realise your kitchen cupboards are going to be fully diarised from now on. He'll teach you all about his recycling schedules, and for God's sake, don't leave a label on a tin or life won't be worth living.'

'*Erika!*'

'What, David? I'm being honest. Even second-hand cars come with a handbook. So, you're the reason he's been shaving his dick?'

Monica and David exchanged a look.

'The Man Mower? I found it in the garage with your tooth whitening kit. I take it that was from Anya? You can understand why I thought it was her he was chasing this time around.'

'Mum?' Matt said. 'The razor's mine. It was with the phone?'

'Oh…'

'*Yeah*,' Matt said. 'Awkward…'

'Oh, and holidays, you can forget —' Erika stopped herself mid-sentence. 'What an idiot. The work trips. Silly me. You went with him? In fact, there were no work trips, were there? All that penny-pinching so you could keep Monica in the manner to which she's accustomed.'

David averted his gaze, increasingly florid.

'Well, this has been very informative,' Erika said. 'And very civilised.'

'Civilised? Galivanting about with your ex-boyfriend?' David said. 'You're no angel.'

'I think it's time we were all honest, Erika,' Monica said. 'You can blame David as much as you like if it makes you feel any better, but you're not entirely innocent.'

'Really? Well, thanks for your opinion, Monica,' Erika said. She was struck by a sudden realisation. 'It was you, wasn't it? You contacted Enzo.'

'What's she talking about?' David asked.

'David, someone had to say something,' Monica said. 'Enzo deserved to know.'

'Deserved to know what?' Matt said, getting to his feet. 'You've been cheating on dad with Enzo?'

'Years ago, but *we were on a break*!' Erika mimicked the *Friends* catchphrase. 'You told her?' Erika said, keeping her eyes on David. 'You kept everything from me, but you told her?'

'I didn't expect her to take matters into her own hands!'

'Well, in that case, David, she might give you a run for your money, this one.'

'David,' Monica said, bringing him to heel. 'I lost everything for you.'

'Hold on, what did you lose?' Erika said. 'I'm the one he's leaving.'

'Victor rewrote his will before he died,' Monica said. 'He found out about David.'

'Victor knew? How long's this been going on?' Erika demanded, thinking of that old song.

'Well,' David said, looking flummoxed, 'it was a gradual —'

'How long?'

'Just over two years,' Monica said. 'We're in love.'

'So you said. And you thought you'd bring Enzo into this, to speed things along?'

'You know exactly why I brought Enzo into this.'

Erika and Monica locked eyes.

'So,' Matt said, sitting back down, typing away on his phone, 'Dad's with Monica, and you've got something going with Enzo. I mean, all things seem pretty equal to me.'

'Perfect. That'll suit your mother,' David said. 'Never to blame.'

'You rendered us null and void years ago,' Erika said. 'I can't begin to tell you how relieved I am that you're not my problem anymore.'

'I think there are quite a few problems, Erika,' Monica said. 'Don't you?'

'What's with the intrigue?' Matt said, looking up from his screen.

'She's talking about Enzo.'

'For God's sake,' Matt said. 'What about Enzo?'

CHAPTER TWENTY-EIGHT

David and Monica left Erika to talk to Matt. She agreed to tell him the whole story, answering his questions about Enzo and divulging the almost non-existent chances of David fathering a child.

'You know, it's almost romantic,' Matt said. 'The return of Enzo Morelli in the Emerald Isle. Your handsome, Italian lover showing up in Dublin as if fate was knitting the two of you together. Until you threw in the part about being pissed up and possibly conceiving me during a hen do.' He stood. 'So, that's it? I'm not Dad's kid?'

'I'm sorry.'

'Don't be. Let's not pretend I have some wonderful relationship with Dad,' he said, wiping his face on his sleeve.

'Your dad loves you, Matt. You know he does, and I know you love him.'

'Yeah? Then where the fuck is he?'

Erika ordered the DNA test kit the next morning. Swabs would be needed from Enzo and Matt, and the result would be emailed the next day. As much as she wanted to be entirely truthful, Erika couldn't bring herself to tell her son about Enzo's illness, and how it could directly affect him.

Matt wanted to go and speak to Tyler, to take a breath before they faced the answer of his paternity. She and Enzo had agreed it was entirely up to him when they read the result. Six days went by, and Matt still hadn't opened the email attachment.

As for David, there had been no contact since the day he'd left with Monica. Despite her frustration at the way he'd abandoned Matt to the truth, no part of Erika regretted his absence.

Meanwhile, as Ursula monitored the Stable Demin campaign, Richard Harrington was becoming something of a legend as the Dad Jeans wearer in the ads.

'I think it all comes down to being relatable,' he told the attractive TV anchor on Breakfast TV, Erika and Ursula tuning in from the office. 'I'm just a regular guy, doing my job. I never intended to put myself out there, but I'd like to think I'm up for a laugh. The whole thing's been crazy. Massively flattering, but it's kind of embarrassing, people fancying me. I mean, I'm not even a dad, not yet.' And was that a hopeful look, appealing to the maternal instincts of his female fans?

'Oh, get fucked, Richard,' Ursula said, chucking half a croissant at the screen.

After a spate of similarly cloying TV appearances, and the possibility of a range of Dad Jean merch being rushed out in time for Christmas, Richard was currently debating whether to sign up for *Endangered Species: Celebrities Dating in Captivity*. It was a scripted reality TV show that involved being flown out to the island of Mustique with a selection of well-known, cosmetically enhanced faces. He would supposedly be searching for the love of his life, while subtly promoting Stable Demin, and he was already pacifying Ursula about his entirely professional intentions.

Left with half a household and with no mention of what was happening with the house itself just yet, Erika set about packing. Leafing through old photograph albums, she found herself scrutinising Matt's features. People often commented on how much Matt took after her, with his hazel eyes and dark hair. He also had the pale complexion of the Karter family. Studying one photo of him, Erika thought she recognised David's straight eyebrows, slightly freckled nose and narrow shoulders. However, Matt's height couldn't be traced back to either her or David's distant relatives.

Enzo kept a low profile, happy to leave the notoriety to Richard when it came to working with Stable Denim. He'd also told Erika that he didn't want to get his hopes up about Matt.

'If he finds out he's mine, where does that get him?' he said. 'He could have what I have. This diagnosis is about all we'll have in common. I feel like a lone wolf, circling someone else's family. It's not a good place to be.'

There was no cure or current treatment for Kennedy's disease. Medically, it was described as the degeneration of motor neurons between the brain and spinal cord. It led to muscle cramps and muscle wastage, and as it continued to take hold, it could affect the sufferer's ability to swallow, speak, and breathe. Erika couldn't believe what was happening to Enzo, nor the fact nothing could be done.

Eventually, Matt, Erika and Enzo all agreed that the three of them would get together to read the test result. Erika and Enzo were invited to join Matt and Tyler in Manchester, where she noticed the easy-going affection, the tangible attraction, between them.

The four of them sat around the table. They made pleasant conversation about the earthenware pasta bowls, linen placemats and tinted glasses bought by Polly during her visit.

'I wasn't sure whether I should cook Italian. Mum said you're a good cook,' Matt told Enzo as he served lunch. 'I've already downloaded a *Beginner's Guide to Italiano*. So, if this is my heritage, with a family restaurant and everything, I should be able to put together a fairly decent risotto.'

'I made the ciabatta,' Tyler said, offering Erika a slice. 'Mum's recipe.'

Erika had told Polly everything, her friend expressing understandable disbelief at what had gone on between her and David, and unapologetic excitement at the prospect of her and Enzo.

'I don't want to make anyone uncomfortable, but it's a big deal, a huge deal, today,' said Matt. He turned to Enzo. 'I know we don't know each other very well yet, but no matter what, I know you make Mum happy.' He picked up his phone. 'I don't know how to do this, so is it okay if we just go ahead and read the result? Sorry to pause lunch, but I think it's obvious that no one's exactly in the mood to eat right now.' Tyler put his arm around Matt. 'One second to download the attachment…'

They all watched as Matt scanned his phone.

'You good?' Enzo said to Erika.

'I'm good,' she said. As Tyler took Matt's hand, Erika kissed Enzo's shoulder.

'Nothing's changed,' said Matt. 'Dad is my biological father.'

CHAPTER TWENTY-NINE

Despite her excitement during the flight, Erika didn't utter a word as she and Enzo reached Marina del Cantone. She was happy to surrender to the hush of the sea, as they stood overlooking the Gulf of Salerno.

'You never said how beautiful this place was.'

'I wouldn't have brought you here otherwise, would I?' Enzo said, gripping the top of the weather-worn fence. 'Hey, Erika, fancy spending a week someplace best described as average?' He smiled. 'You needed to see it for yourself.'

This was where Italian families came on holiday, far from the tourist track, he'd said. There was a tiny church, striped yellow and white, a pink gelato parlour, and candlelit terraces illuminating the incline, each a distinct stitch in a delicate, unspoilt tapestry. She was in love.

'Look, he's fishing,' Erika said, noticing a wonderfully aged-looking man hauling his catch from one of three coloured boats on the water.

A freshly salted scent, purified by the waters. Erika felt purified, too. Those kneaded rows of cobbled rocks. She couldn't wait to step out across them, surrounded by quietened hillside. This was where Enzo belonged, she decided. Something about the solitude made sense, as if here was the origin of his deepest thoughts.

'We'll head out to Sorrento one of the days,' Enzo said. 'I prefer it here, personally, but you'll probably like it. Full of tourists and shops,' he added, teasing. 'Everything you've ever wanted, as long as it's lemon-scented, flavoured or shaped, or actual lemons.'

The place was timeless. Standing on the peninsula, an almost daunting sense of remoteness in stark contrast to the embrace of his family.

The Morelli family restaurant, L'Oliva Blu, was set a little higher on the hillside. It had a white and navy façade with billowing canopies. Walking past gnarled, earth-grazing trees as they approached, Erika and Enzo heard orders being issued in the open kitchen.

Enzo's Uncle Pietro and his aunties, Lorena and Aurura, greeted him like a young prince. Valeria, his mum, took Erika in her arms as if she were still a child, though they had only shared a smile here and there when Erika was growing up.

Lorena, a tall, angular woman with a mass of silver hair and shrewd, dark eyes, had given up her house and now lived with Aurura, the older, quieter sister who wore gold-rimmed glasses and kept her hair tightly bound in a plait. They both insisted that Erika should stay with them. Enzo would stay with Val, of course, who was seeing a nice man named Danilo, an artist from one of the neighbouring towns.

His grandmother had died a couple of years back, Enzo explained, and his Uncle Pietro had taken over the restaurant. The old lady's picture was framed on a table in reverence, with candles and flowers. L'Oliva Blu had been her family's creation, Valeria explained. Pietro had a lot to live up to, as far as Enzo's grandfather — his nonno — was concerned.

Erika perused the dishes and ordered a seafood linguine.

'The fish were caught by local fishermen, like the ones you saw before,' Enzo told her. He chose a type of pasta Erika had never heard of, paccheri, with white fish and zucchini.

Enzo's nonno soon found him and gripped him by the elbows, planting firm kisses on each cheek. The elderly gentleman placed an unsteady kiss on Erika's hand, then said something in Italian, which made the rest of the family laugh. Enzo and Erika looking to Val for translation.

'Beautiful women are the songs we sing in our hearts,' Val said. 'This is what keeps Nonno's heart beating so strongly after all these years.' She gave them a knowing look.

Over the next couple of leisurely days, Enzo became the man she remembered, vivid and relaxed. She bought a bikini especially and headed into the water, encouraged by clusters of families, waist-deep in the blue. Enzo reclined on a lounger with one arm folded behind his head. As her feet curved around rocks, nearing the water, Erika sensed his eyes on her. She looked back. She was right. Dressed only in his gaze, Enzo watched her as if she existed within memory. Erika turned back to the sun, wondered what else he sensed in her. She fought against it, as if everything unknown to her was known to him.

One night, encouraged by Valeria, they volunteered to work in the kitchen. Enzo was concentrating and confident, but Erika found herself distracted. There was an intimacy between them as they worked, brushing past each other, ever aware of his proximity.

Valeria joined them, and Enzo reiterated promises to return with his brother very soon.

'I worry,' Val said, placing a hand on his shoulder as he prepared another board of abundant green vegetables: zucchini, artichoke, fennel. 'I want someone to love him the way I love him.' At this, Enzo met Erika's eye, raising his eyebrows. 'But I couldn't go back to England, not now.'

'I wouldn't want you to,' Enzo said with warm amusement, before he went in search of further instructions from Pietro.

'I came here to look after his father, Val said to Erika, checking Enzo was out of earshot. Erika nodded. 'It's a terrible thing. I wish he'd come home, be with us, here. Enzo is stubborn, like me. He didn't want to come to his father's funeral. We found out about his father's illness. There were no symptoms until he got much older. Perhaps it will be the same for Enzo.' She crossed her fingers.

The last night before Erika and Enzo were due to return, they walked to the neighbouring bay, roaming the strip of pebbled coastline. Another interlude of confusion; they had not so much as kissed since that night at his apartment. Erika felt quietly content with the friendly affection between them, or maybe it was the effects of the wine. Not a day went by without wine at lunch and dinner, not forgetting the wine in between. She was peacefully disorientated in this sacred place, with this family who welcomed her like their own.

Enzo had made a reservation at a place he knew Erika would love. They took a table on the balcony, with white linen, wildflowers and candles.

'What is it with you and balconies?' Erika said, holding a generous, lime-soaked gin. 'This is how I picture you now, you know.'

'This is how you picture me?' Enzo said. 'Been picturing me often, have you?'

'Only late at night,' she said, enjoying the flirtation.

'You seem different.'

'Do I?' she said, attempting an intriguing look for dramatic effect.

'It's good to see.'

'Thank you. It's good, feeling different. Do you?'

'Feel different?' He gave a slight shake of the head. 'No, why?'

'I like it, seeing you with your family.' She waved her empty glass. 'Am I drinking too much? This is what'll happen after divorce. First the drink, then the dance classes.'

'Well, you're on holiday,' Enzo said, with a smile and a shrug. 'I quite enjoy watching you sink the entire bottle. Still waiting for that revealing dress phase you mentioned. You'll have to keep me posted.'

'Keep you posted?'

She had wondered, over dinner, if he might finally kiss her at some point that night. Now, she found herself growing restless, suddenly out of step with this newly contrived, old friendship of theirs.

They stared ahead, as if ignoring everything between them.

'Erika,' he said, finally breaking the impasse. 'I can't be more.'

'Why not?' she said.

'You know why. That's just the way it is.'

'But we're together now,' she said. 'We're here now.'

'I'm glad you're here. I wanted to spend time with you after the last few weeks.'

'The last few weeks — meaning Matt? What about everything else? What about us?'

'Erika, you know how I feel about you. I never expected any of this, not after all this time. The attraction has always been there — neither of us has much choice in that. But our friendship is important to me. You're important to me, but I didn't bring you out here, expecting anything else.'

'Our *friendship*. So, we can still be friends. Decent of you.'

'Erika, I'm not rejecting you, but you understand my circumstances?'

'Your prognosis?'

'My prognosis?' He drew back in his seat. 'Someone's been doing their research.'

'Don't be so defensive. This could easily have been Matt. So, yes, I did my research. I'm here for you.'

'I don't want you to be *here for me*,' he said. 'I'm not interested in using you as a distraction. You know how this thing's going to play out.'

'No one knows that,' Erika said. 'You don't know that.'

'I only know what I've been told to expect. I'm not interested in having *someone special* around to shoulder the burden.'

'Did your ex know about it? The one who cheated on you?'

'Yes, and she got out once she knew. I didn't appreciate how she went about it, but I don't blame her. No one wants to be saddled with this. I don't want anyone around, waiting for this disease to kick in.'

'So, you're going to base the rest of your life on something that hasn't happened yet?'

'It's happening right now, slowly but surely.'

'But I know about it. You already told me. I choose not to walk away.'

'I'm not walking away from you, either. Give me a while and I won't have much choice, not without someone's help.'

'That's supposed to be funny?' she said. 'Fine. Feel sorry for yourself. All you've got to do is adjust *if* and *when* things change.'

'Really, Erika?' he said, folding his arms. 'That's good to know. Why don't you tell me all about how I should stop moping and learn to adjust to my *new normal…*'

'I was going to say it's *us* who'll adapt.'

'That's very kind of you, Erika, but I don't want *us* adapting.'

'I don't care what the doctors said, do you hear me? I'm not afraid of it.'

'Good for you,' he said. 'I'll get the bill.'

'Very impressed with the stone-cold silence,' Erika said, carrying her shoes and lagging behind on the footpath. 'It must feel great, not having the guts to want anybody.'

'Gutless and spineless. There you go, just what you want in a partner. It's nothing personal, Erika.'

'I know,' she said. 'You specialise in keeping things impersonal, these days.'

'You'll meet someone…'

'Is that what you think?' She came to a halt in the middle of the trail. 'I'm desperate? In search of some knight in shining armour?'

'Jesus,' he said, pulling on his jacket. 'Next time you tell me not to let you drink, remind me to listen.'

'Drinking's got nothing to do with it,' she said, holding onto the wooden fence with one hand and pulling on her shoes. 'Do you think for one minute that I actually believe my life, my plans, come down to some man, *or you*, after everything it's taken to start over? You can be so patronising at times, do you know that?'

'Well, thanks for clearing that up. And, sorry to be patronising, but your shoes are on the wrong feet.'

She looked down. He was right. 'This is us,' she said, covering her grin and pointing at them. 'These shoes, this is how we always end up — going off in opposite directions. But we're the same pair — don't you get it?'

'We're a pair. I think we are, yes,' Enzo smiled, helping her to keep her balance as she swapped shoes. 'A pair of what, I couldn't say.'

'I don't want to do this again, Enzo,' she said, both feet on the ground. 'Not being with you has always been a mistake. I want to stay like this.'

'It's not going to stay like some holiday, Erika,' he said, as they continued arm-in-arm towards the village. 'I wish it could, but I can't tell you what to expect.'

'I expect to be with you,' she said, looking at him. 'That's all I expect.'

They walked on in silence, finally coming to a stop outside Aunt Lorena's house. As they reached the top of the stoop, he wrapped his arm around her waist. 'Erika, you can do so much better than this, than me.'

'I know, but let's face it, you can't, so...' She placed her arms around his neck. 'Call it a distraction if you want, but some people spend half their lives looking for this kind of distraction.'

'You,' he said, blue eyes beaming, 'are very distracting.'

'Good,' she said. 'That's exactly what I intend to be...'

'Yes,' he said, stepping closer, their bodies meeting. 'I can tell.'

Us, she thought. *Finally, we get to be us.*

A NOTE TO THE READER

Dear Reader,

Thank you so much for reading *When We Were Us*. If you enjoyed the novel, please share a review on my **Amazon** or **Goodreads** pages. You can also find me on **Facebook**, **Instagram** or follow me on **Twitter**. To fully delve into the Caliskaniverse, make your way over to **www.patriciacaliskanauthor.com**.

I'll be sharing the inspiration behind the story of WHEN WE WERE US and how much I've loved spending so much time with these characters. You can also take a deep dive into my writing process, and find out how I begin to develop ideas into working novels. Spoiler alert: lots of coffee, research, and late nights.

Make yourself at home and take a look around. It's always lovely to hear from you, and as long as you keep reading, I'll keep on writing.

Until next time,

Patricia

Sapere Books is an exciting new publisher of brilliant fiction and popular history.

To find out more about our latest releases and our monthly bargain books visit our website:
saperebooks.com